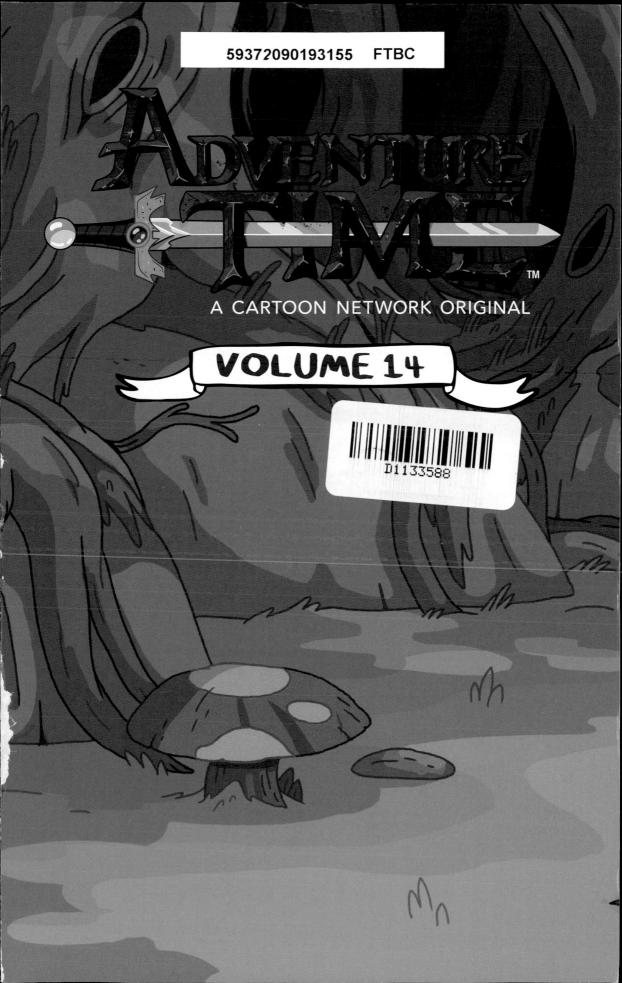

ADVENTURE TIME

A CARTOON NETWORK ORIGINAL

VOLUME 14

ROSS RICHIE CEO & Founder • MATT GAGNON Editor-in-Chief • FILIP SABLIK President of Publishing & Marketing • STEPHEN CHRISTY President of Development • LANCE KREITER VP of Licensing & Merchandising • PHIL BARBARO VP of Finance
ARUNE SINGH VP of Marketing • BRYCE CARLSON Managing Editor • SCOTT NEWMAN Production Design Manager • KATE HENNING Operations Manager • SIERRA HAHN Senior Editor • DAFNA PLEBAN Editor, Talent Development • SHANNON WATTERS Editor
ERIC HARBURN Editor • WHITNEY LEOPARD Editor • CAMERON CHITTOCK Editor • CHRIS ROSA Associate Editor • MATTHEW LEVINE Associate Editor • SOPHIE PHILIPS-ROBERTS Assistant Editor • AMANDA LaFRANCO Executive Assistant
KATALINA HOLLAND Editorial Administrative Assistant • JILLIAN CRAB Production Designer • MICHELLE ANKLEY Production Designer • KARA LEOPARD Production Designer • MARIE KRUPINA Production Designer • GRACE PARK Production Design Assistant
CHELSEA ROBERTS Production Design Assistant • ELIZABETH LOUGHRIDGE Accounting Coordinator • STEPHANIE HOCUTT Social Media Coordinator • JOSÉ MEZA Event Coordinator • HOLLY AITCHISON Operations Coordinator • MEGAN CHRISTOPHER Operations Assistant
RODRIGO HERNANDEZ Mailroom Assistant • MORGAN PERRY Direct Market Representative • CAT O'GRADY Marketing Assistant • LIZ ALMENDAREZ Accounting Administrative Assistant • CORNELIA TZANA Administrative Assistant

ADVENTURE TIME Volume Fourteen, April 2018. Published by KaBOOM!, a division of Boom Entertainment, Inc. ADVENTURE TIME, CARTOON NETWORK, the logos, and all related characters and elements are trademarks of and © Cartoon Network. (S18) Originally published in single magazine form as ADVENTURE TIME No.62-65. © Cartoon Network. (S17) All rights reserved. KaBOOM!™ and the KaBOOM! logo are trademarks of Boom Entertainment, Inc., registered in various countries and categories. All characters, events, and institutions depicted herein are fictional. Any similarity between any of the names, characters, persons, events, and/or institutions in this publication to actual names, characters, and persons, whether living or dead, events, and/or institutions is unintended and purely coincidental. KaBOOM! does not read or accept unsolicited submissions of ideas, stories, or artwork.

For information regarding the CPSIA on this printed material, call: (203) 595-3636 and provide reference #RICH – 779489.

BOOM! Studios, 5670 Wilshire Boulevard, Suite 400, Los Angeles, CA 90036-5679. Printed in USA. First Printing.

ISBN: 978-1-68415-144-8, eISBN: 978-1-61398-883-1

CREATED BY
Pendleton Ward

WRITTEN BY
Mariko Tamaki

ILLUSTRATED BY
Ian McGinty

COLORS BY
Maarta Laiho

LETTERS BY
Mike Fiorentino

COVER BY
Shelli Paroline & Braden Lamb

DESIGNER
Chelsea Roberts

ASSISTANT EDITORS
Katalina Holland
Michael Moccio

EDITOR
Whitney Leopard

With Special Thanks to Marisa Marionakis, Janet No, Curtis Lelash, Conrad Montgomery, Kelly Crews, Scott Malchus, Adam Muto and the wonderful folks at Cartoon Network.

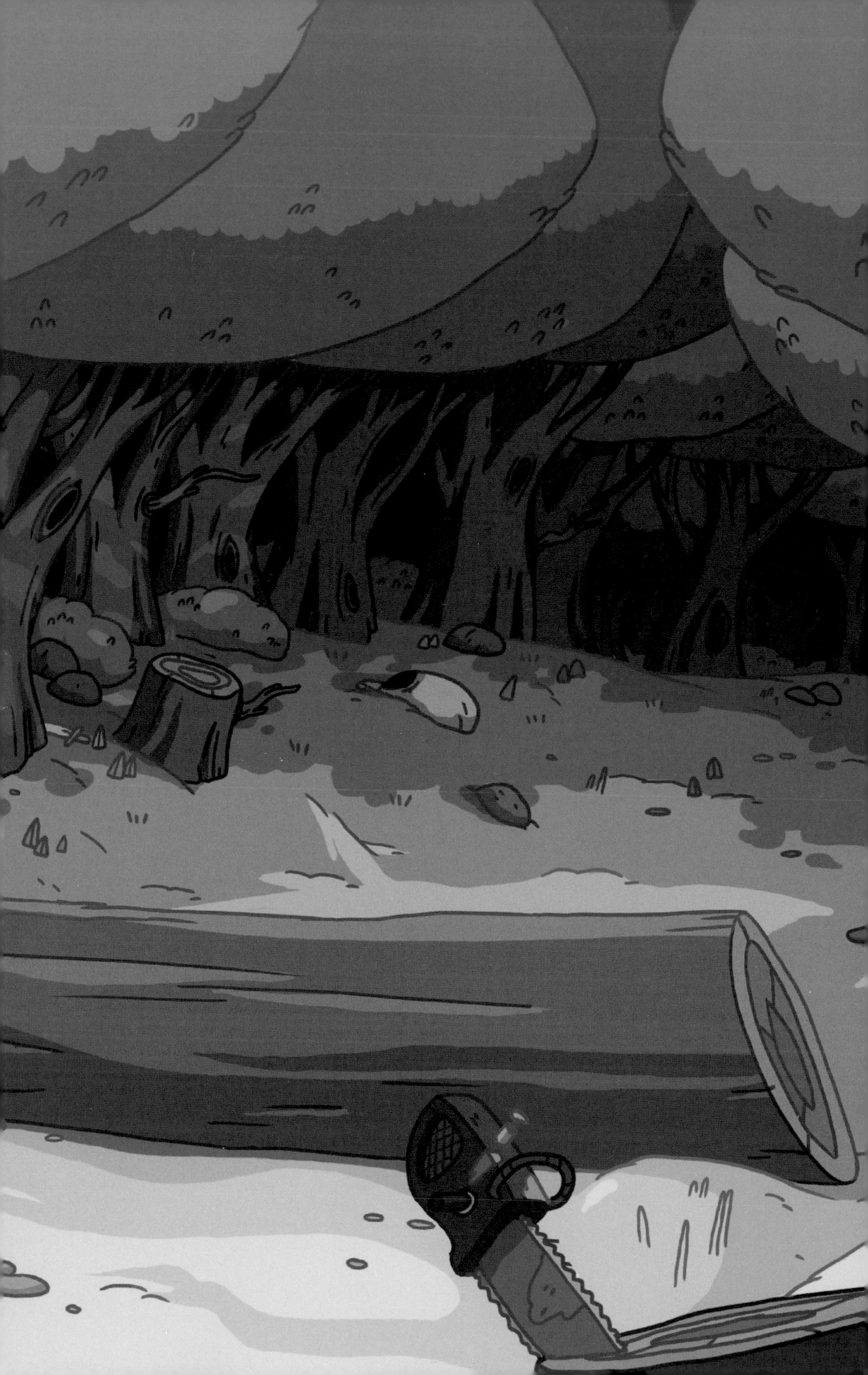

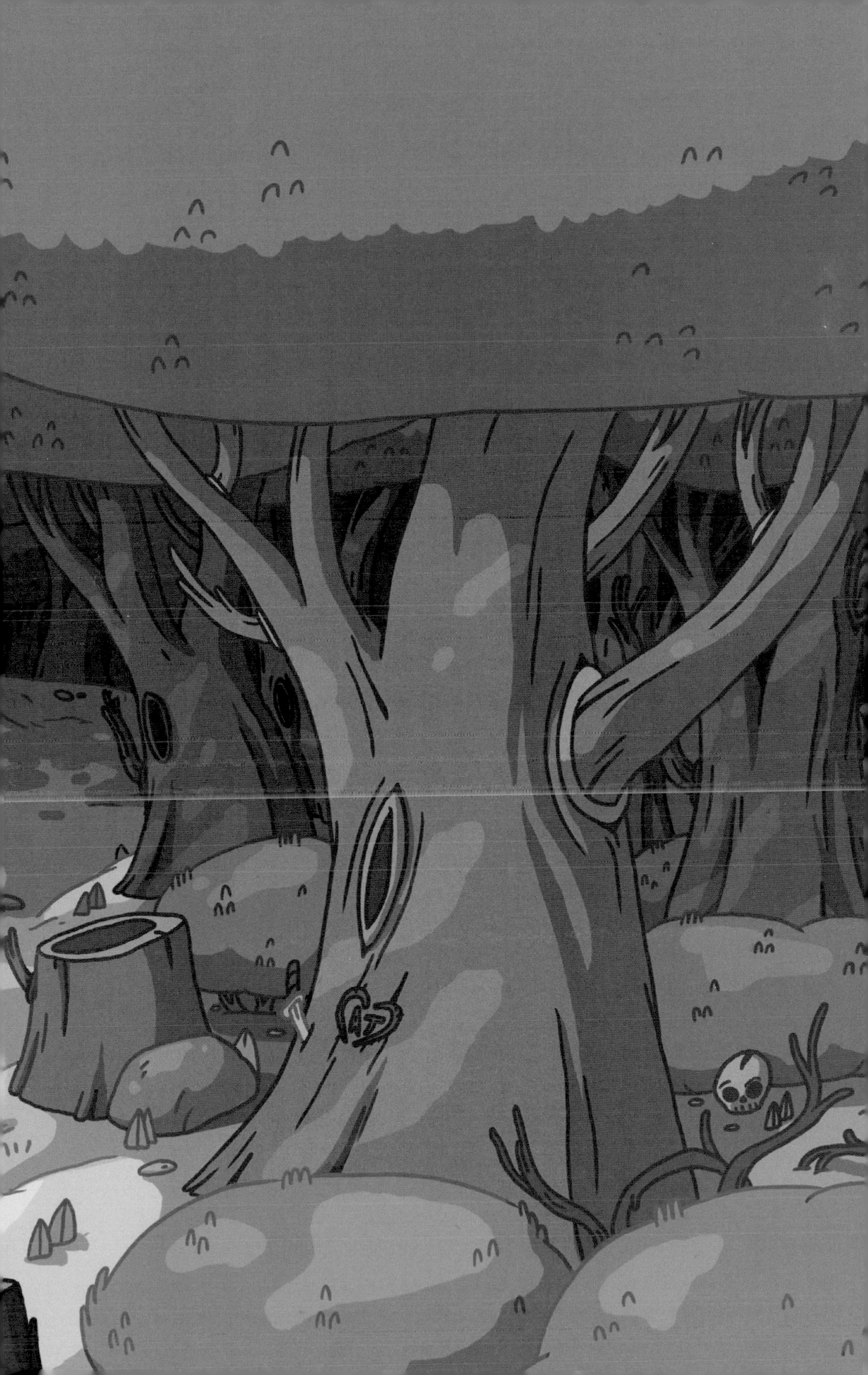

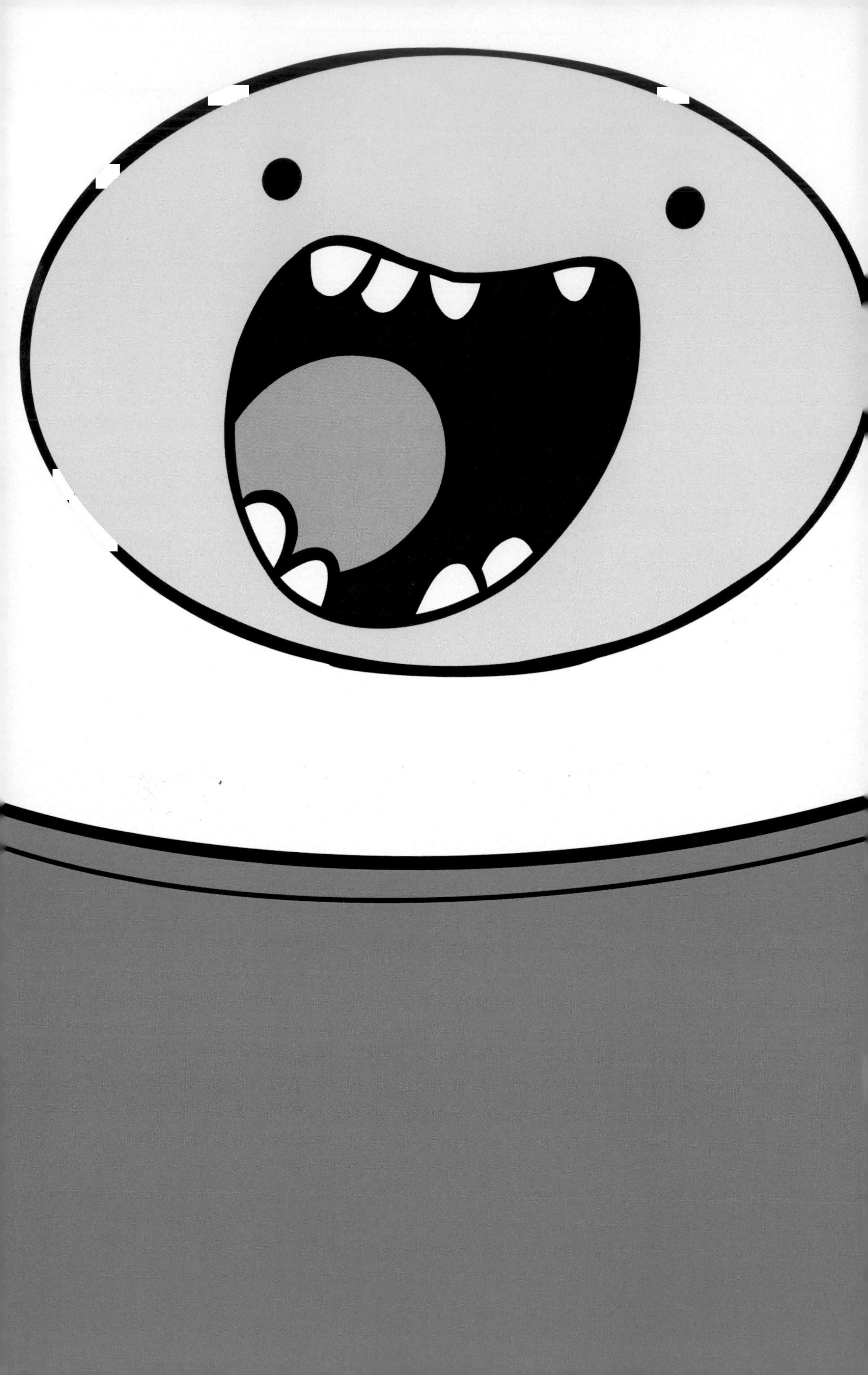

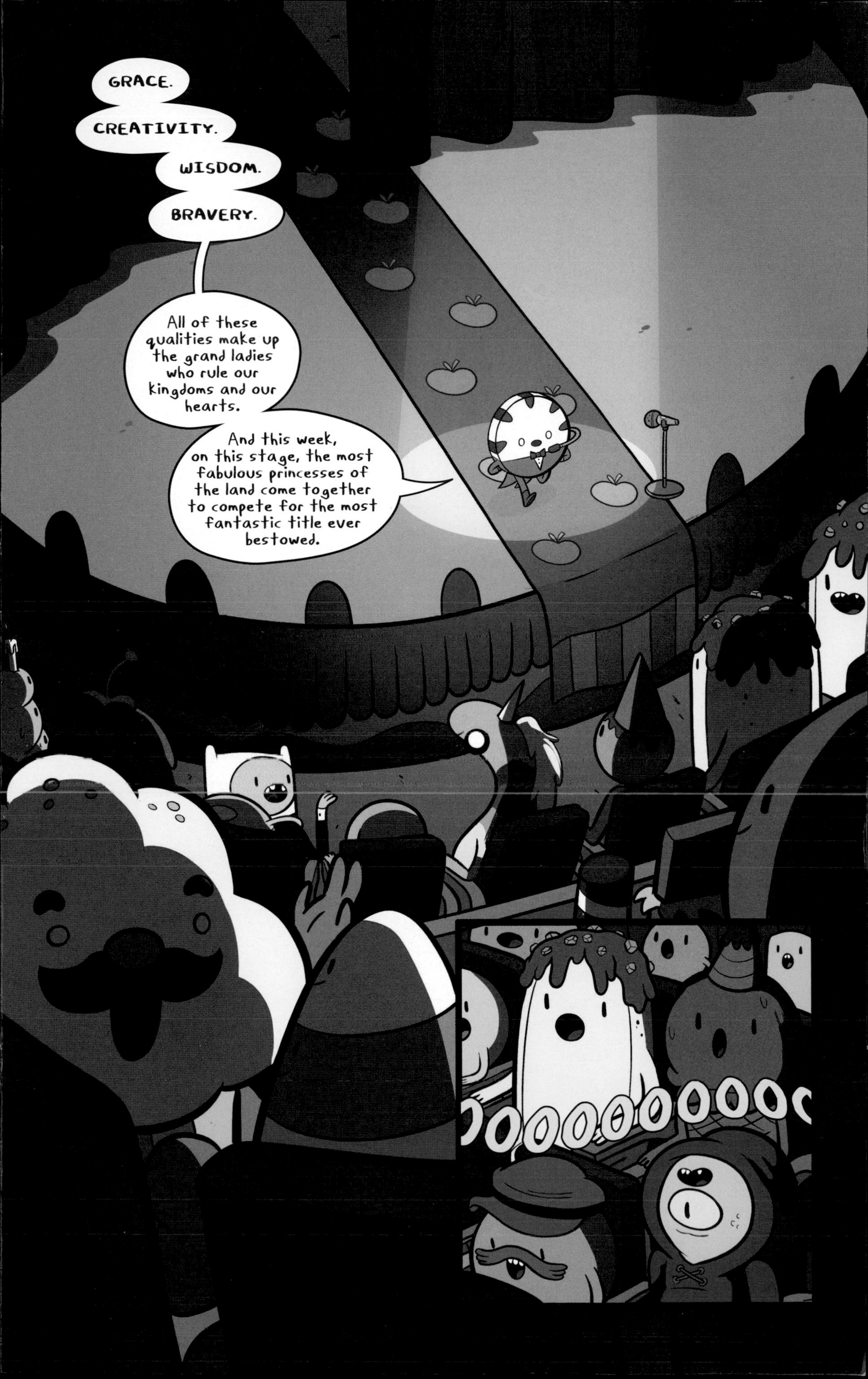
GRACE.
CREATIVITY.
WISDOM.
BRAVERY.
All of these qualities make up the grand ladies who rule our kingdoms and our hearts.
And this week, on this stage, the most fabulous princesses of the land come together to compete for the most fantastic title ever bestowed.
OOOOOOOOOOO

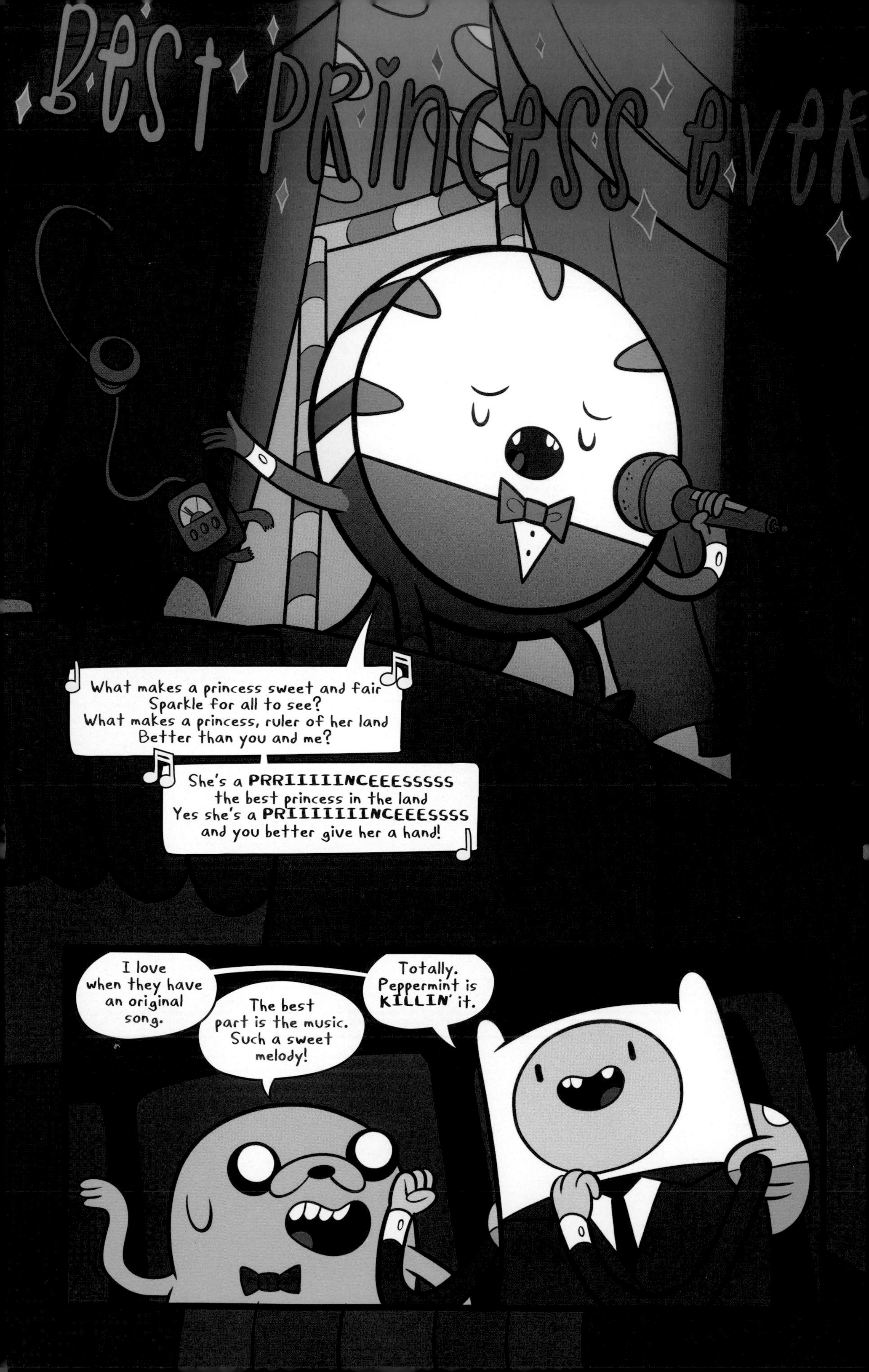
Best Princess Ever
What makes a princess sweet and fair
Sparkle for all to see?
What makes a princess, ruler of her land
Better than you and me?
She's a PRRIIIIINCEEESSSS
the best princess in the land
Yes she's a PRIIIIIIINCEEESSSS
and you better give her a hand!
I love when they have an original song.
The best part is the music. Such a sweet melody!
Totally. Peppermint is KILLIN' it.

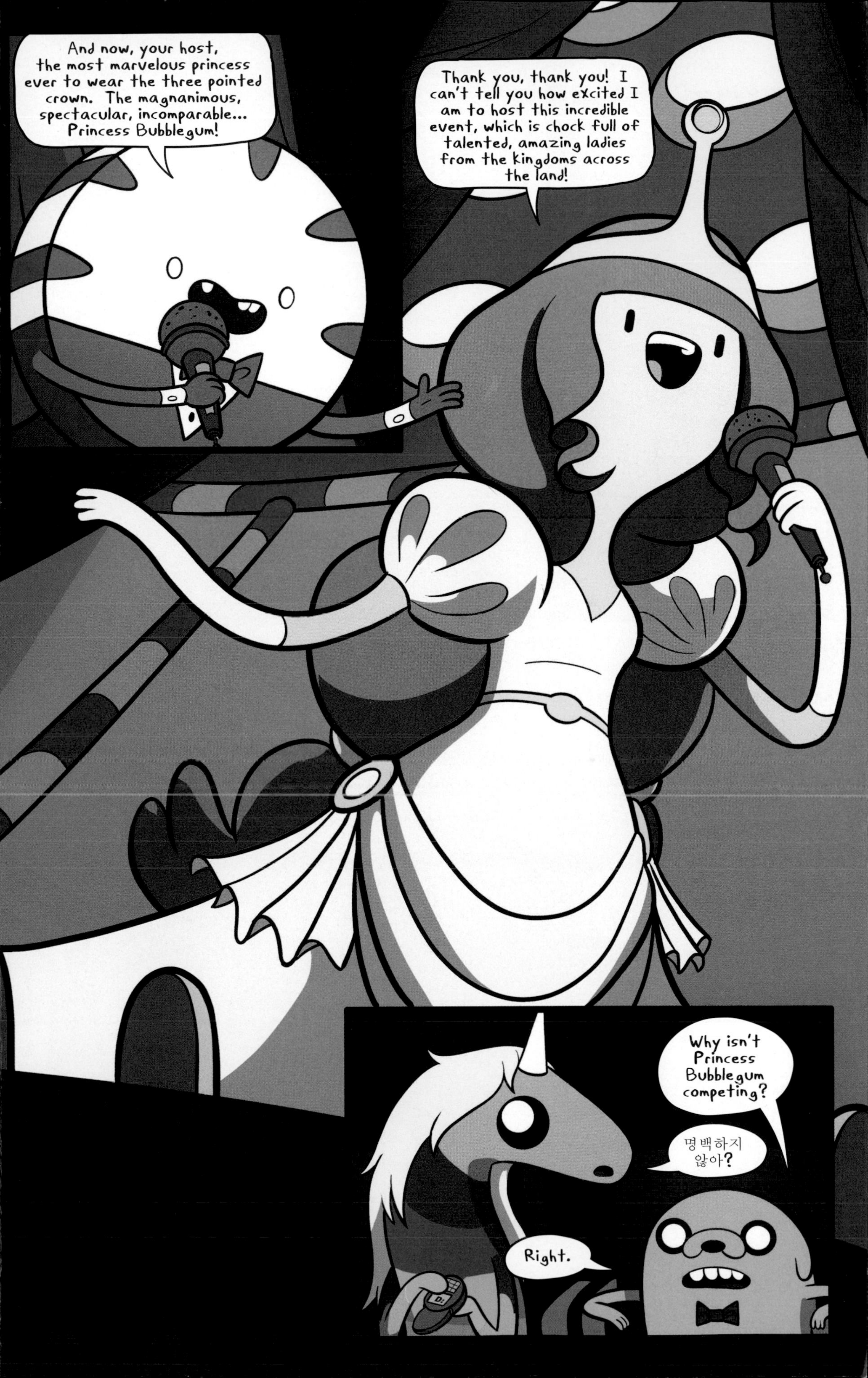
And now, your host, the most marvelous princess ever to wear the three pointed crown. The magnanimous, spectacular, incomparable... Princess Bubblegum!
Thank you, thank you! I can't tell you how excited I am to host this incredible event, which is chock full of talented, amazing ladies from the kingdoms across the land!
Why isn't Princess Bubblegum competing?
명백하지 않아?
Right.

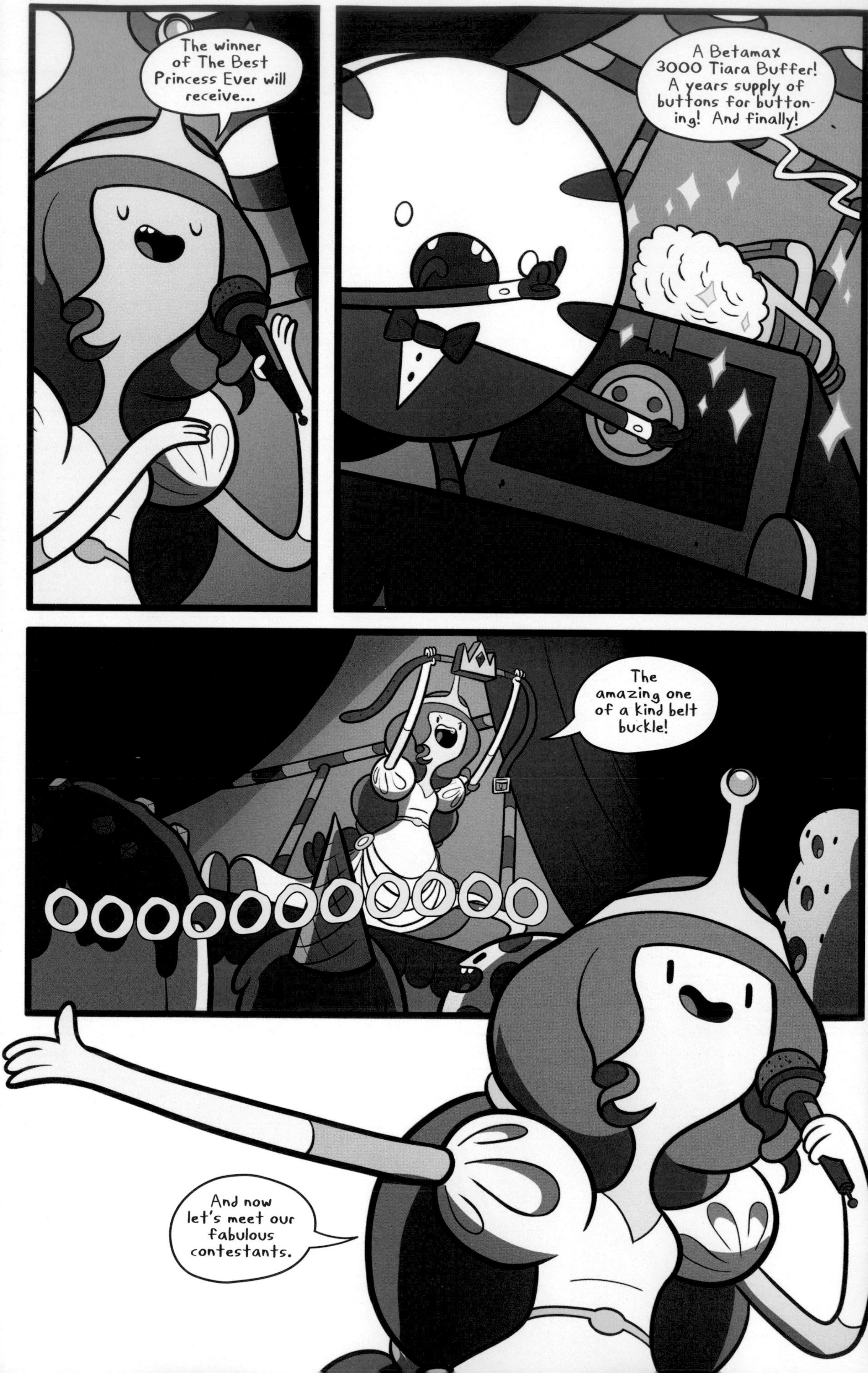
The winner of The Best Princess Ever will receive...
A Betamax 3000 Tiara Buffer! A years supply of buttons for button-ing! And finally!
The amazing one of a kind belt buckle!
And now let's meet our fabulous contestants.

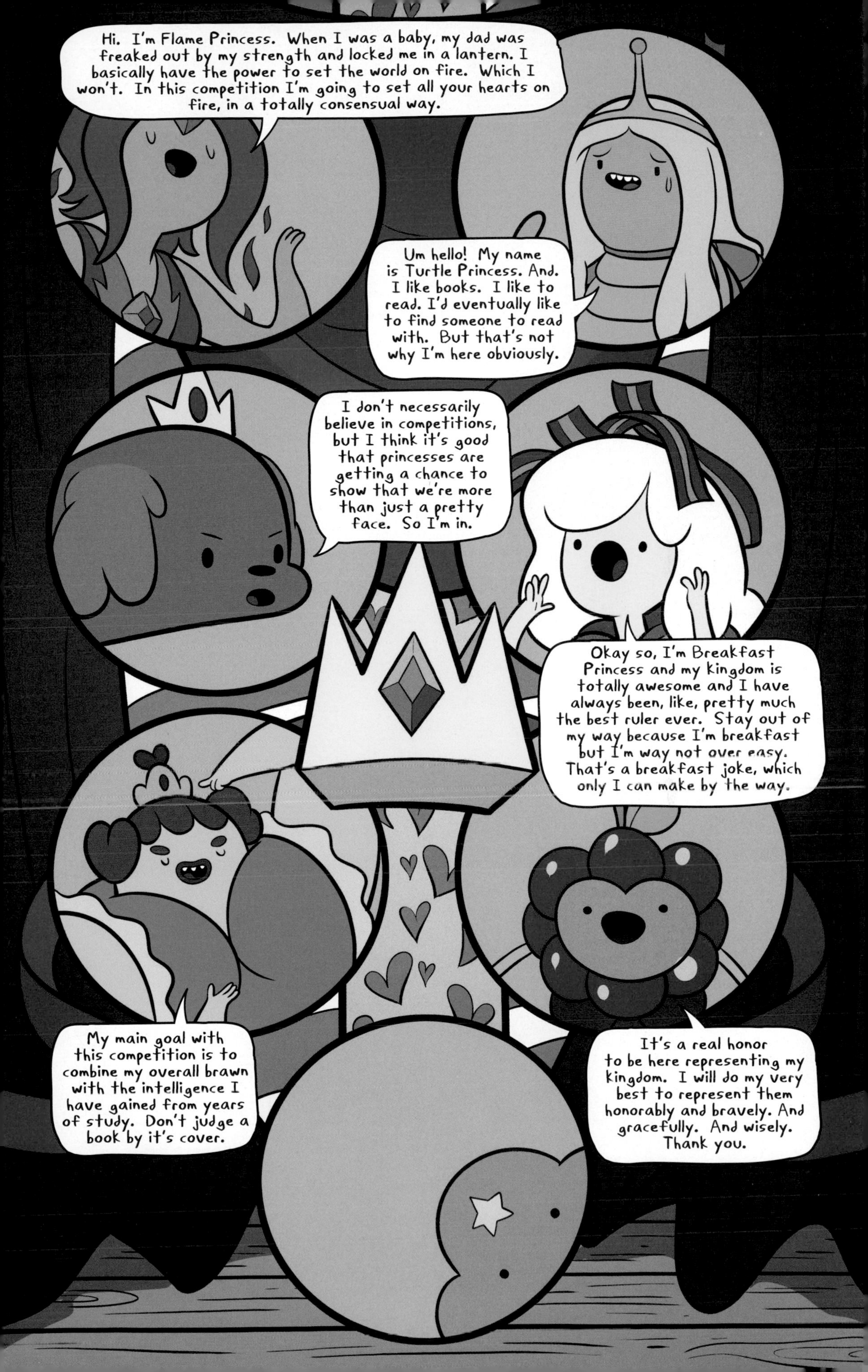

Hi. I'm Flame Princess. When I was a baby, my dad was freaked out by my strength and locked me in a lantern. I basically have the power to set the world on fire. Which I won't. In this competition I'm going to set all your hearts on fire, in a totally consensual way.
Um hello! My name is Turtle Princess. And. I like books. I like to read. I'd eventually like to find someone to read with. But that's not why I'm here obviously.
I don't necessarily believe in competitions, but I think it's good that princesses are getting a chance to show that we're more than just a pretty face. So I'm in.
Okay so, I'm Breakfast Princess and my kingdom is totally awesome and I have always been, like, pretty much the best ruler ever. Stay out of my way because I'm breakfast but I'm way not over easy. That's a breakfast joke, which only I can make by the way.
My main goal with this competition is to combine my overall brawn with the intelligence I have gained from years of study. Don't judge a book by it's cover.
It's a real honor to be here representing my kingdom. I will do my very best to represent them honorably and bravely. And gracefully. And wisely. Thank you.

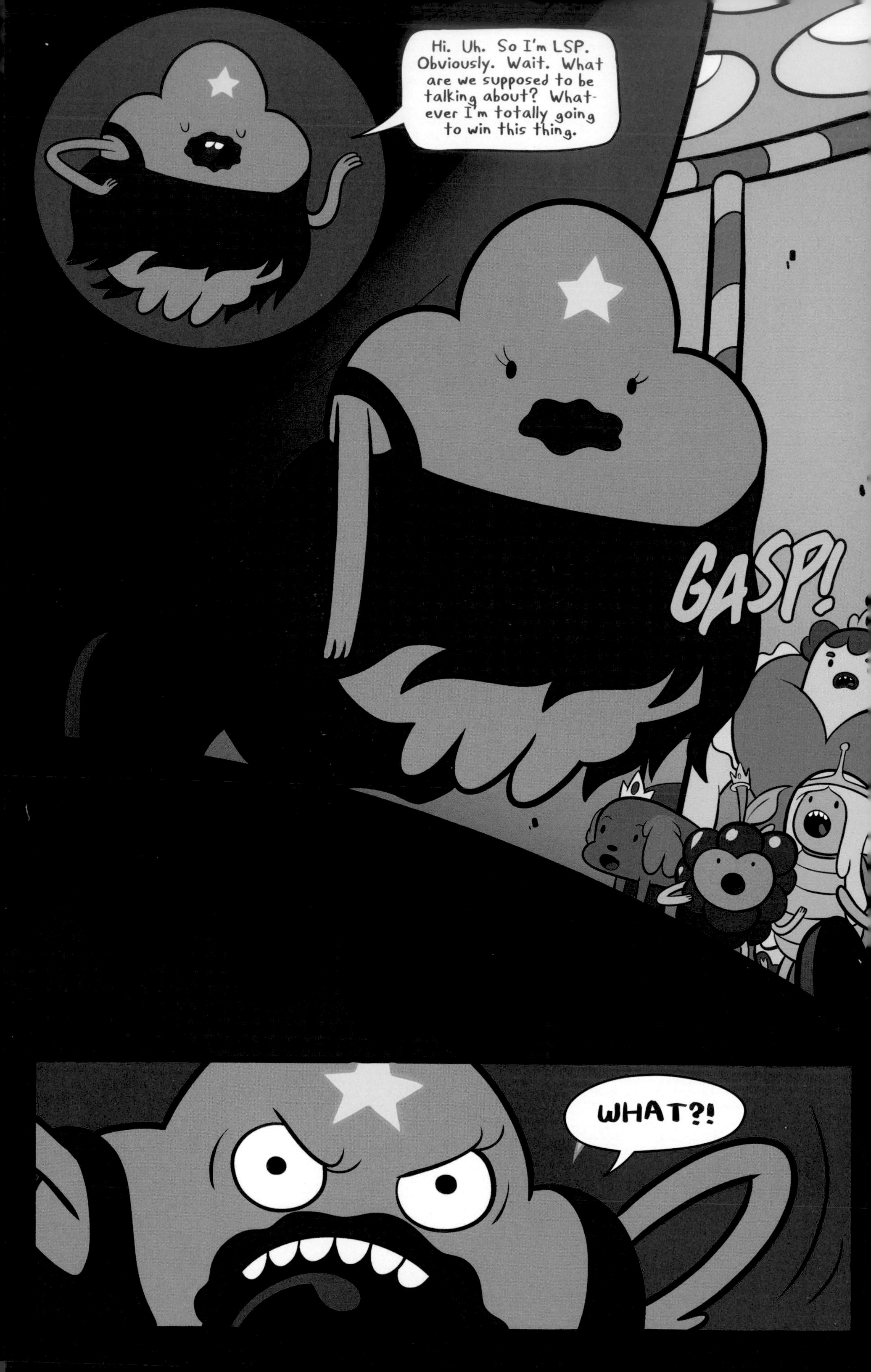
Hi. Uh. So I'm LSP. Obviously. Wait. What are we supposed to be talking about? Whatever I'm totally going to win this thing.
GASP!
WHAT?!

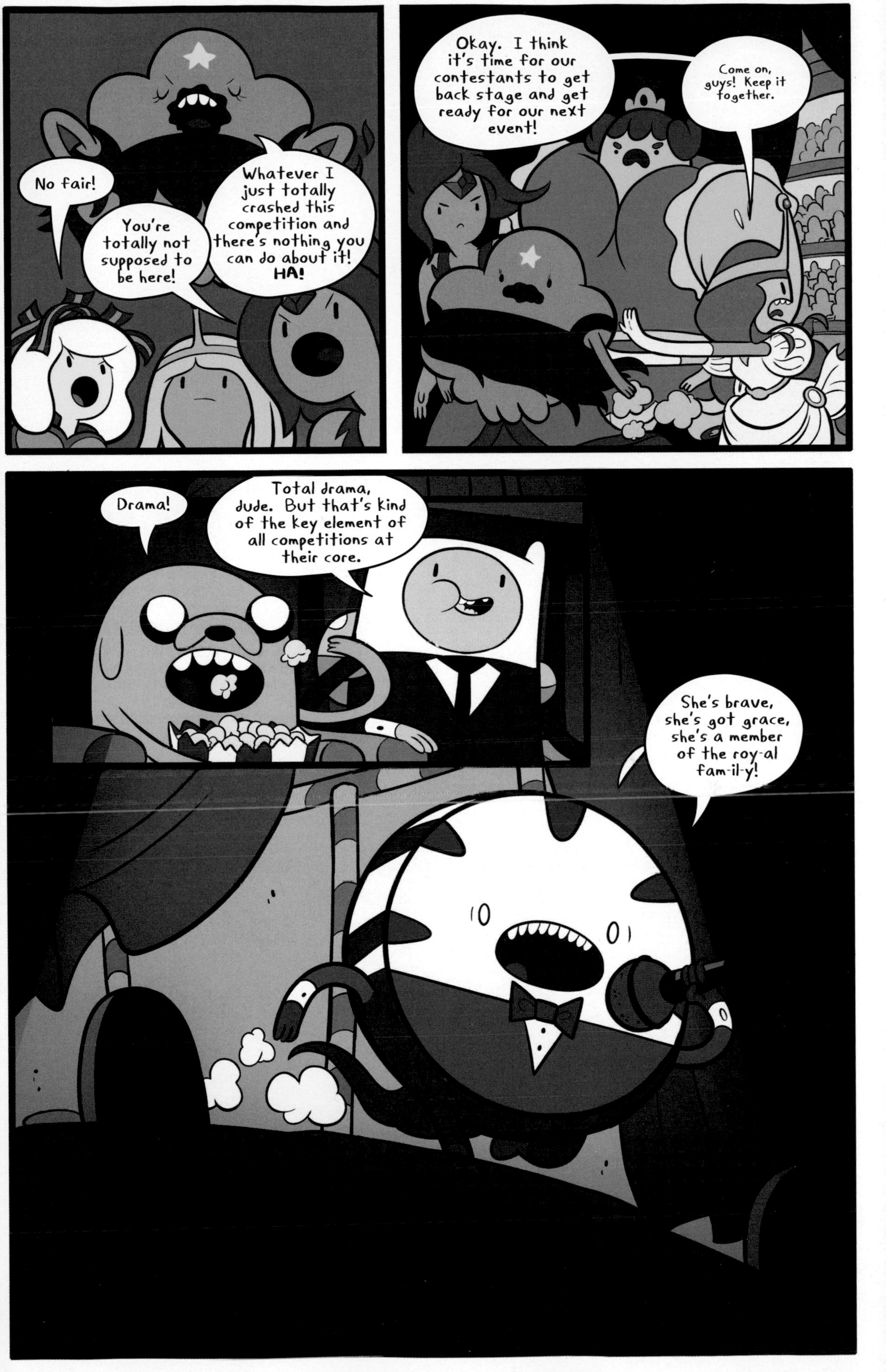
No fair!
You're totally not supposed to be here!
Whatever I just totally crashed this competition and there's nothing you can do about it! HA!
Okay. I think it's time for our contestants to get back stage and get ready for our next event!
Come on, guys! Keep it together.
Drama!
Total drama, dude. But that's kind of the key element of all competitions at their core.
She's brave, she's got grace, she's a member of the roy-al fam-il-y!

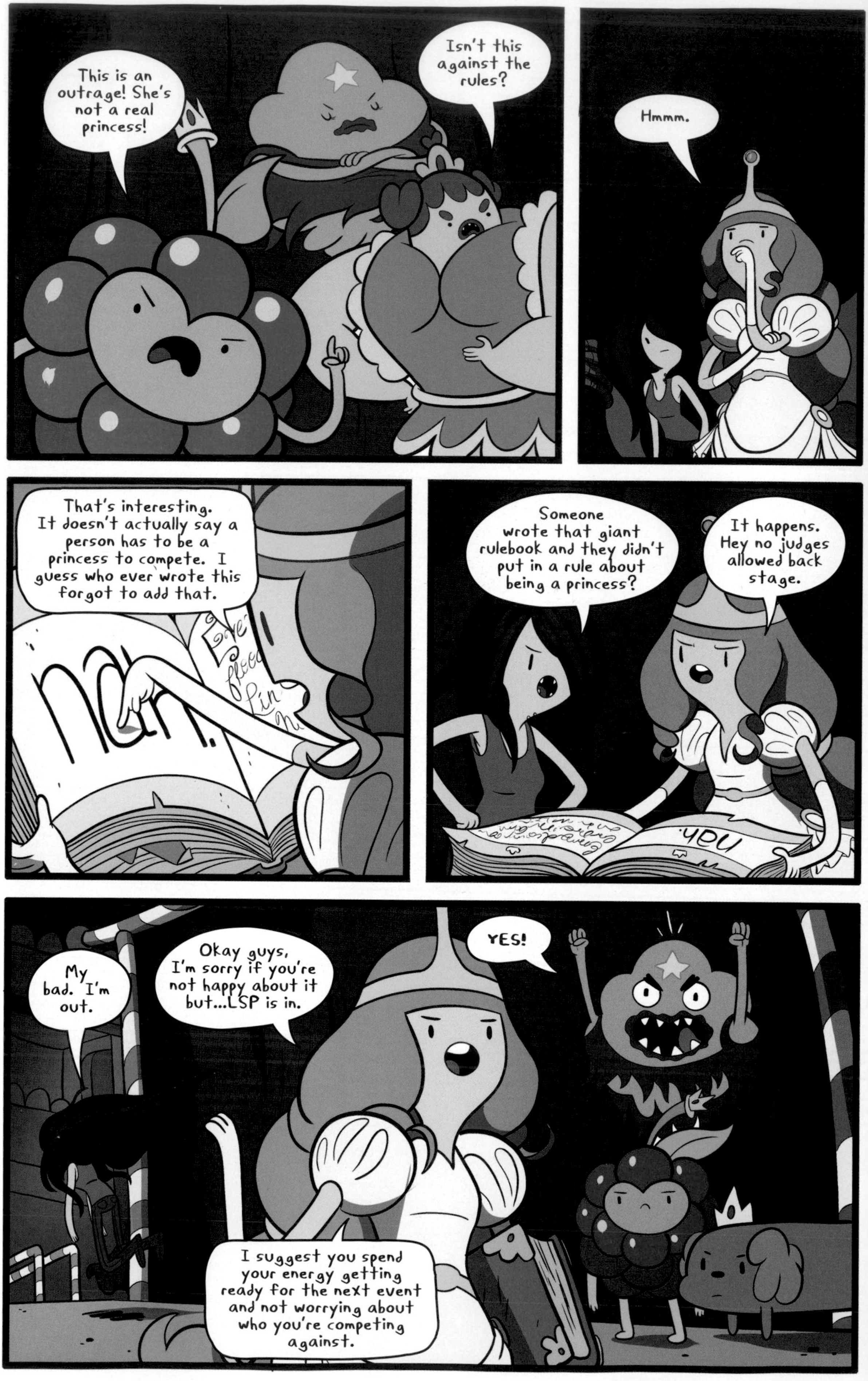

This is an outrage! She's not a real princess!
Isn't this against the rules?
Hmmm.
That's interesting. It doesn't actually say a person has to be a princess to compete. I guess who ever wrote this forgot to add that.
nah.
Someone wrote that giant rulebook and they didn't put in a rule about being a princess?
It happens. Hey no judges allowed back stage.
My bad. I'm out.
Okay guys, I'm sorry if you're not happy about it but...LSP is in.
YES!
I suggest you spend your energy getting ready for the next event and not worrying about who you're competing against.

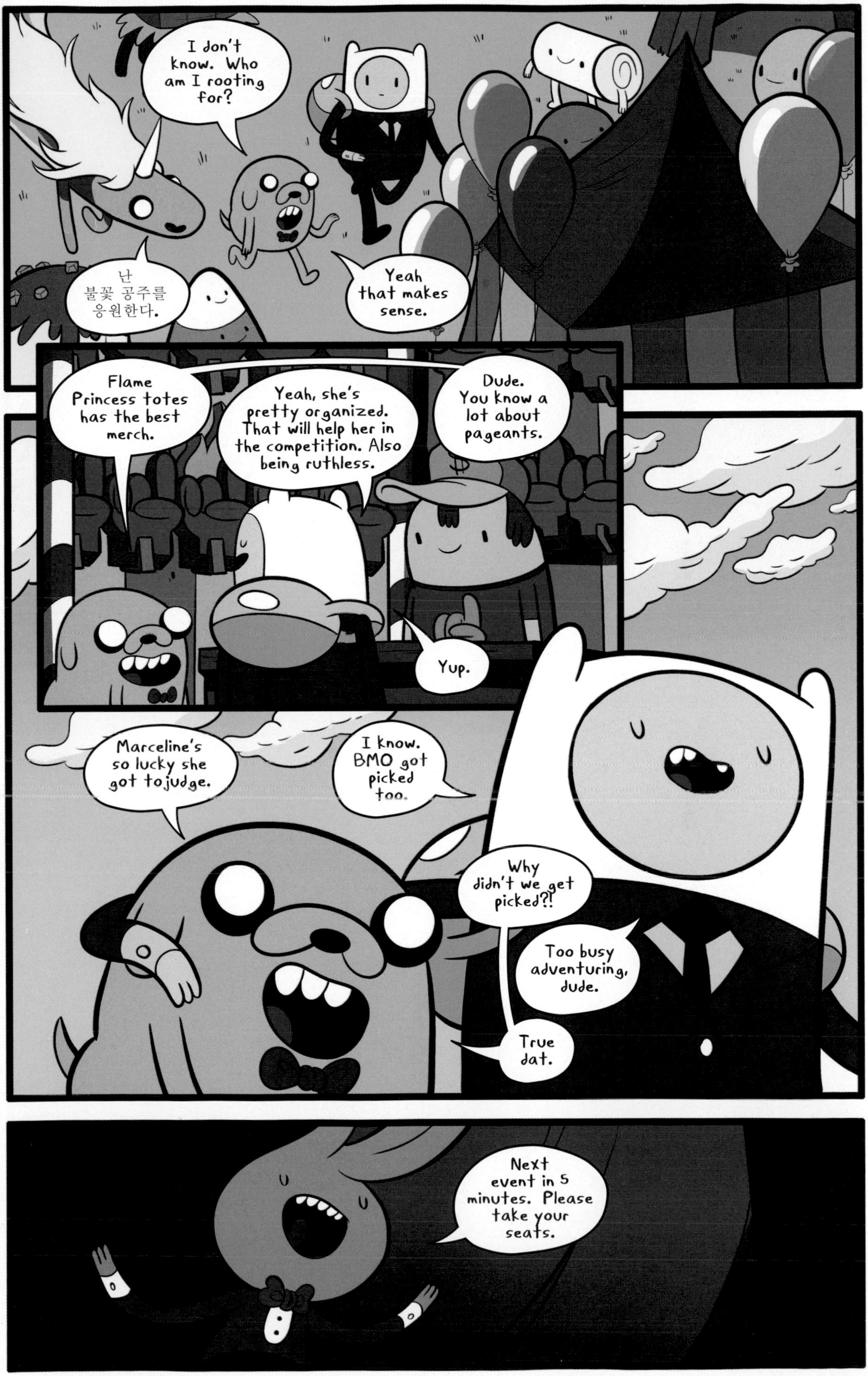

I don't know. Who am I rooting for?
난 불꽃 공주를 응원한다.
Yeah that makes sense.
Flame Princess totes has the best merch.
Yeah, she's pretty organized. That will help her in the competition. Also being ruthless.
Dude. You know a lot about pageants.
Yup.
Marceline's so lucky she got to judge.
I know. BMO got picked too.
Why didn't we get picked?!
Too busy adventuring, dude.
True dat.
Next event in 5 minutes. Please take your seats.

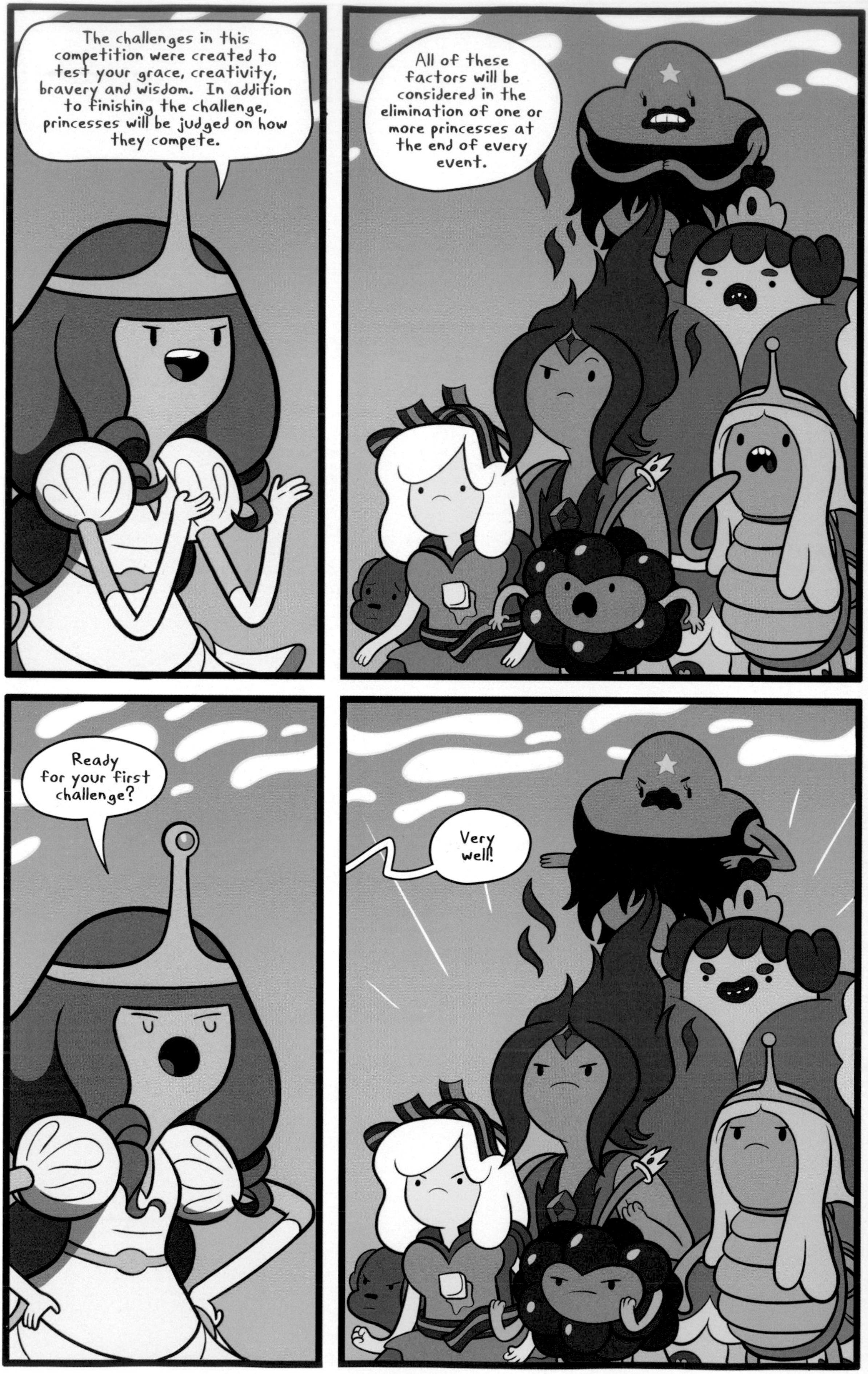
The challenges in this competition were created to test your grace, creativity, bravery and wisdom. In addition to finishing the challenge, princesses will be judged on how they compete.
All of these factors will be considered in the elimination of one or more princesses at the end of every event.
Ready for your first challenge?
Very well!

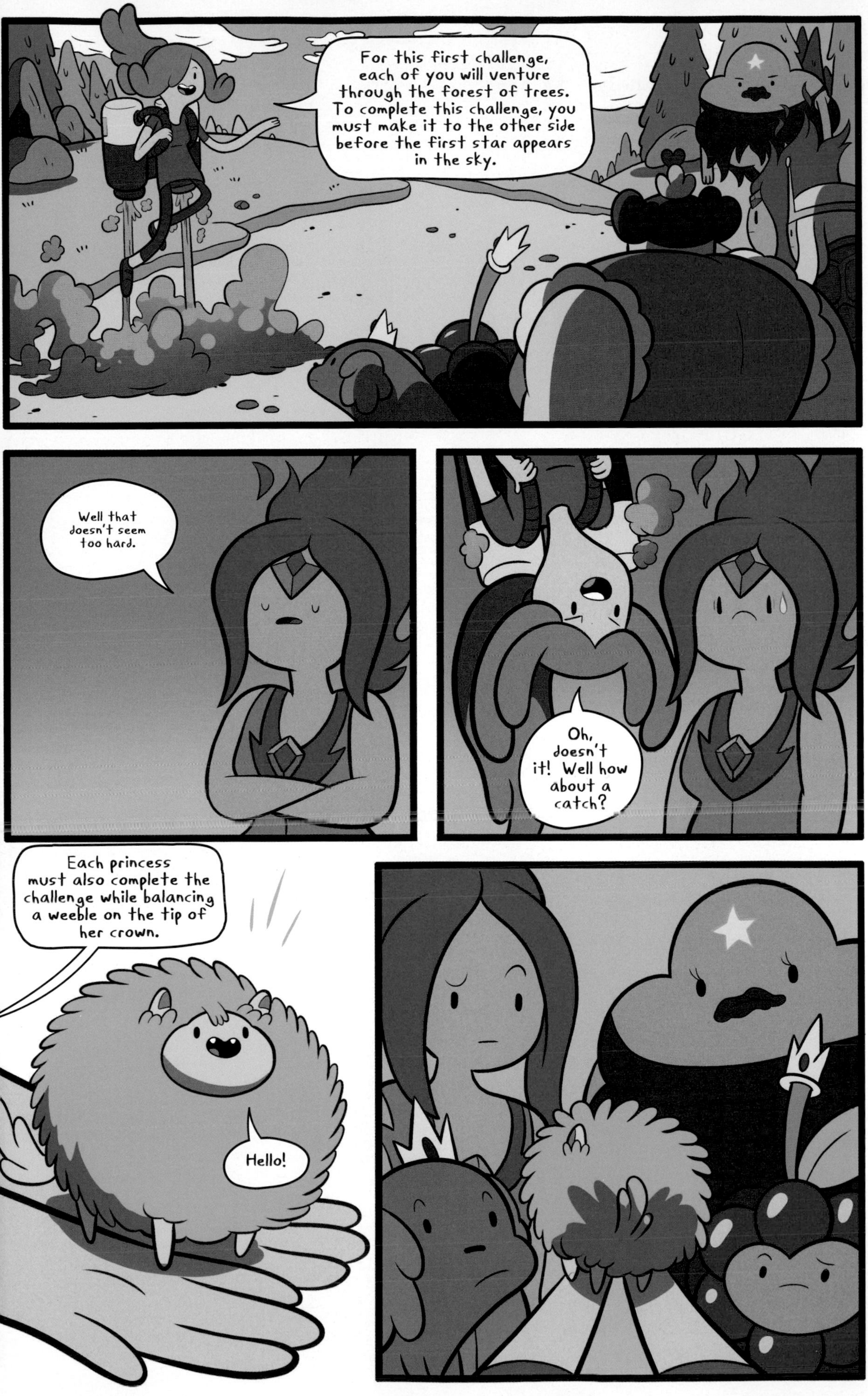
For this first challenge, each of you will venture through the forest of trees. To complete this challenge, you must make it to the other side before the first star appears in the sky.
Well that doesn't seem too hard.
Oh, doesn't it! Well how about a catch?
Each princess must also complete the challenge while balancing a weeble on the tip of her crown.
Hello!

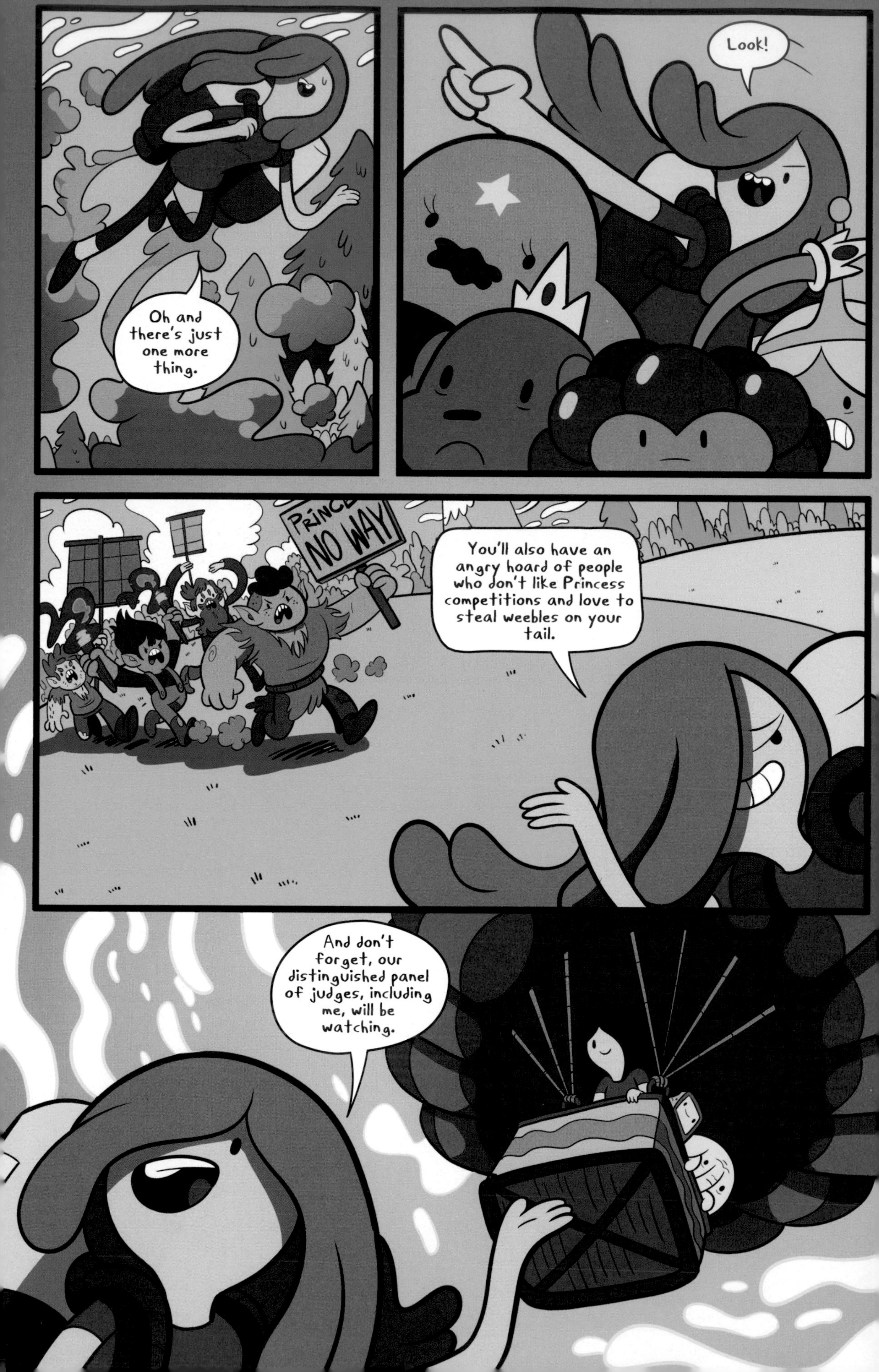
Oh and there's just one more thing.
Look!
PRINCE
NO WAY
You'll also have an angry hoard of people who don't like Princess competitions and love to steal weebles on your tail.
And don't forget, our distinguished panel of judges, including me, will be watching.

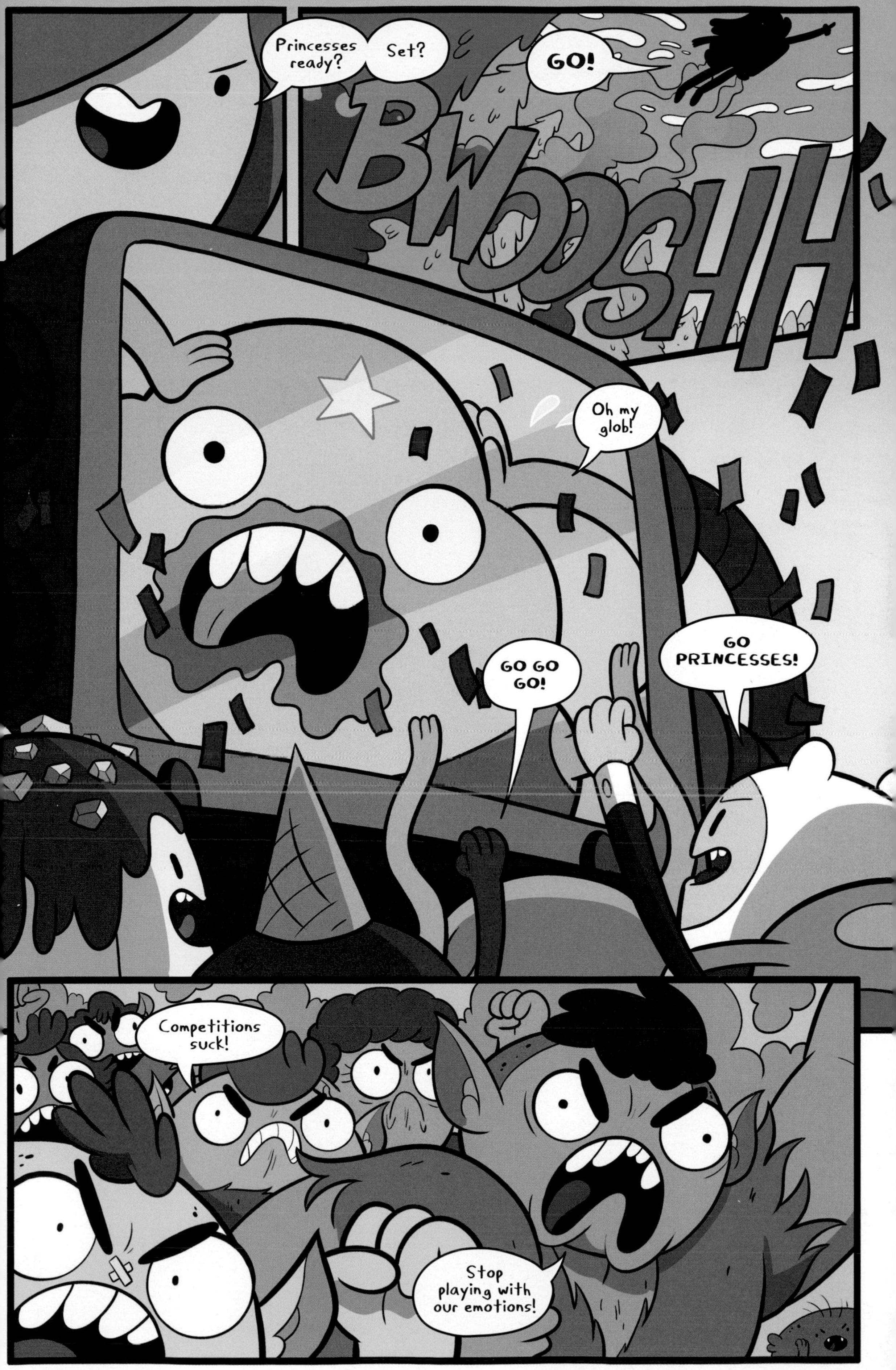

Princesses ready?
Set?
GO!
BWOOSHH
Oh my glob!
GO GO GO!
GO PRINCESSES!
Competitions suck!
Stop playing with our emotions!

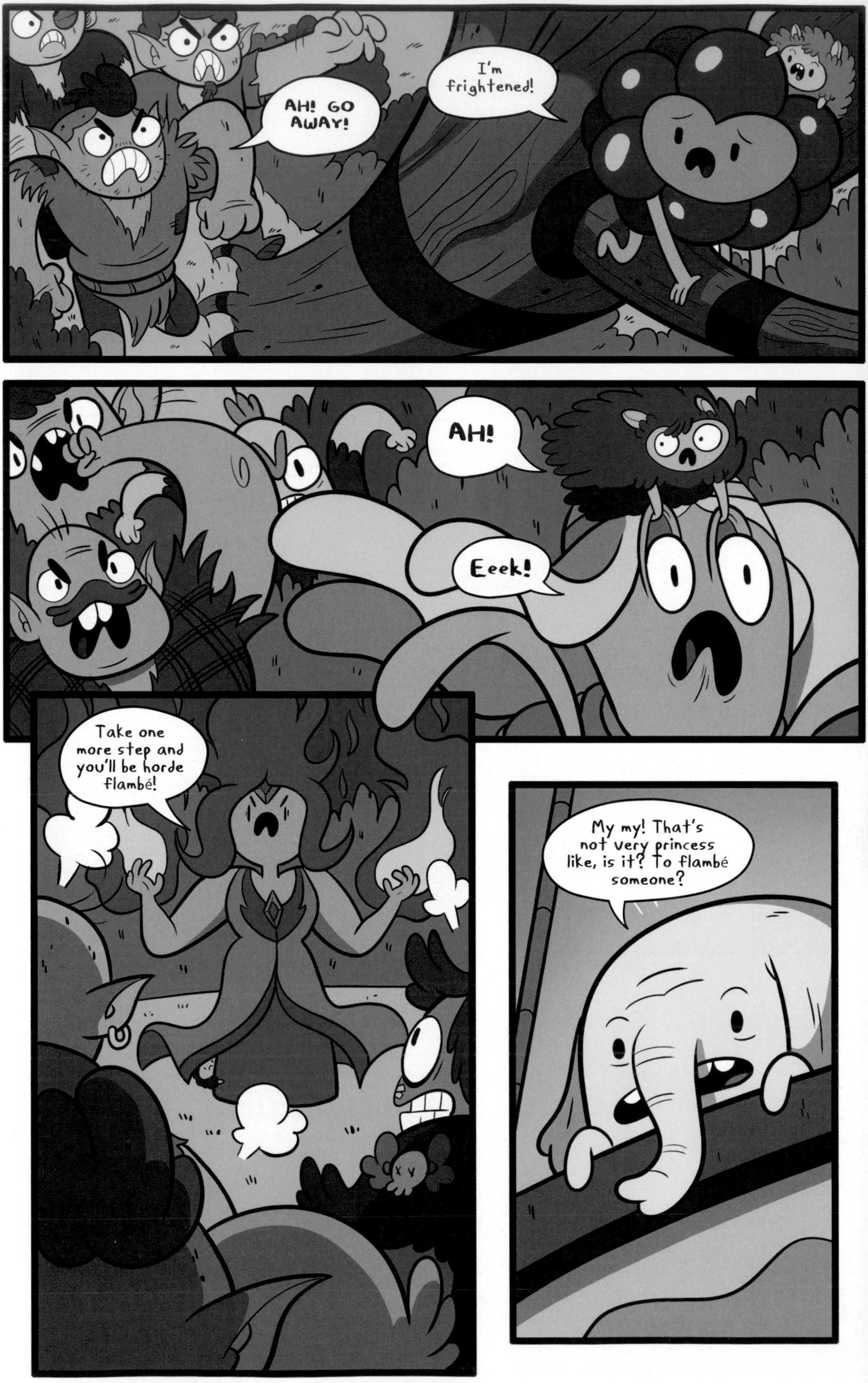
AH! GO AWAY!
I'm frightened!
AH!
Eeek!
Take one more step and you'll be horde flambé!
My my! That's not very princess like, is it? To flambé someone?

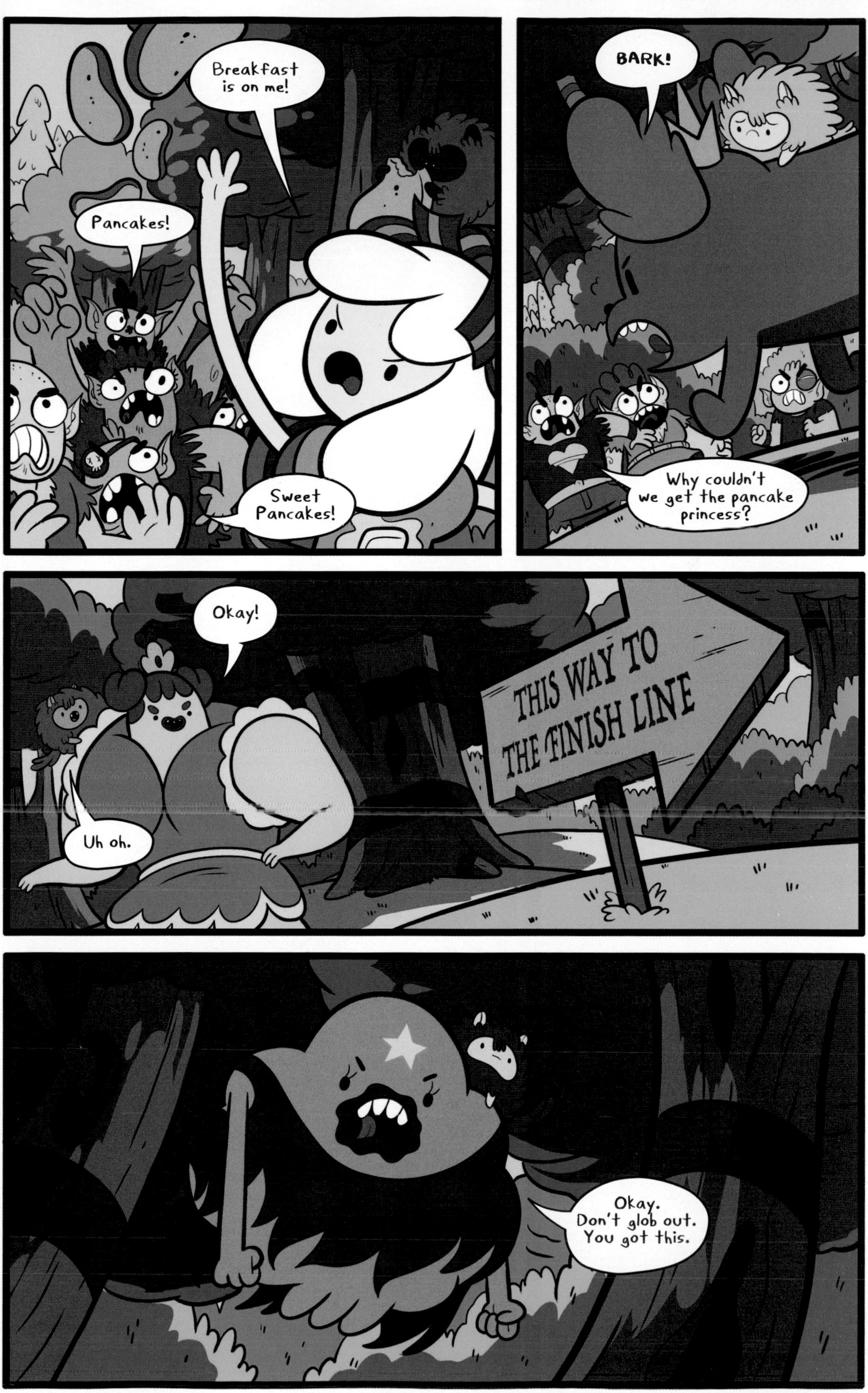
Breakfast is on me!
Pancakes!
Sweet Pancakes!
BARK!
Why couldn't we get the pancake princess?
Okay!
THIS WAY TO THE FINISH LINE
Uh oh.
Okay. Don't glob out. You got this.

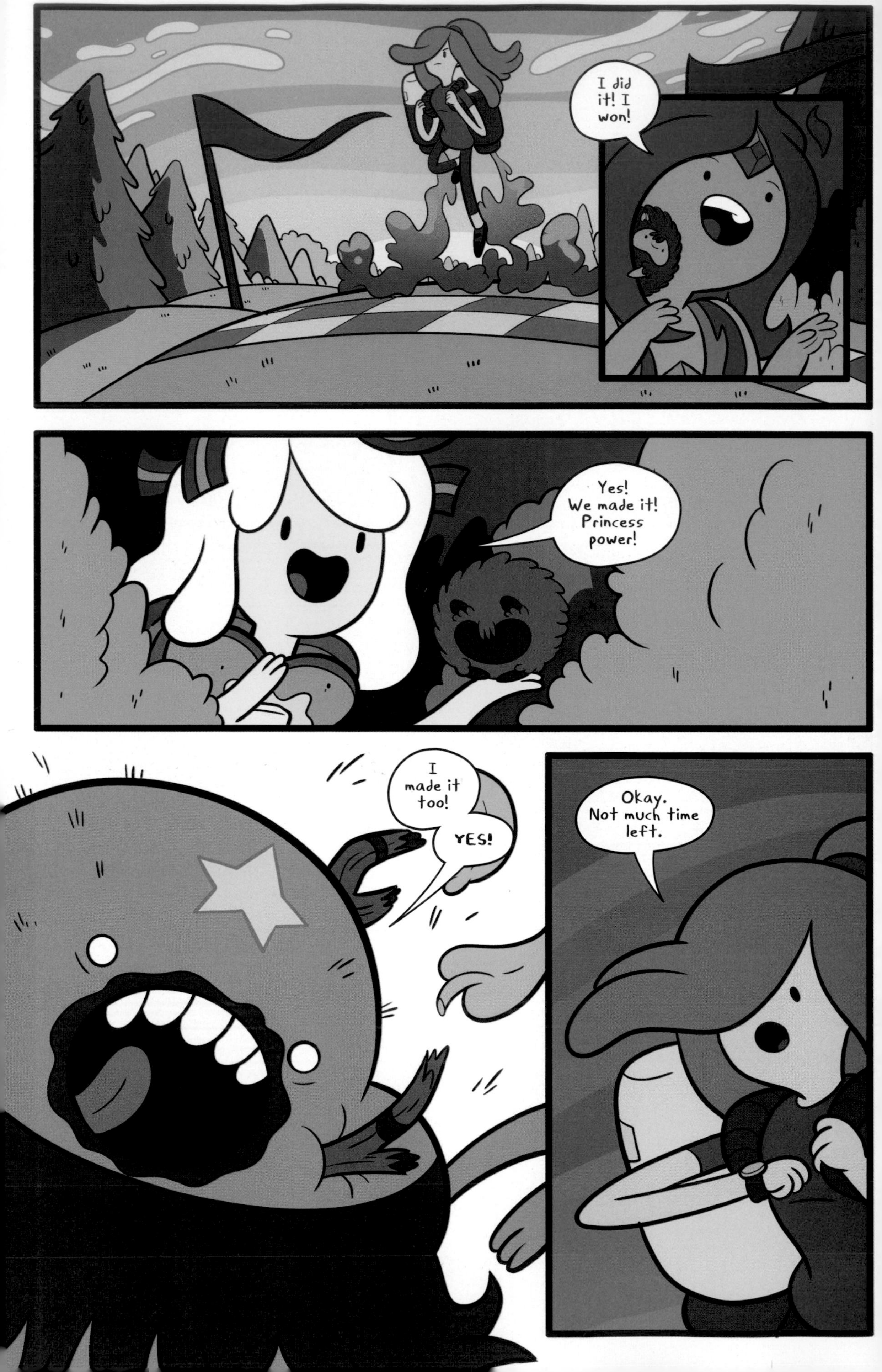
I did it! I won!
Yes! We made it! Princess power!
I made it too!
YES!
Okay. Not much time left.

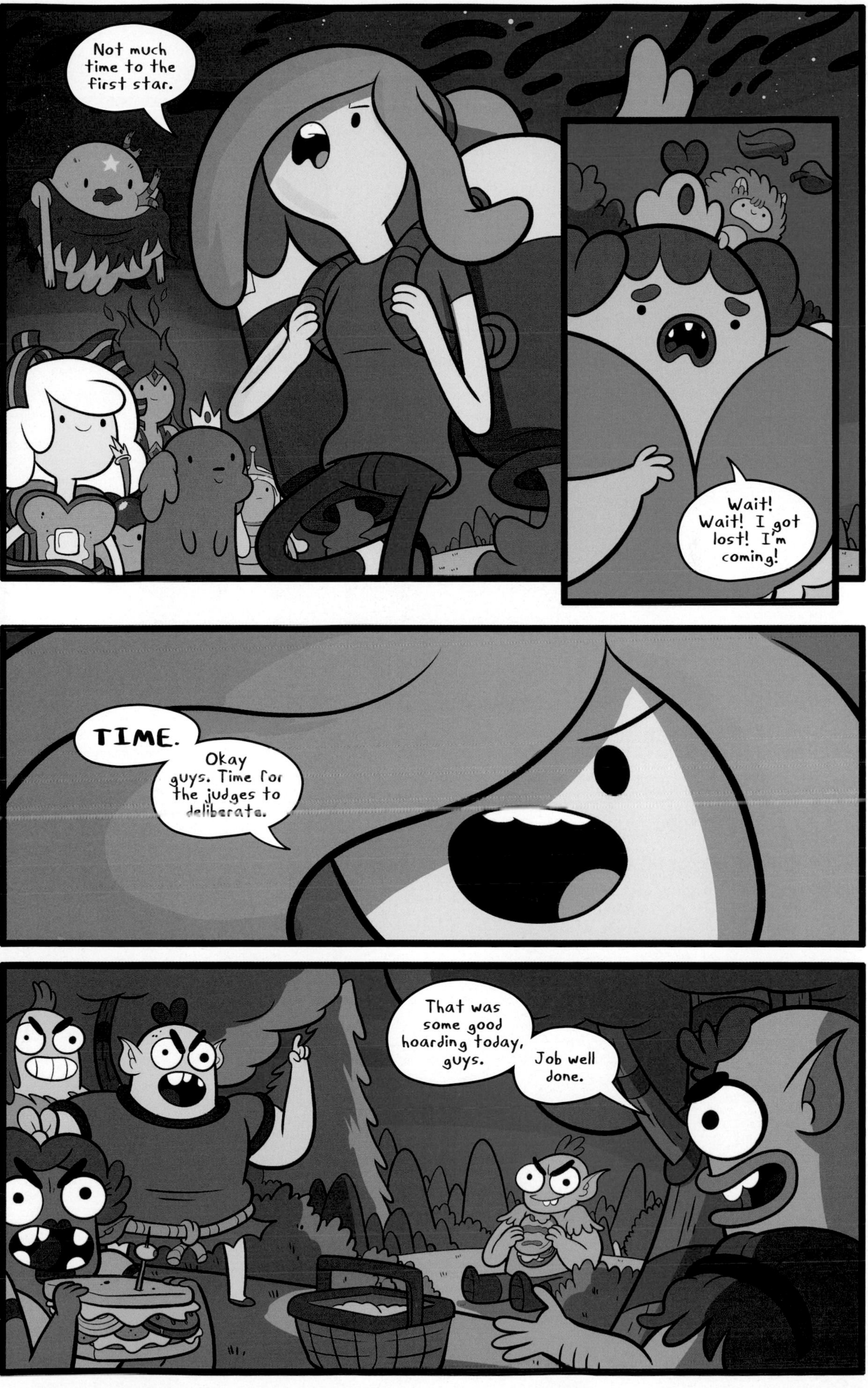

Not much time to the first star.
Wait! Wait! I got lost! I'm coming!
TIME.
Okay guys. Time for the judges to deliberate.
That was some good hoarding today, guys.
Job well done.

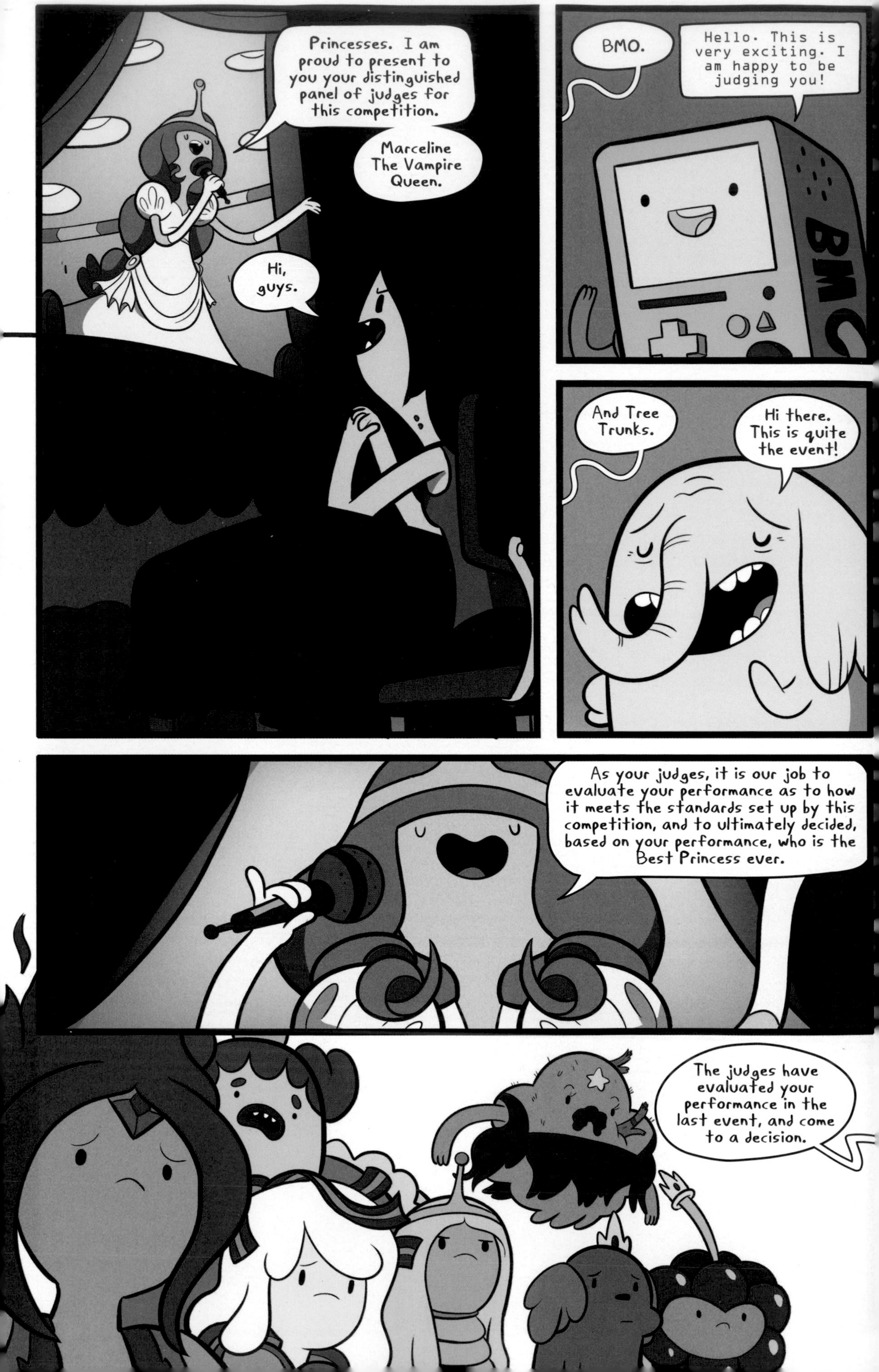

Princesses. I am proud to present to you your distinguished panel of judges for this competition.
Marceline The Vampire Queen.
Hi, guys.
BMO.
Hello. This is very exciting. I am happy to be judging you!
BMO
And Tree Trunks.
Hi there. This is quite the event!
As your judges, it is our job to evaluate your performance as to how it meets the standards set up by this competition, and to ultimately decided, based on your performance, who is the Best Princess ever.
The judges have evaluated your performance in the last event, and come to a decision.

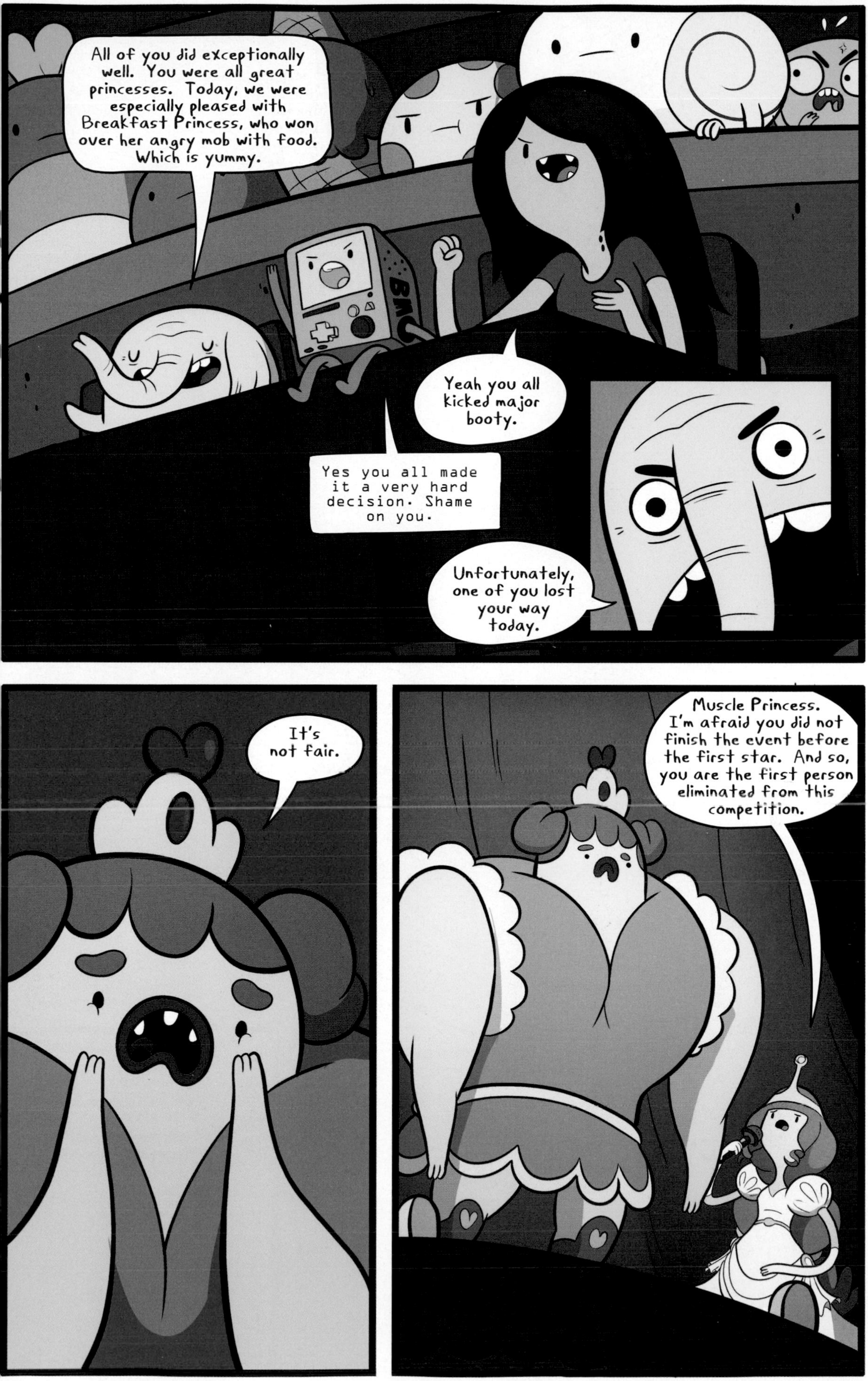
All of you did exceptionally well. You were all great princesses. Today, we were especially pleased with Breakfast Princess, who won over her angry mob with food. Which is yummy.
Yeah you all kicked major booty.
Yes you all made it a very hard decision. Shame on you.
Unfortunately, one of you lost your way today.
BMO
It's not fair.
Muscle Princess. I'm afraid you did not finish the event before the first star. And so, you are the first person eliminated from this competition.

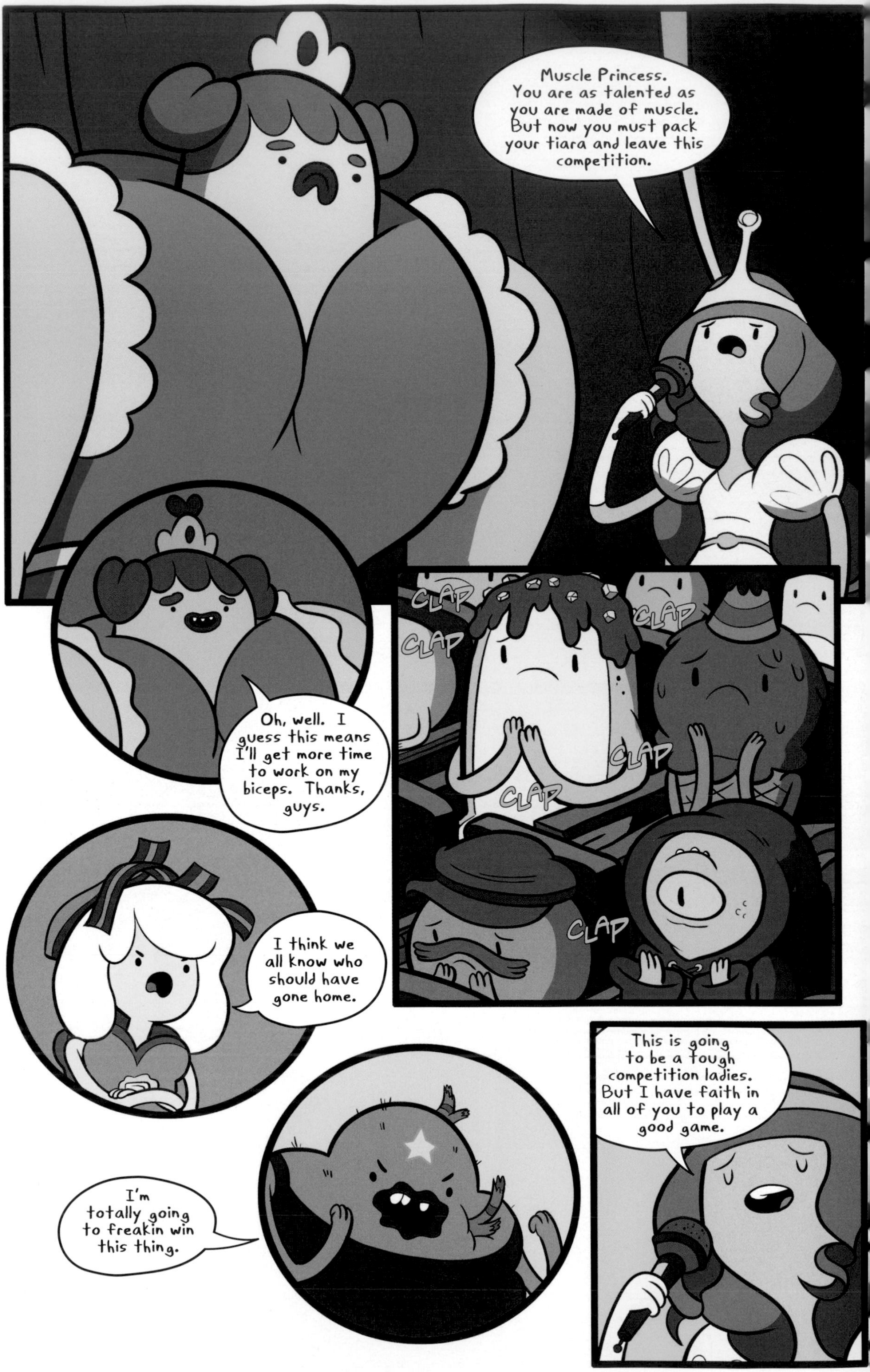
Muscle Princess. You are as talented as you are made of muscle. But now you must pack your tiara and leave this competition.
Oh, well. I guess this means I'll get more time to work on my biceps. Thanks, guys.
CLAP
CLAP
CLAP
CLAP
CLAP
CLAP
I think we all know who should have gone home.
This is going to be a tough competition ladies. But I have faith in all of you to play a good game.
I'm totally going to freakin win this thing.

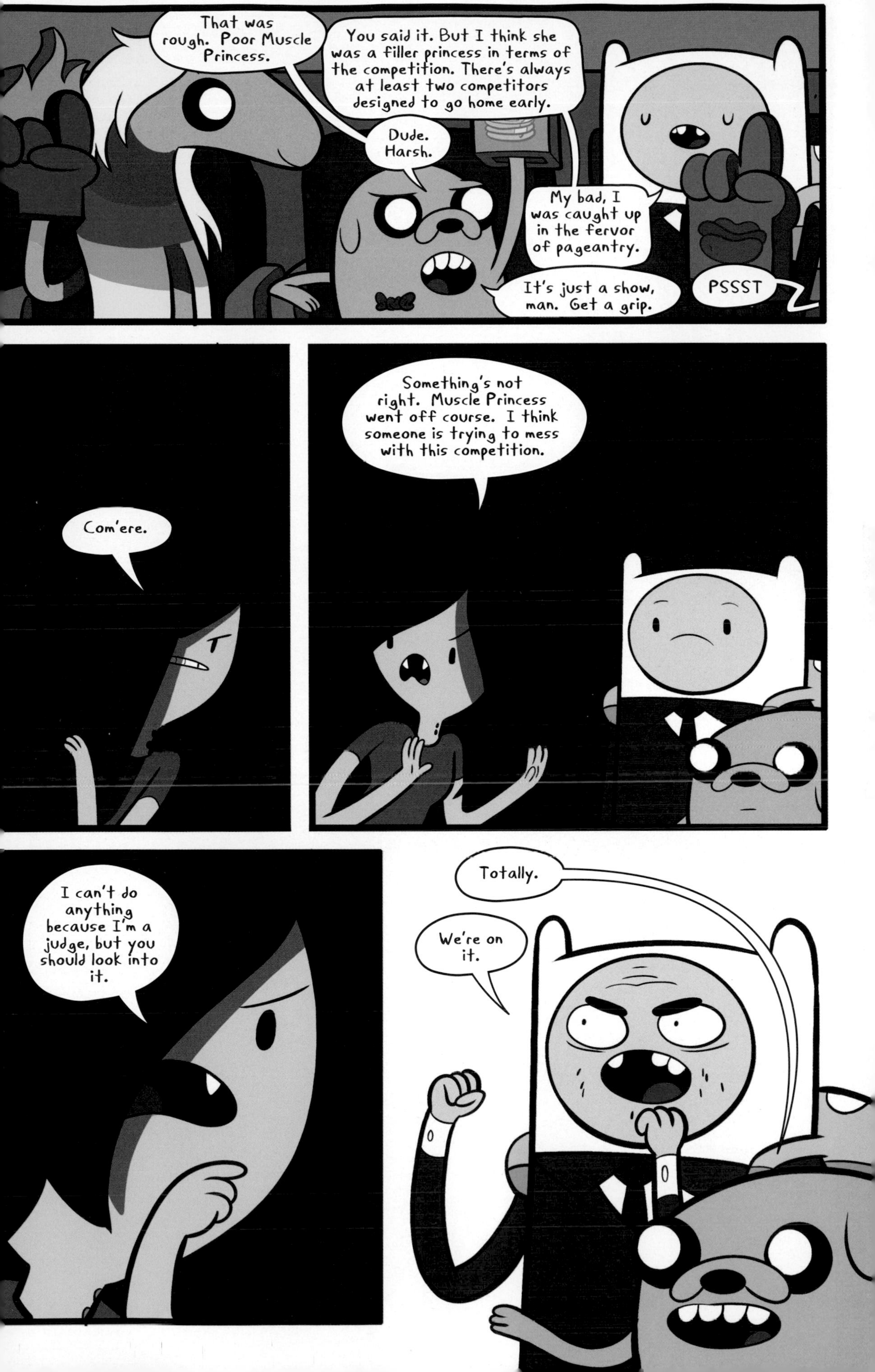
That was rough. Poor Muscle Princess.
You said it. But I think she was a filler princess in terms of the competition. There's always at least two competitors designed to go home early.
Dude. Harsh.
My bad, I was caught up in the fervor of pageantry.
It's just a show, man. Get a grip.
PSSST
Com'ere.
Something's not right. Muscle Princess went off course. I think someone is trying to mess with this competition.
I can't do anything because I'm a judge, but you should look into it.
Totally.
We're on it.

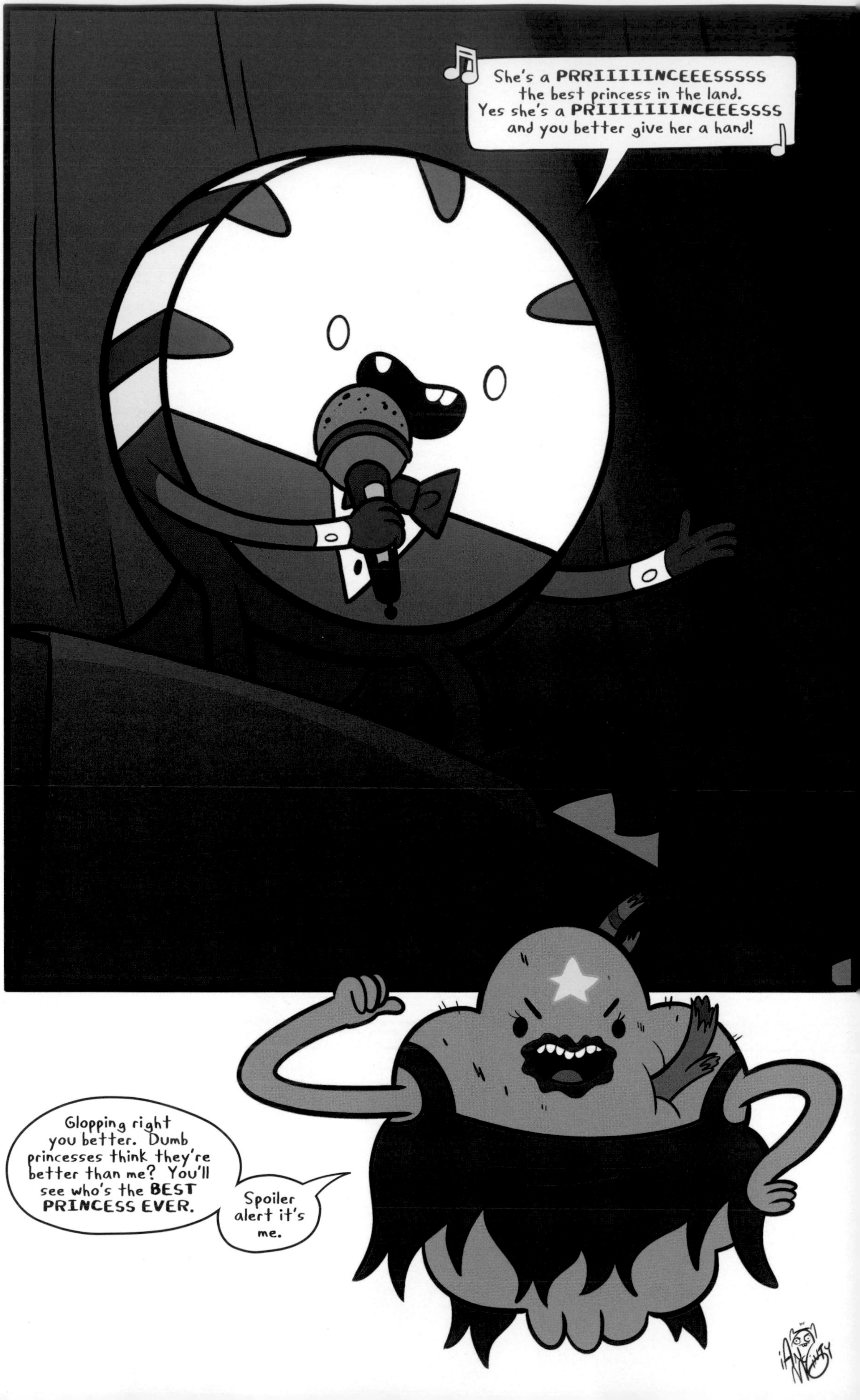

She's a PRRIIIIIINCEEEESSSSS the best princess in the land. Yes she's a PRIIIIIIINCEEEESSSS and you better give her a hand!
Glopping right you better. Dumb princesses think they're better than me? You'll see who's the BEST PRINCESS EVER.
Spoiler alert it's me.

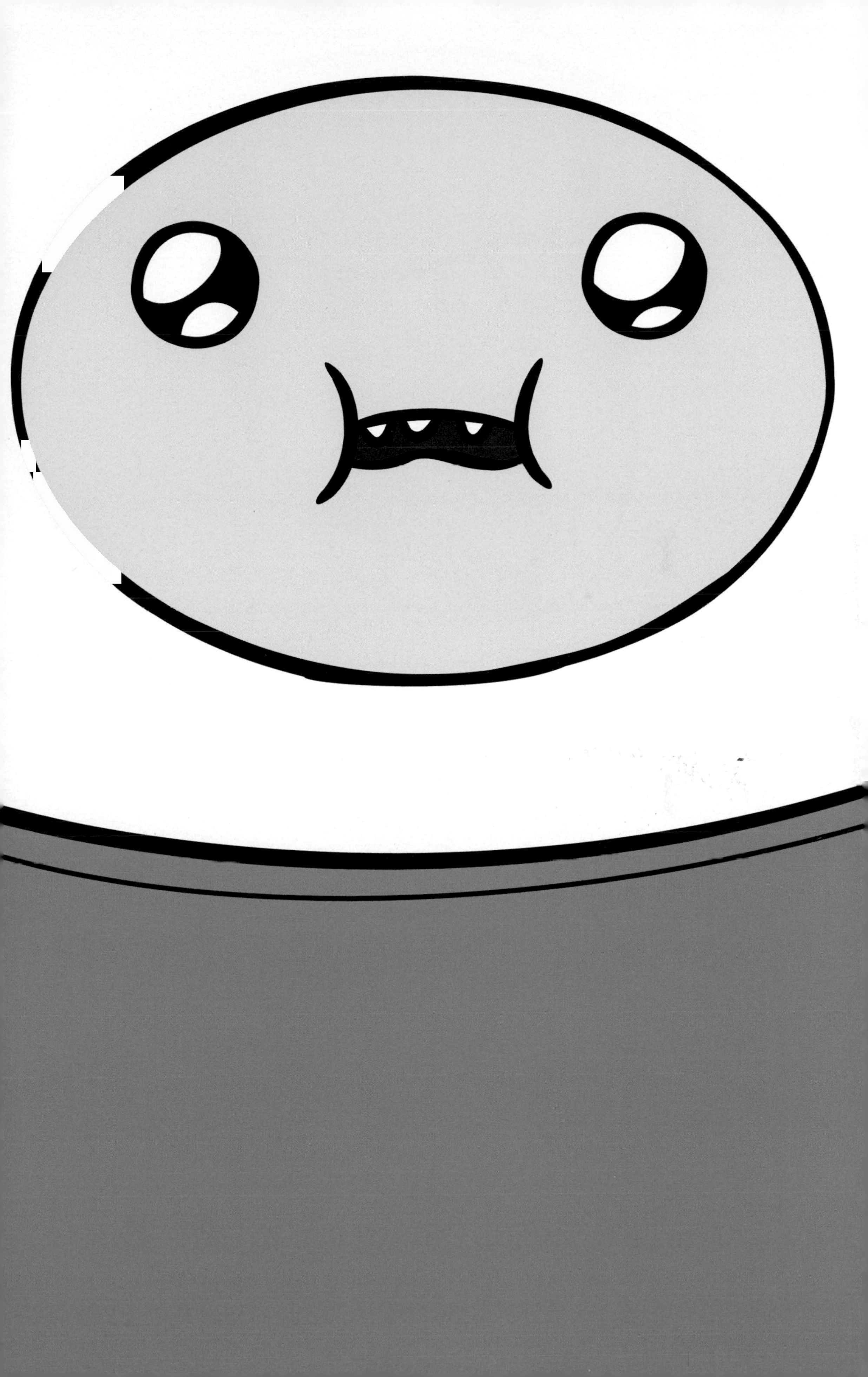

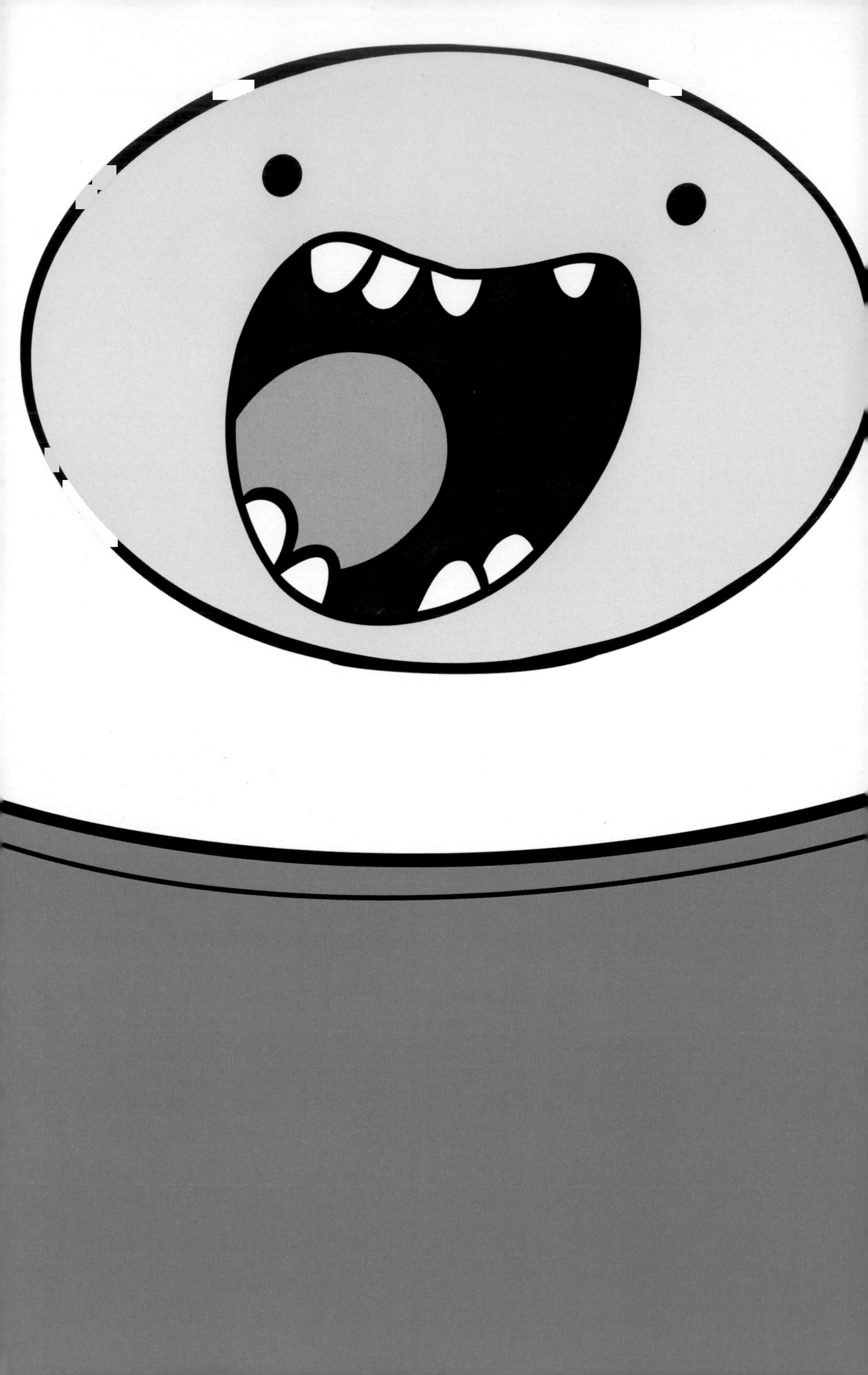

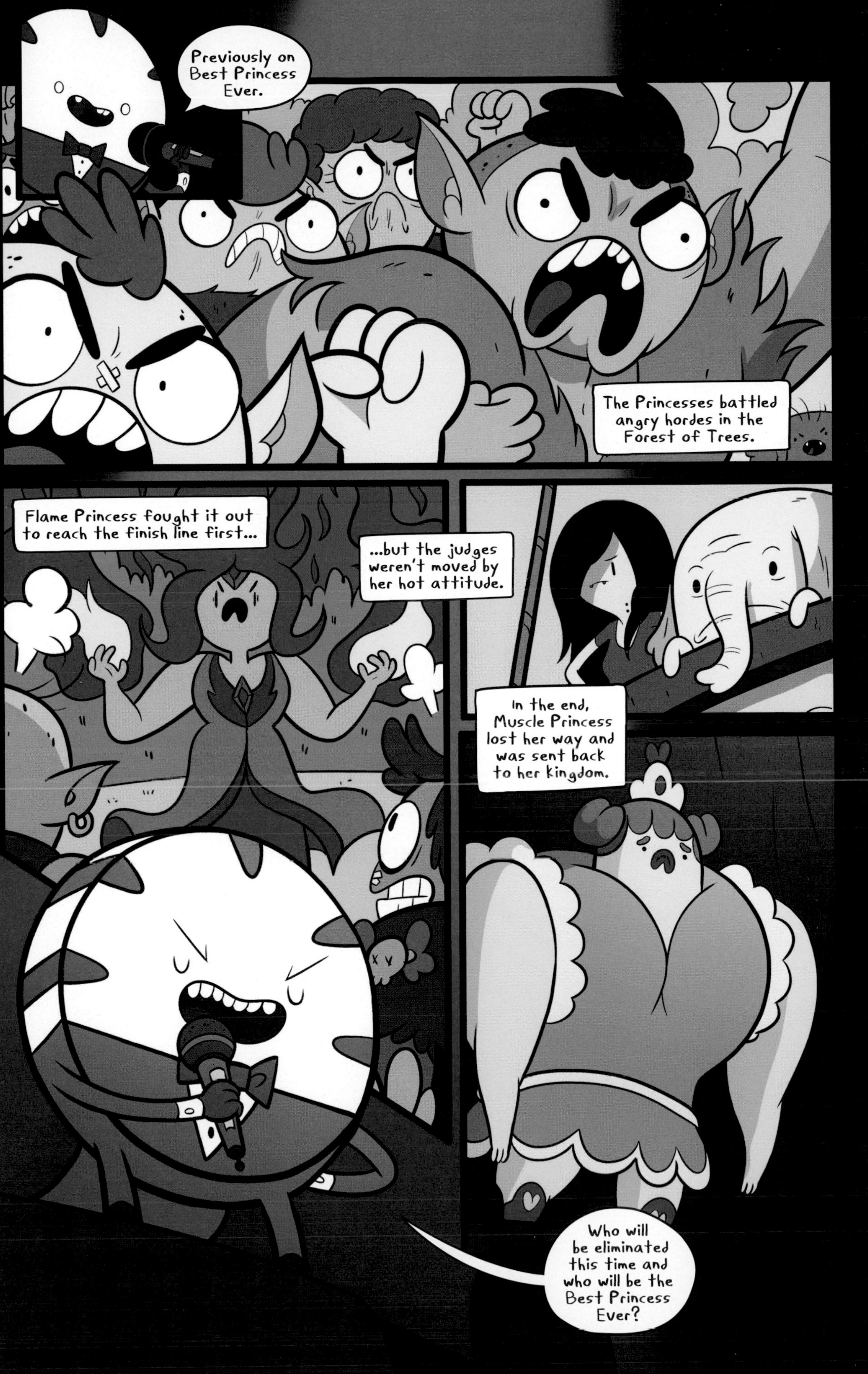
Previously on Best Princess Ever.
The Princesses battled angry hordes in the Forest of Trees.
Flame Princess fought it out to reach the finish line first...
...but the judges weren't moved by her hot attitude.
In the end, Muscle Princess lost her way and was sent back to her kingdom.
Who will be eliminated this time and who will be the Best Princess Ever?

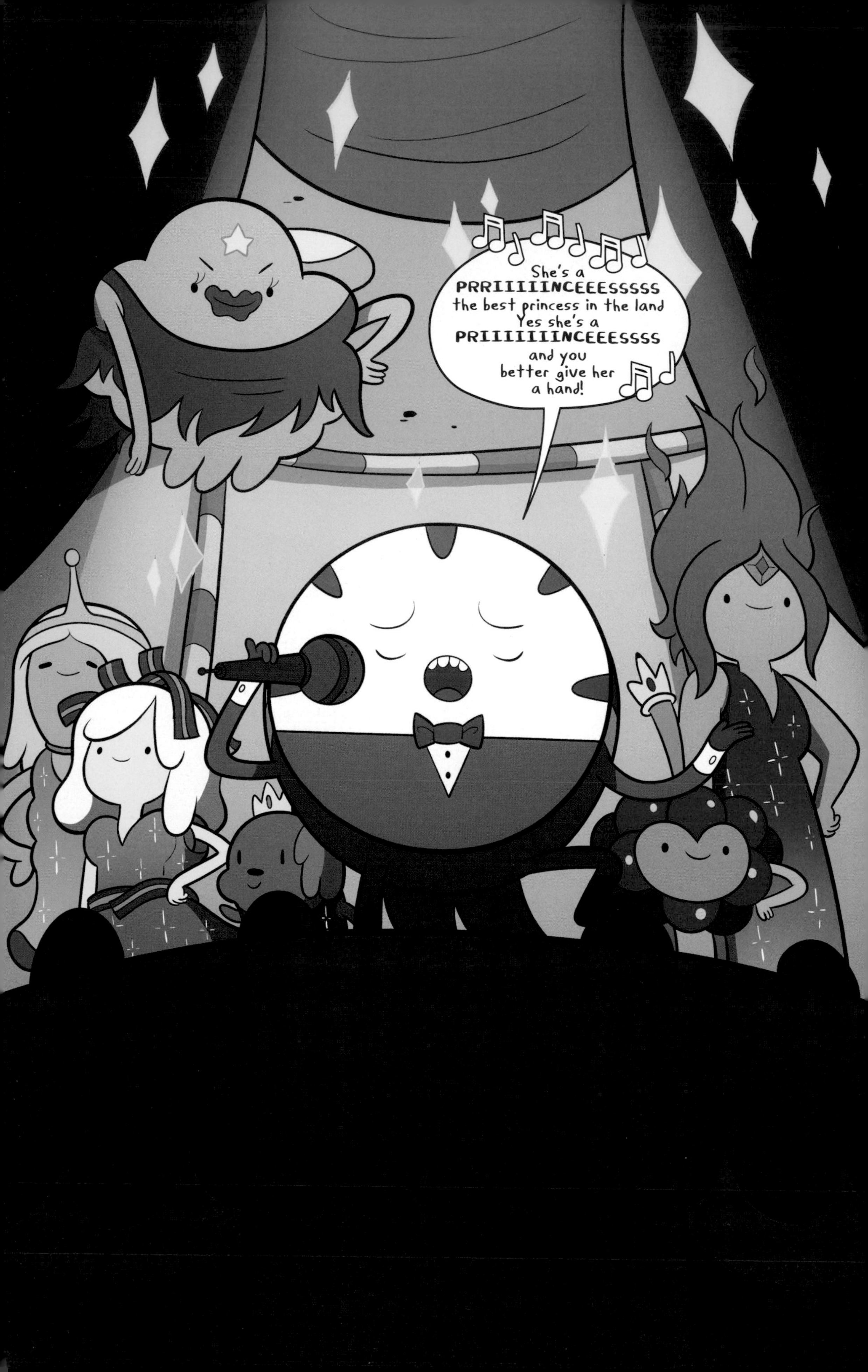
She's a PRRIIIIIINCEEEESSSSS the best princess in the land Yes she's a PRIIIIIIIINCEEEESSSS and you better give her a hand!

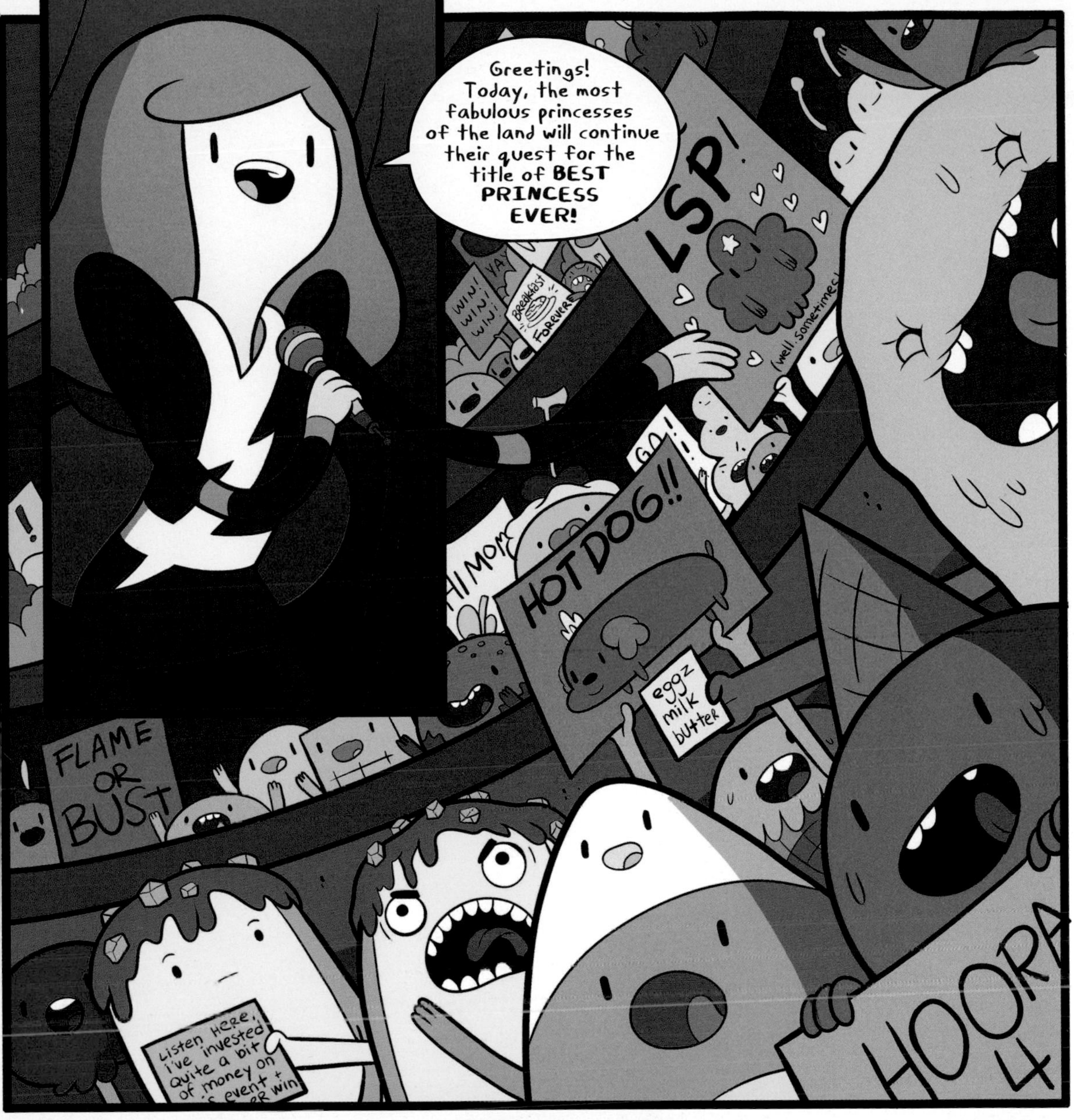
Greetings! Today, the most fabulous princesses of the land will continue their quest for the title of **BEST PRINCESS EVER!**
LSP!
(well, sometimes)
WIN! WIN! WIN!
YAY
Breakfast FOREVER
HOT DOG!!
HI MOM
eggz milk butter
FLAME OR BUST

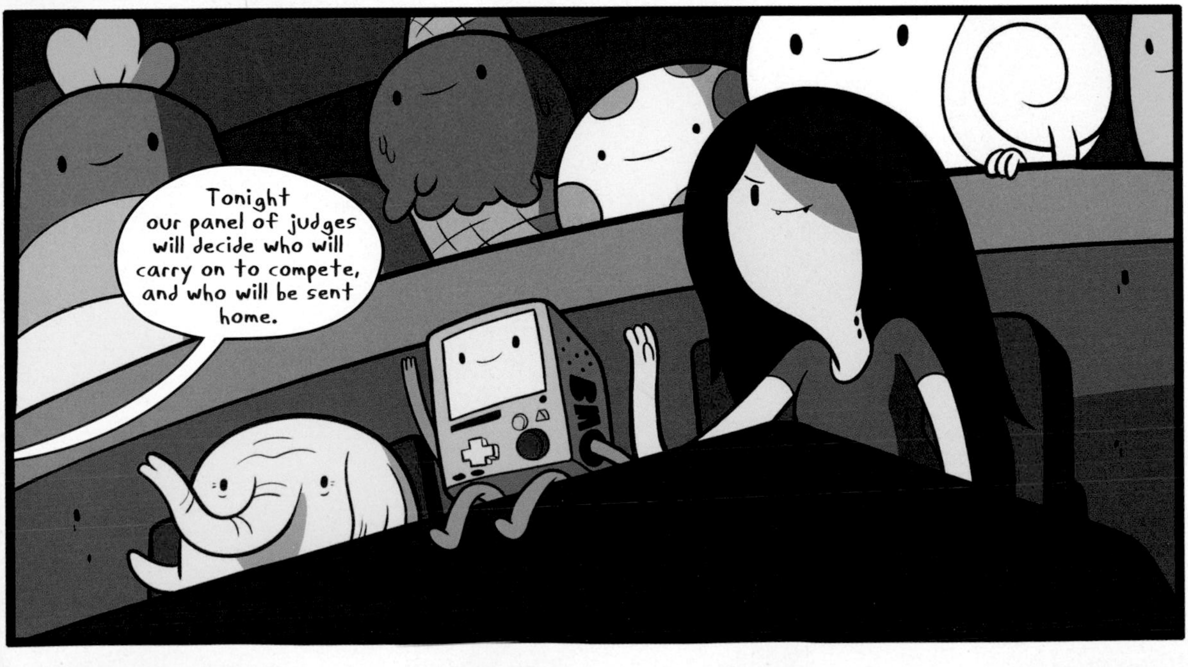
Tonight our panel of judges will decide who will carry on to compete, and who will be sent home.

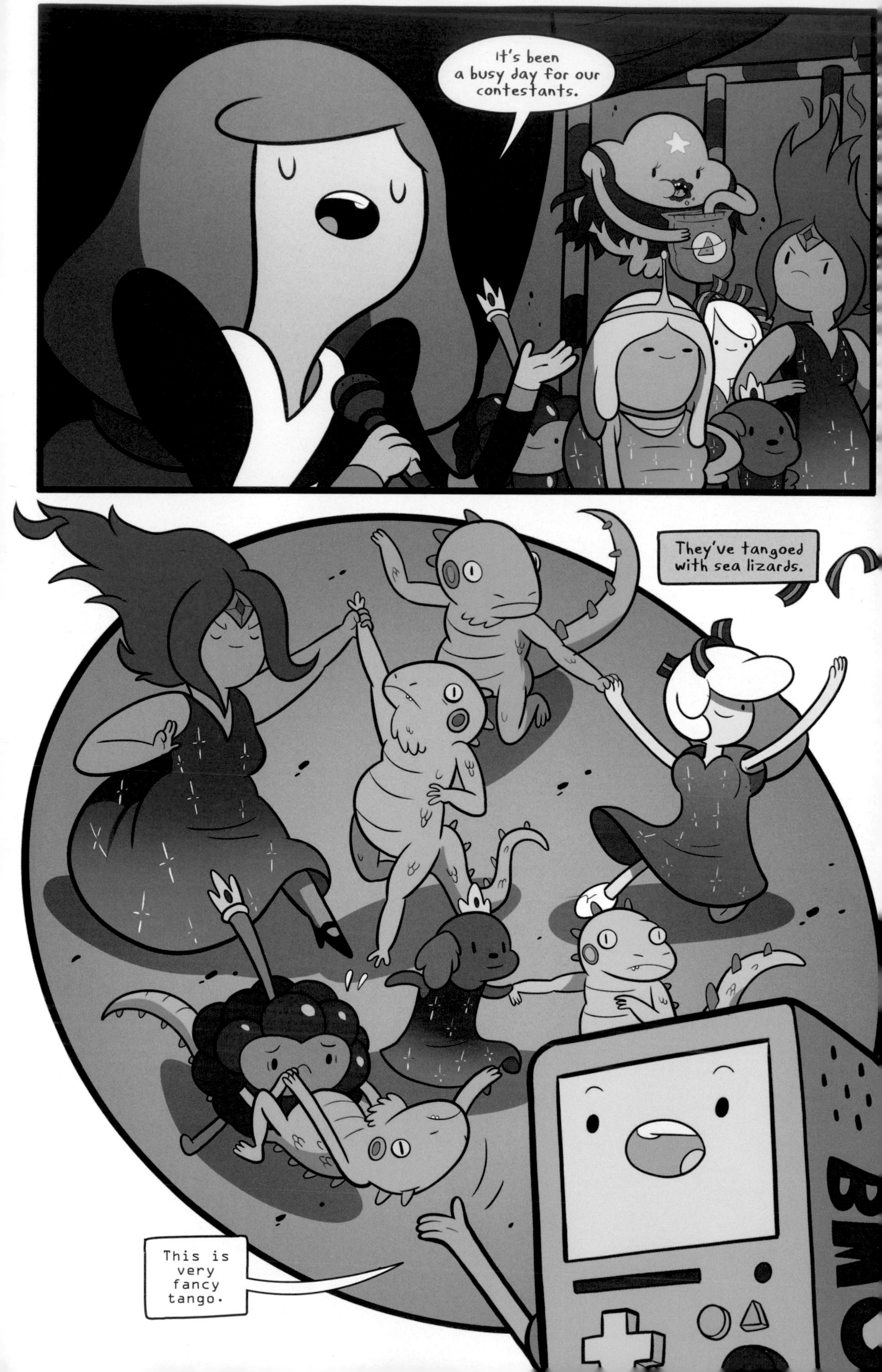
It's been a busy day for our contestants.
They've tangoed with sea lizards.
This is very fancy tango.
BMO

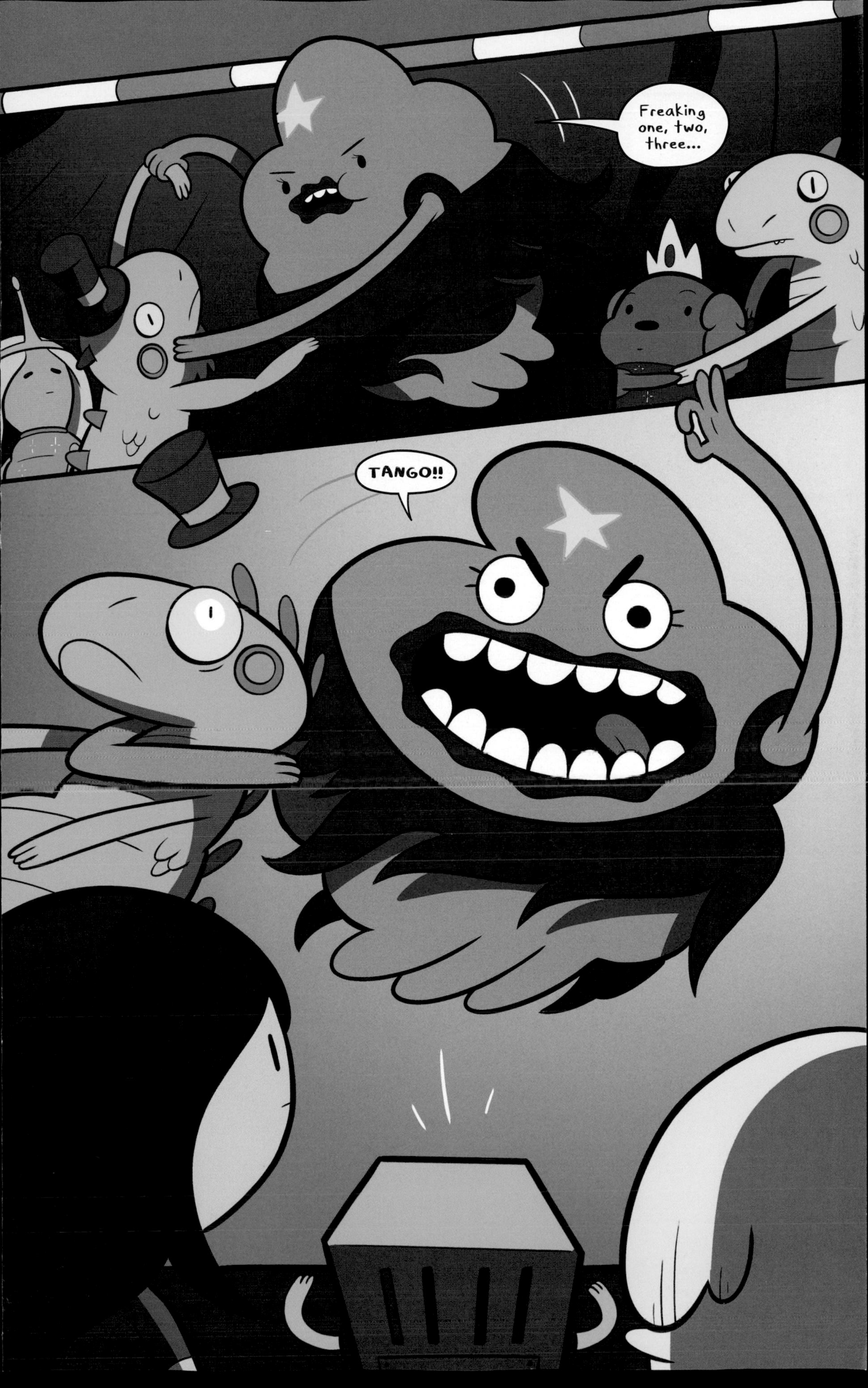

Freaking one, two, three...
TANGO!!

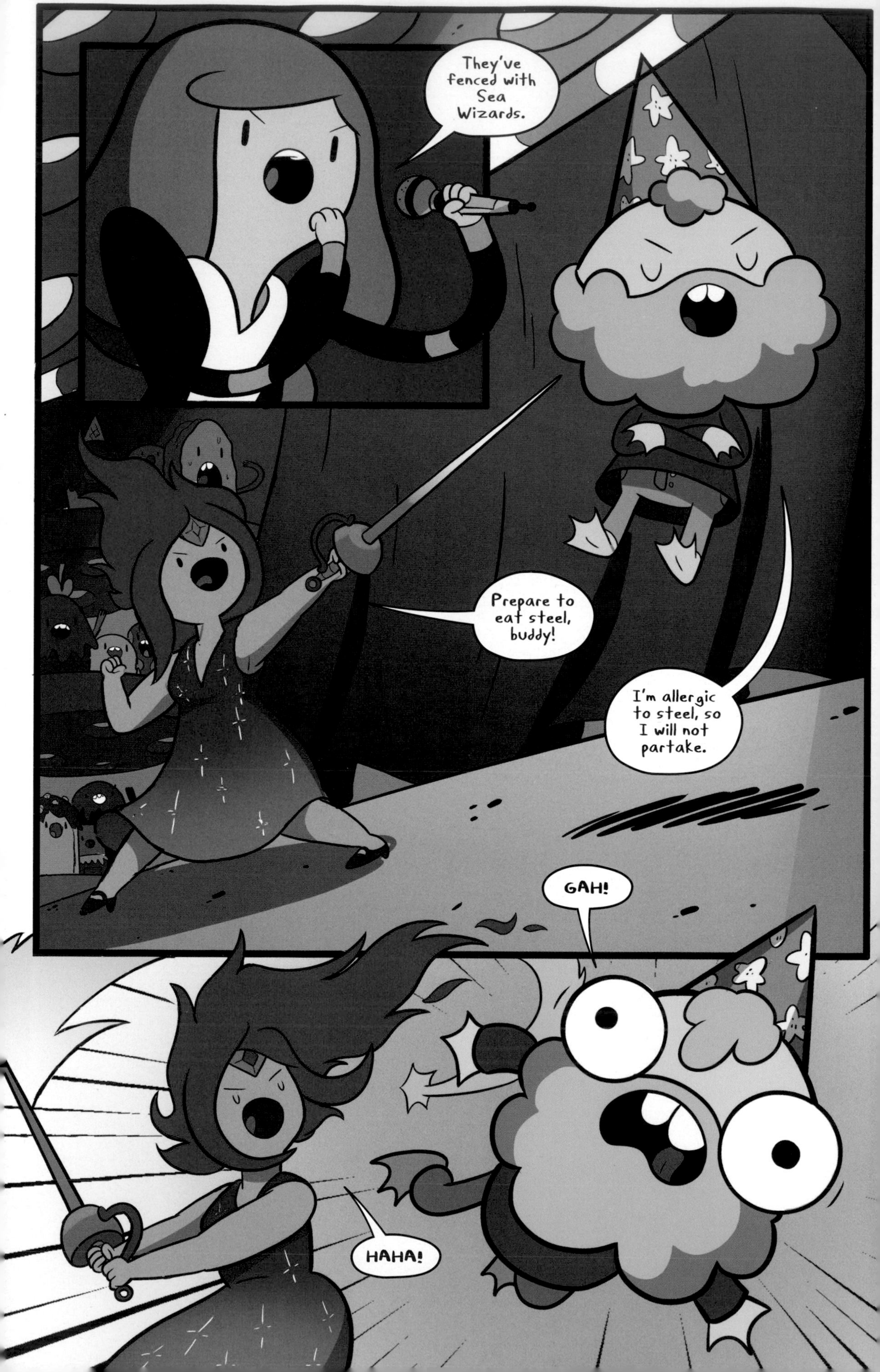
They've fenced with Sea Wizards.
Prepare to eat steel, buddy!
I'm allergic to steel, so I will not partake.
GAH!
HAHA!

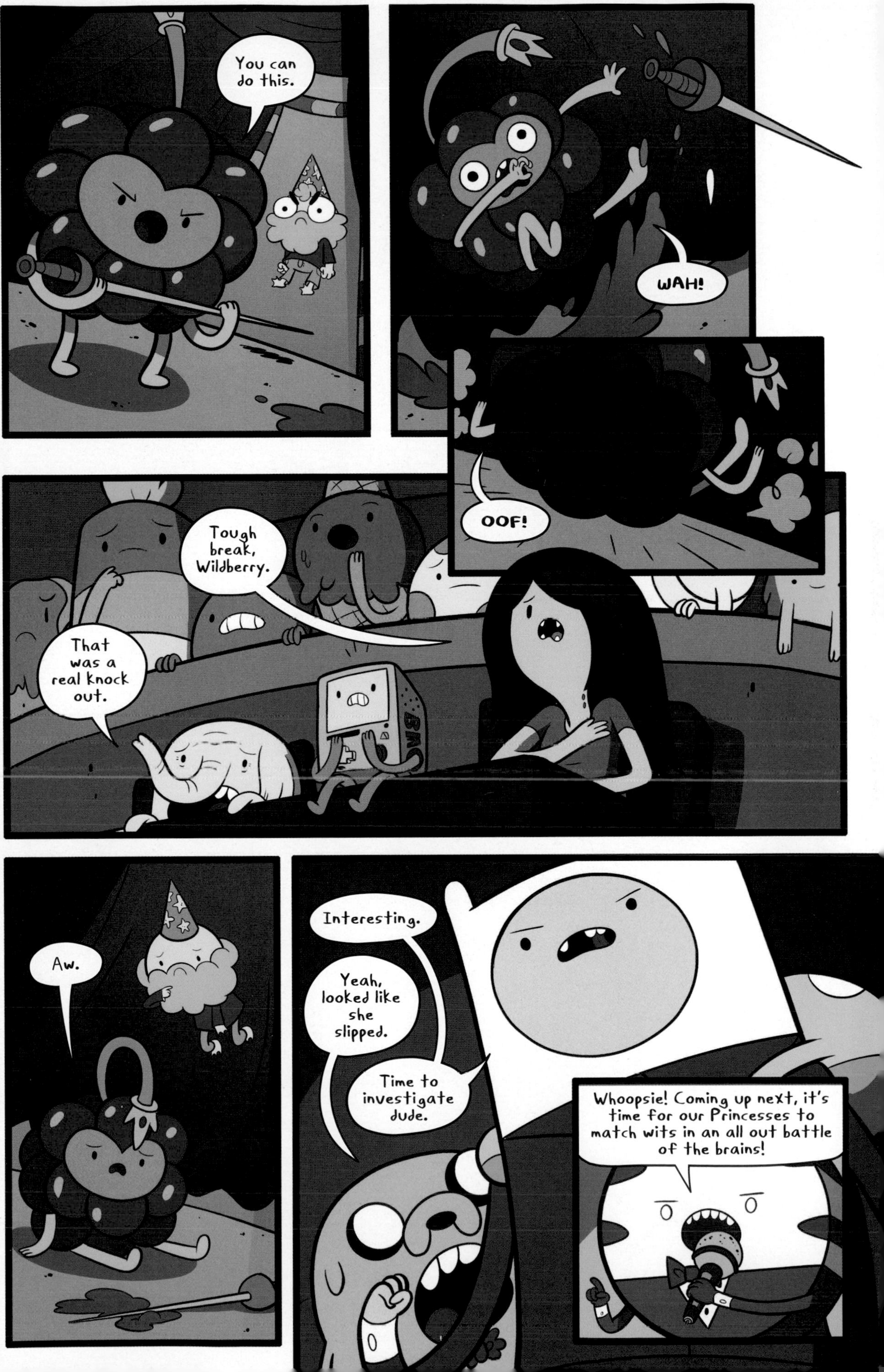
You can do this.
WAH!
OOF!
Tough break, Wildberry.
That was a real knock out.
Aw.
Interesting.
Yeah, looked like she slipped.
Time to investigate dude.
Whoopsie! Coming up next, it's time for our Princesses to match wits in an all out battle of the brains!

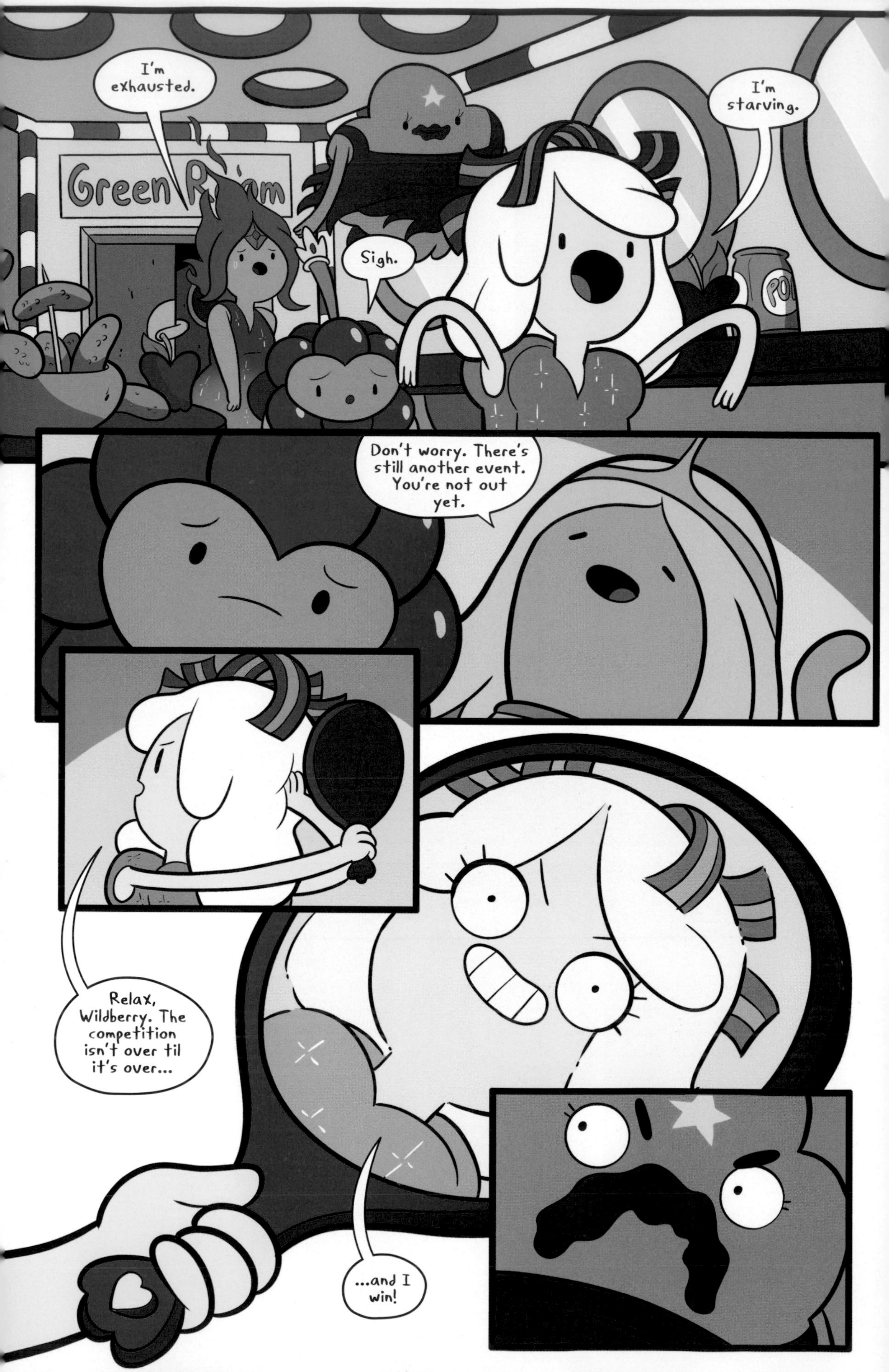
Green Room
I'm exhausted.
Sigh.
I'm starving.
Don't worry. There's still another event. You're not out yet.
Relax, Wildberry. The competition isn't over til it's over...
...and I win!

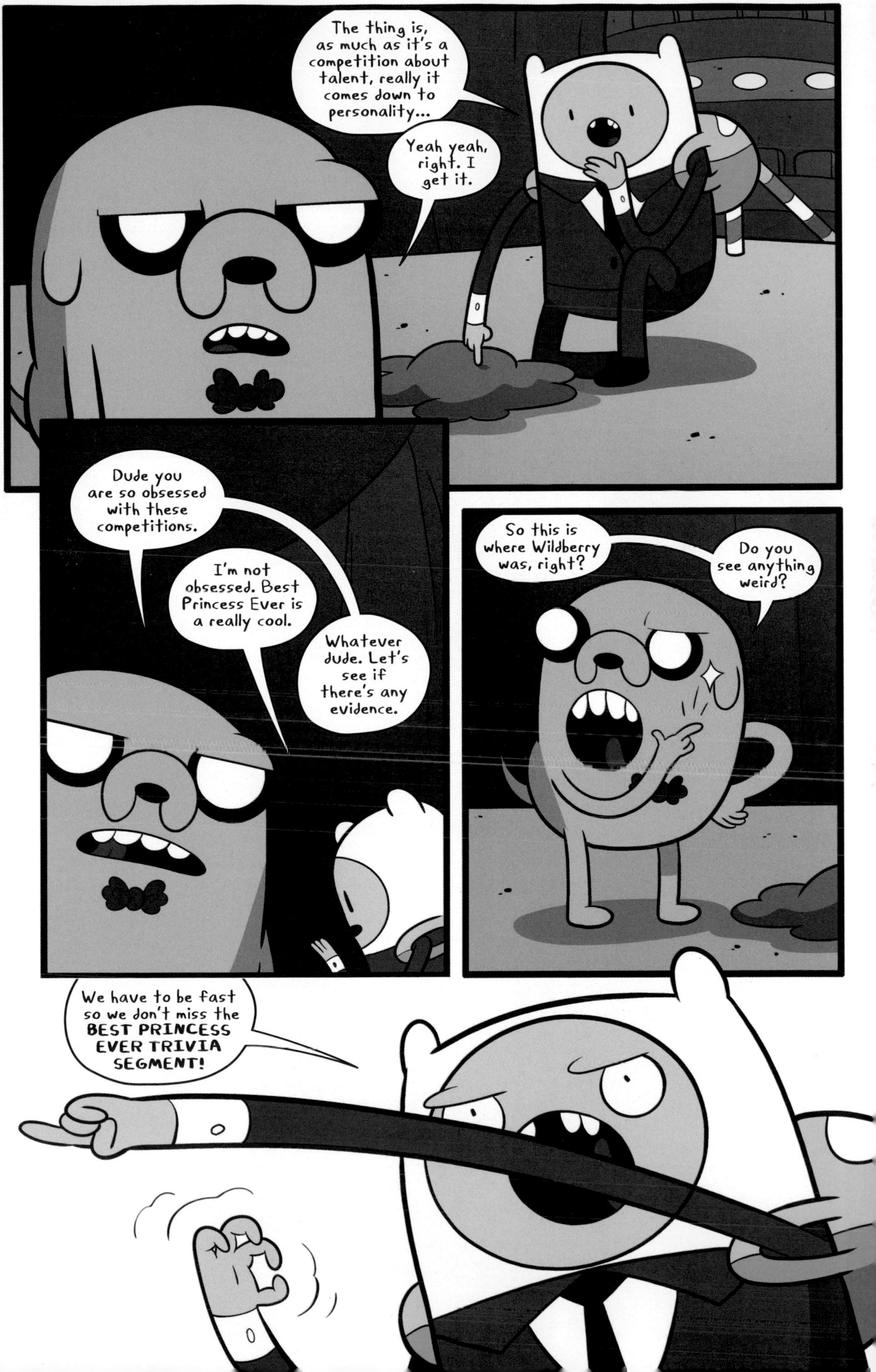
The thing is, as much as it's a competition about talent, really it comes down to personality...
Yeah yeah, right. I get it.
Dude you are so obsessed with these competitions.
I'm not obsessed. Best Princess Ever is a really cool.
Whatever dude. Let's see if there's any evidence.
So this is where Wildberry was, right?
Do you see anything weird?
We have to be fast so we don't miss the BEST PRINCESS EVER TRIVIA SEGMENT!

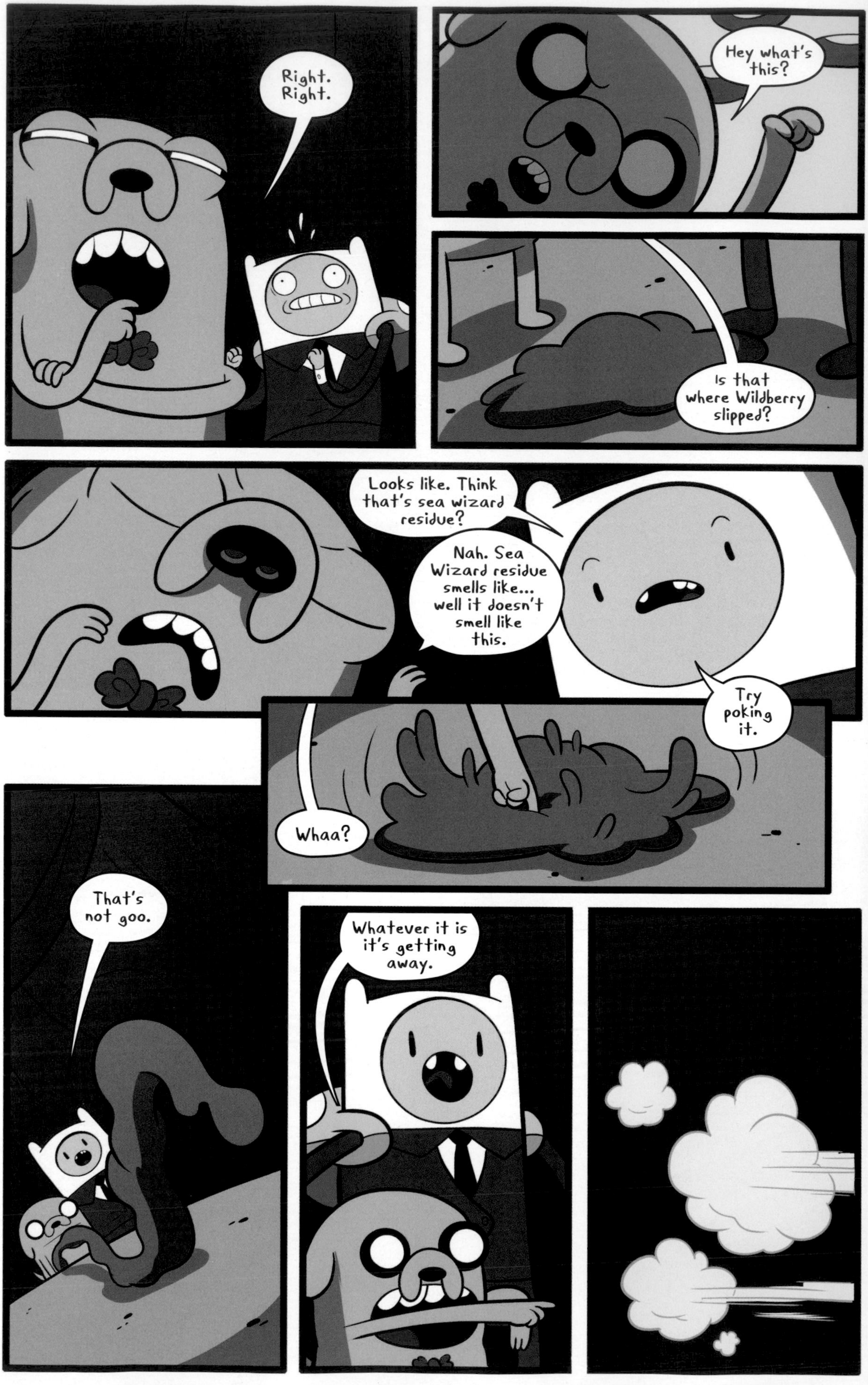
Right.
Right.
Hey what's this?
Is that where Wildberry slipped?
Looks like. Think that's sea wizard residue?
Nah. Sea Wizard residue smells like... well it doesn't smell like this.
Try poking it.
Whaa?
That's not goo.
Whatever it is it's getting away.

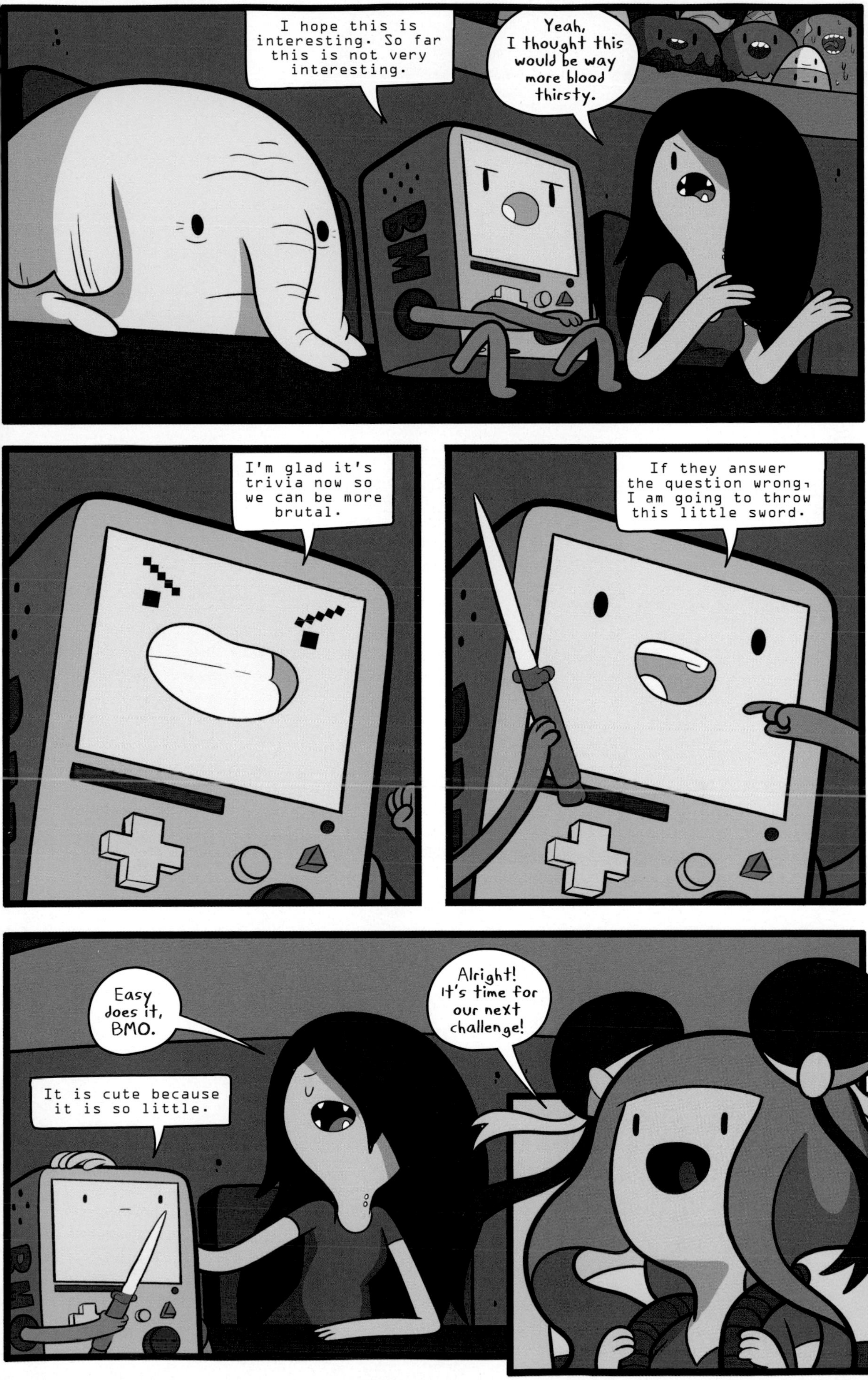
I hope this is interesting. So far this is not very interesting.
Yeah, I thought this would be way more blood thirsty.
I'm glad it's trivia now so we can be more brutal.
If they answer the question wrong, I am going to throw this little sword.
Easy does it, BMO.
It is cute because it is so little.
Alright! It's time for our next challenge!

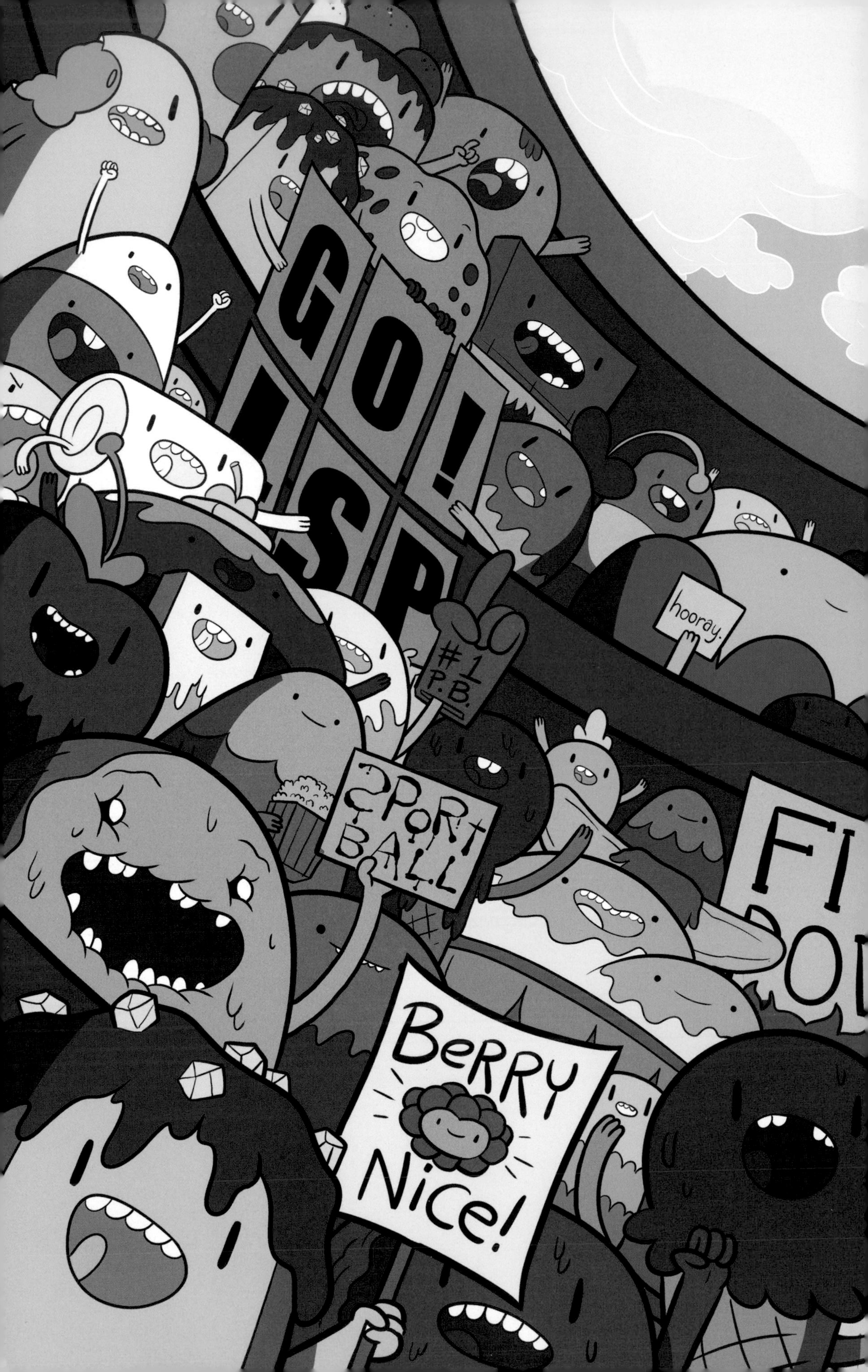
GO! ! SP
hooray.
#1 P.B.
SPORT BALL
Berry Nice!

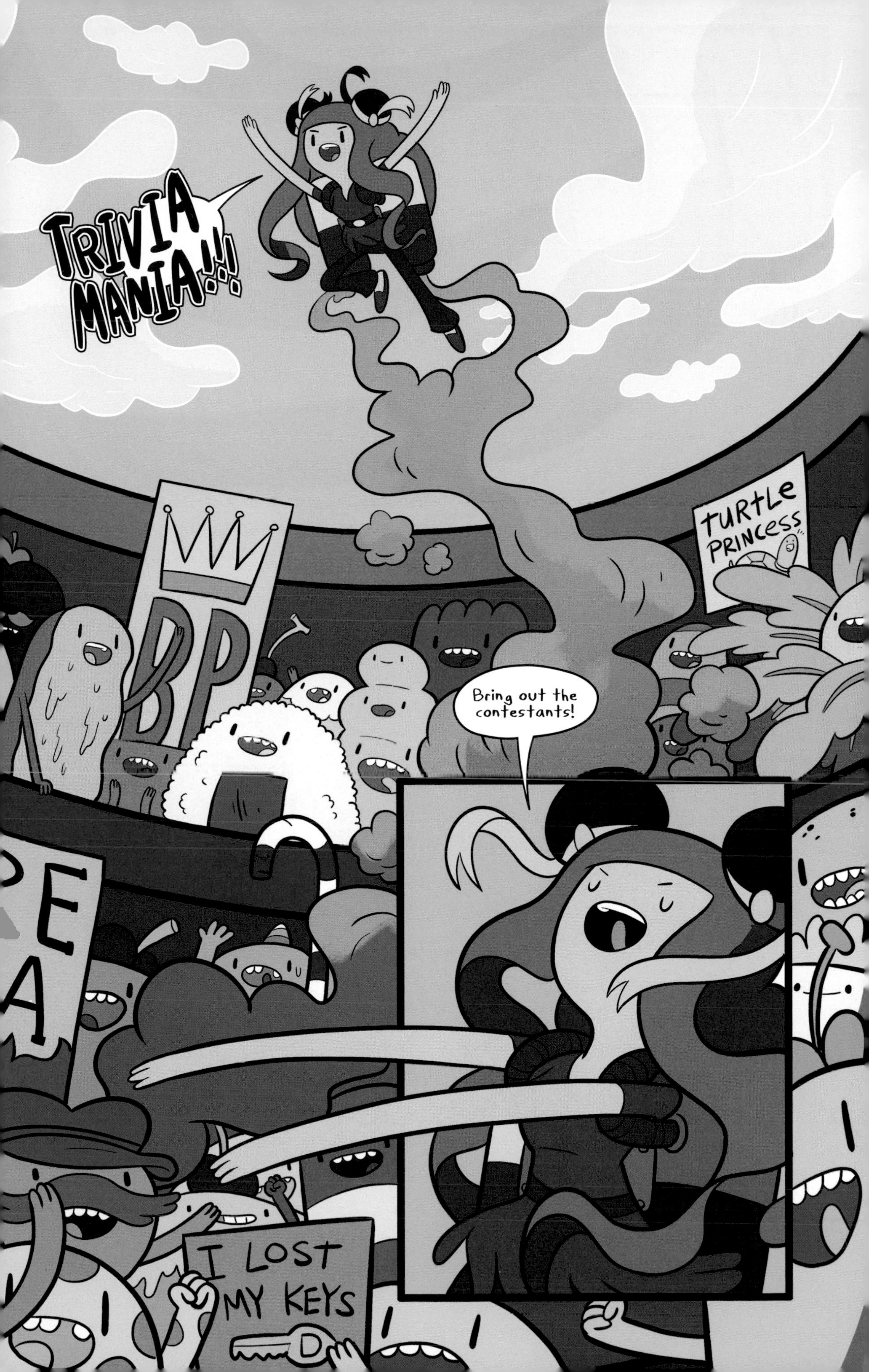
TRIVIA MANIA!!!
TURTLE PRINCESS
BP
Bring out the contestants!
I LOST MY KEYS

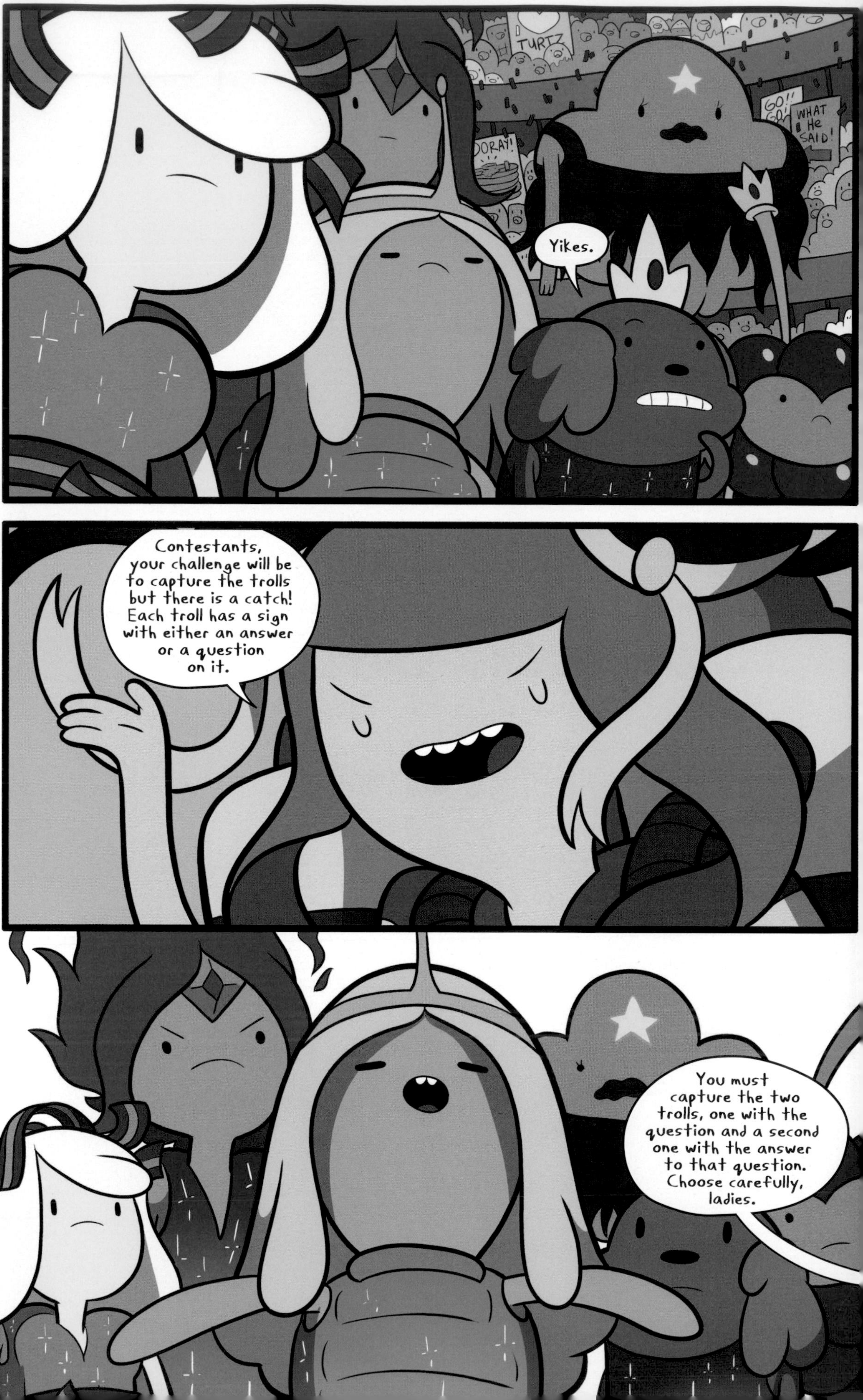
TURTZ
GO!! GO!
WHAT He SAID!
Yikes.
Contestants, your challenge will be to capture the trolls but there is a catch! Each troll has a sign with either an answer or a question on it.
You must capture the two trolls, one with the question and a second one with the answer to that question. Choose carefully, ladies.

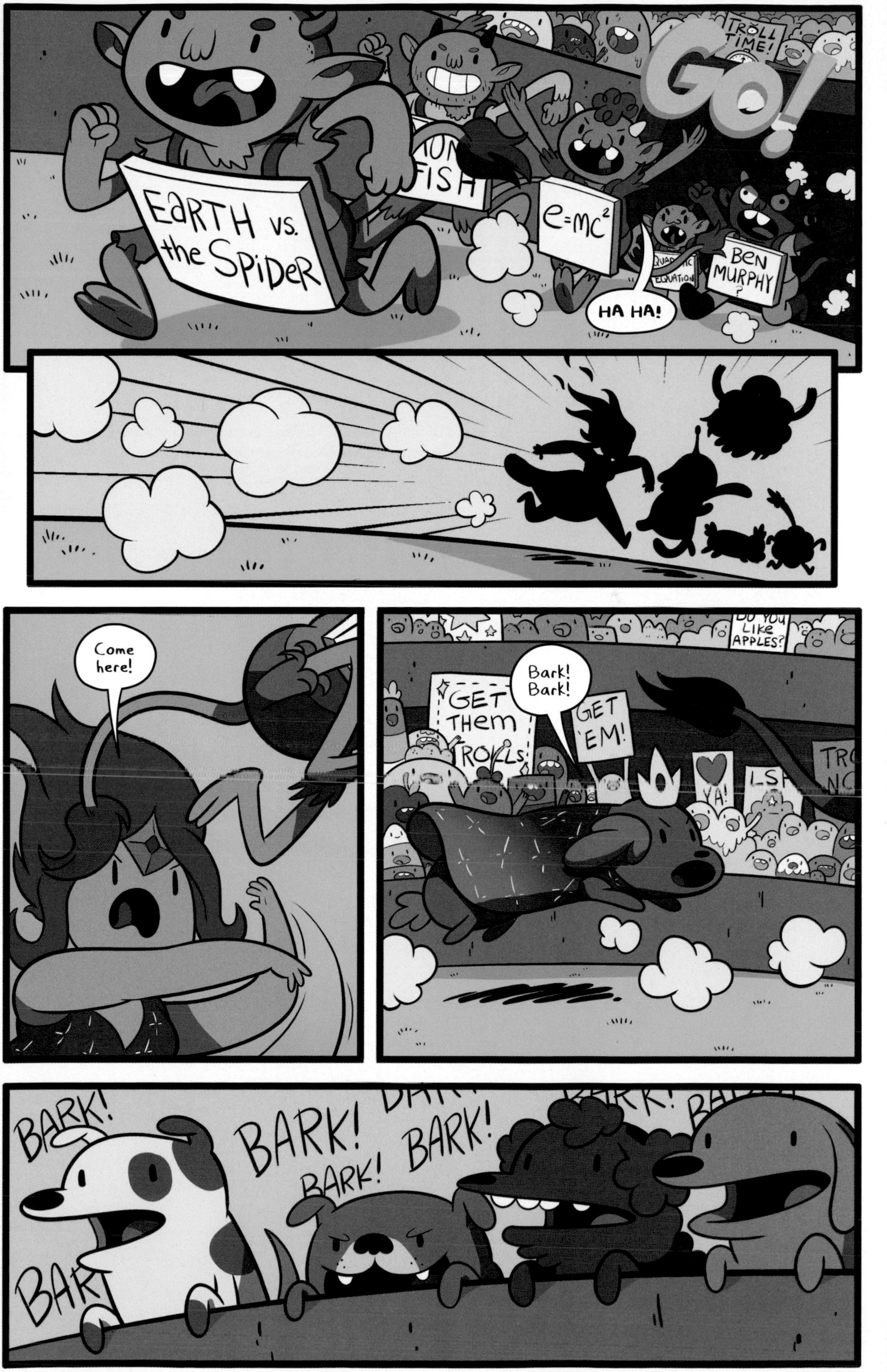
TROLL TIME!
GO!
EARTH vs. the SPIDER
FISH
e=mc²
BEN MURPHY ?
HA HA!
Come here!
DO YOU LIKE APPLES?
GET THEM TROLLS
Bark! Bark!
GET 'EM!
YA!
BARK!
BARK!
BARK!
BARK!

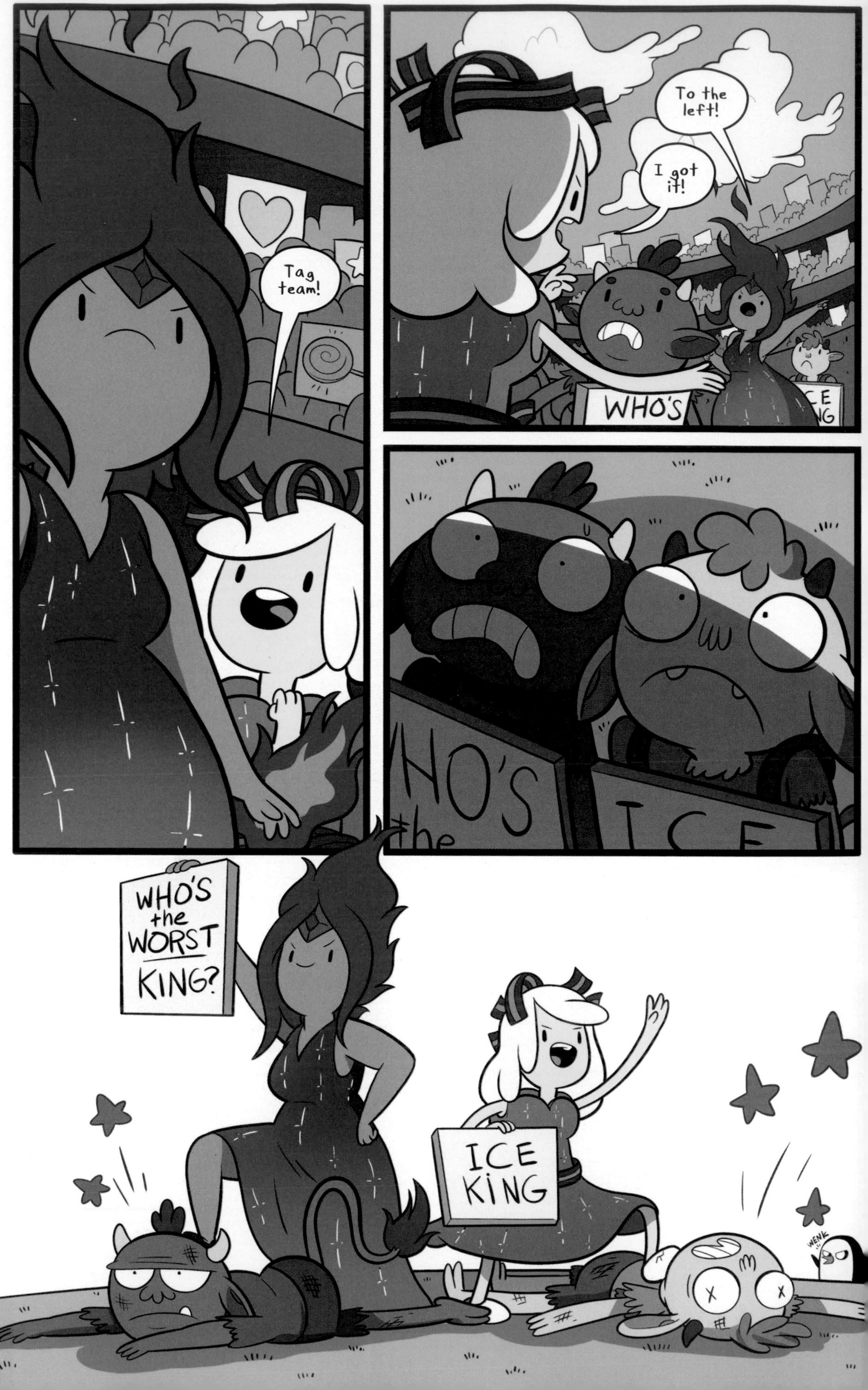
Tag team!
To the left!
I got it!
WHO'S
CE
NG
HO'S
the
ICE
WHO'S the WORST KING?
ICE KING
WENK

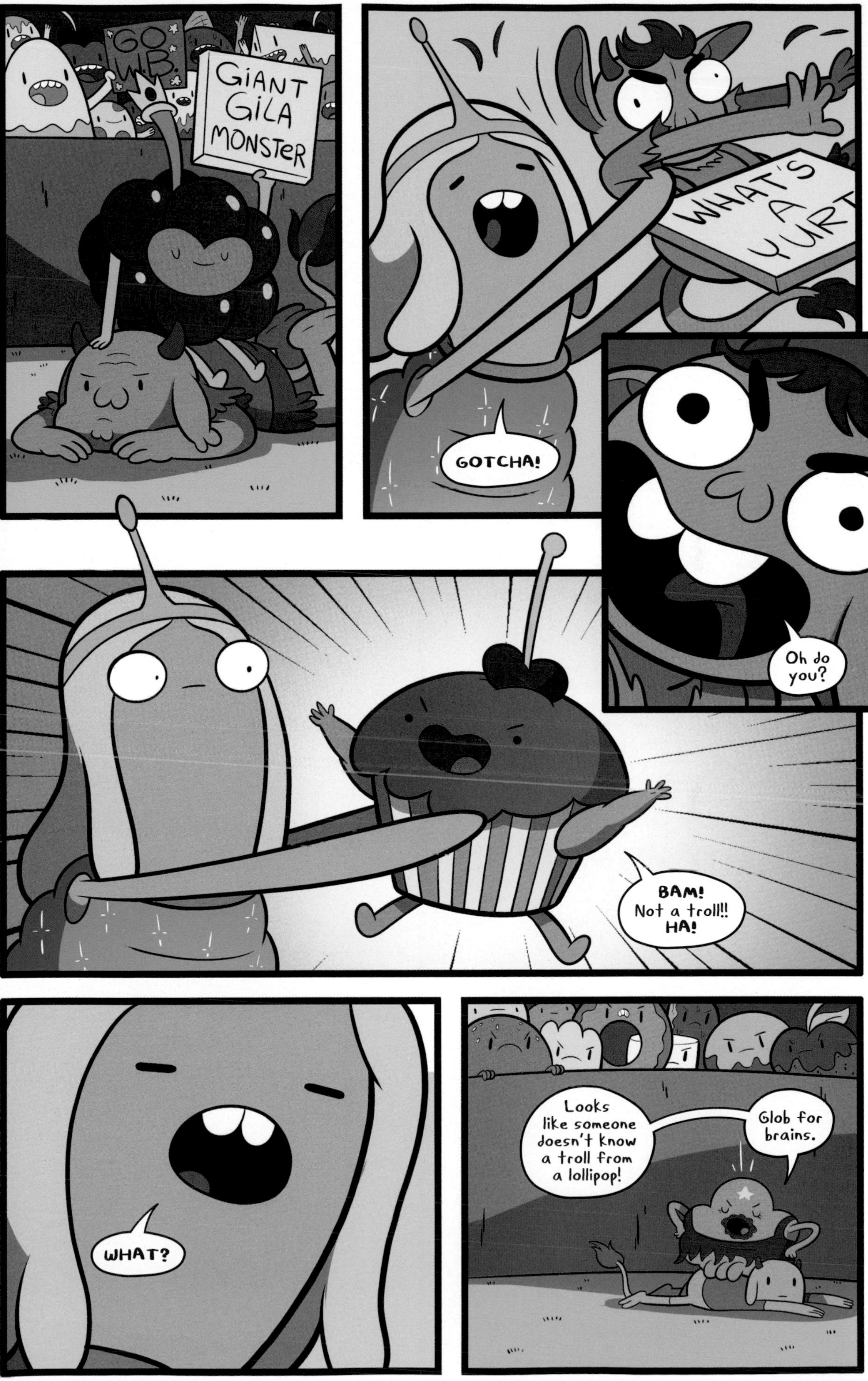
GO W.B.
GiANT GiLA MONSTER
WHAT'S A YURT
GOTCHA!
Oh do you?
BAM! Not a troll!! HA!
WHAT?
Looks like someone doesn't know a troll from a lollipop!
Glob for brains.

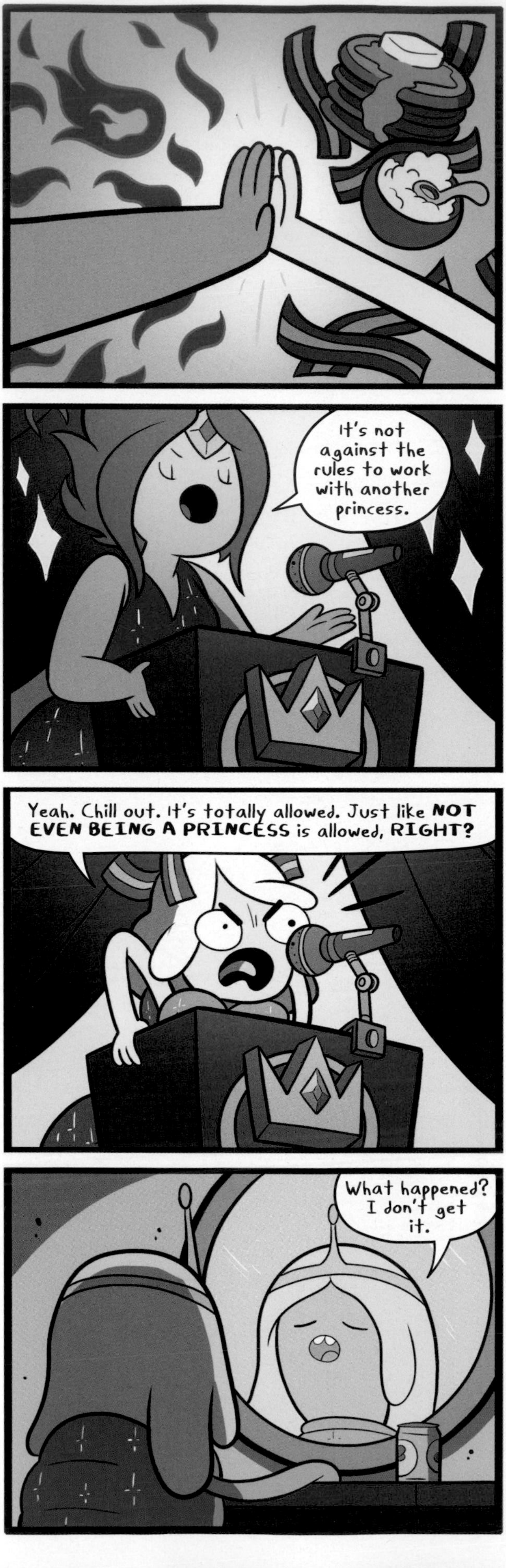
It's not against the rules to work with another princess.
Yeah. Chill out. It's totally allowed. Just like **NOT EVEN BEING A PRINCESS** is allowed, **RIGHT?**
What happened? I don't get it.

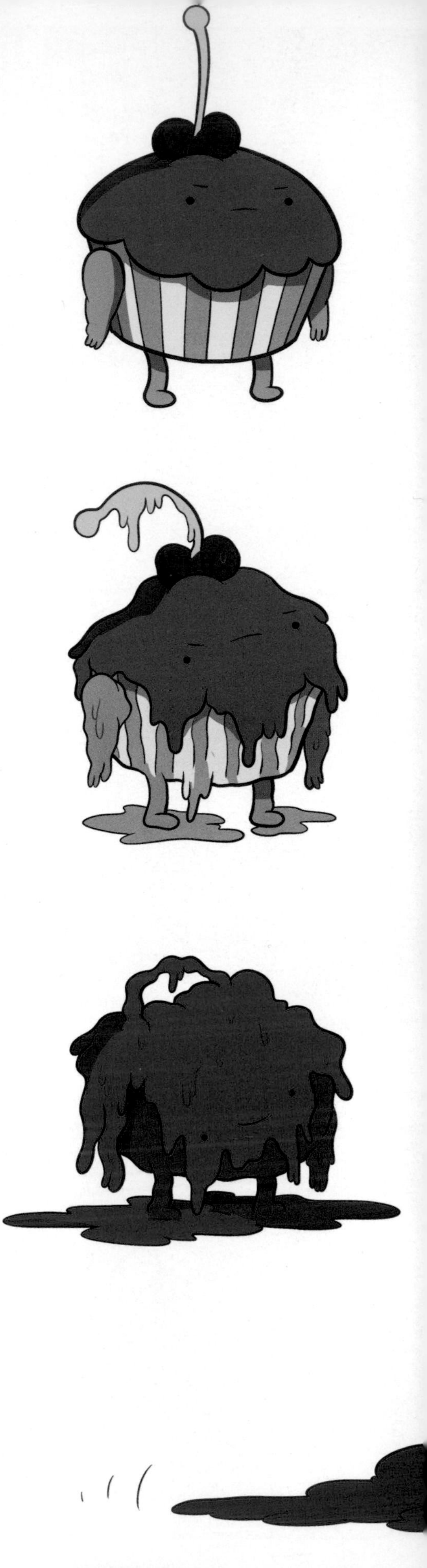

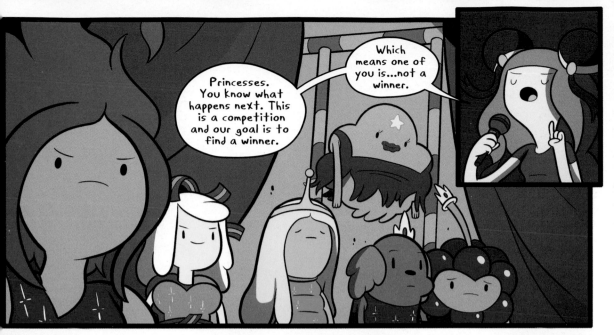

Princesses. You know what happens next. This is a competition and our goal is to find a winner.

Which means one of you is...not a winner.

That's right, man. Cut throat.

Hello. Some of you were not good this week.

This is all still very exciting. Although I am getting a bit sleepy.

Your judges have evaluated your performance as to how it met the standards set up by this competition, and ultimately decided, based on your performance,

...who is NOT the Best Princess ever.

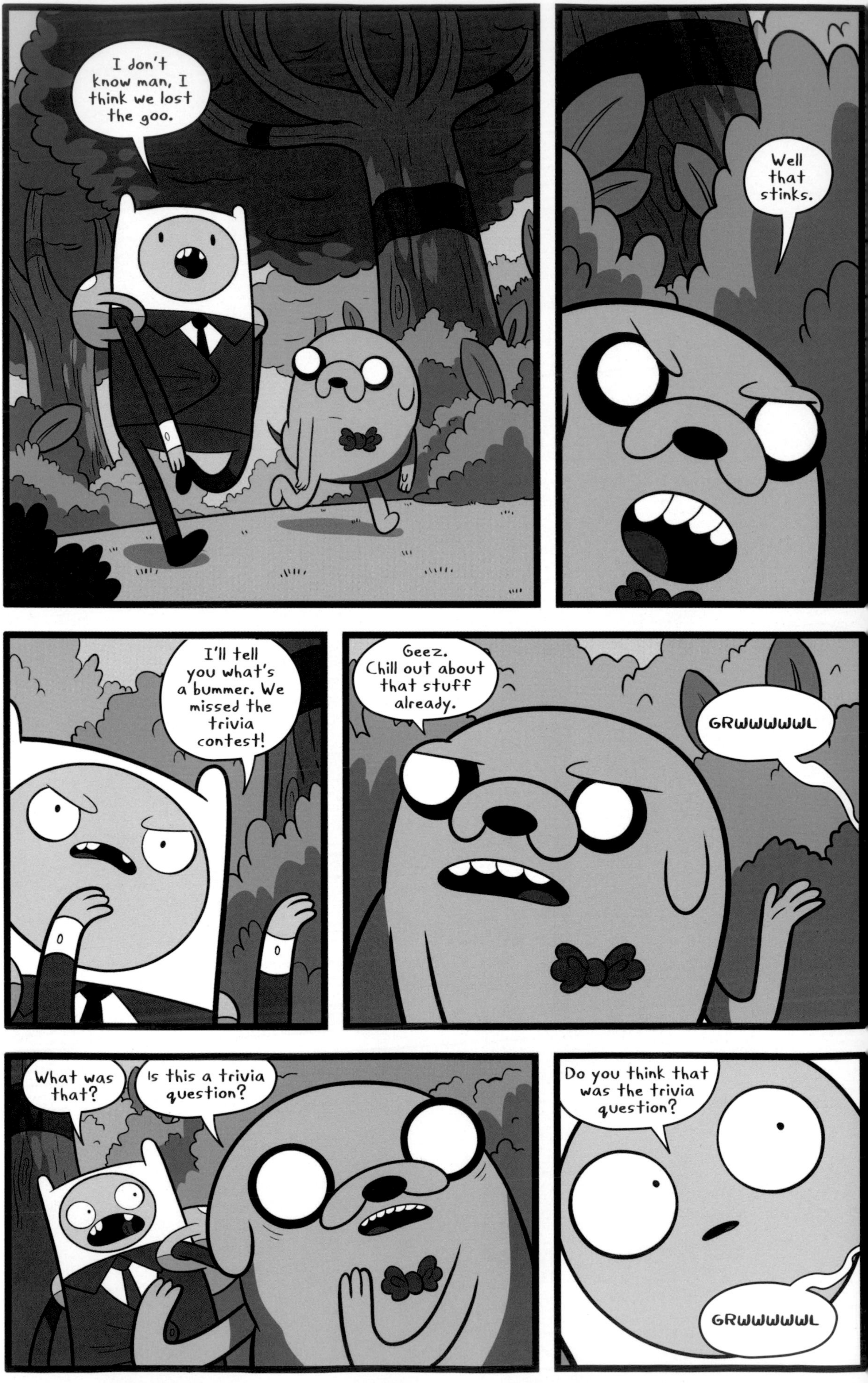
I don't know man, I think we lost the goo.
Well that stinks.
I'll tell you what's a bummer. We missed the trivia contest!
Geez. Chill out about that stuff already.
GRWWWWWL
What was that?
Is this a trivia question?
Do you think that was the trivia question?
GRWWWWWL

Marceline? Can you explain your verdict?

Yeah. Hey you guys. You all kicked it hardcore today. But some of you kind of blew it so one of those two obviously had to go. Even though...

Anyway, drawing out things is weird so we're just going to get to it.

I'm really sorry Turtle Princess. You're not the best princess ever.

That's okay.

Turtle Princess.

You're a smartie and we've all loved seeing you come out of your shell.

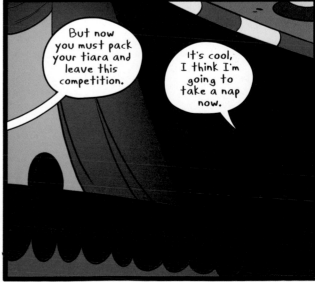

But now you must pack your tiara and leave this competition.

It's cool, I think I'm going to take a nap now.

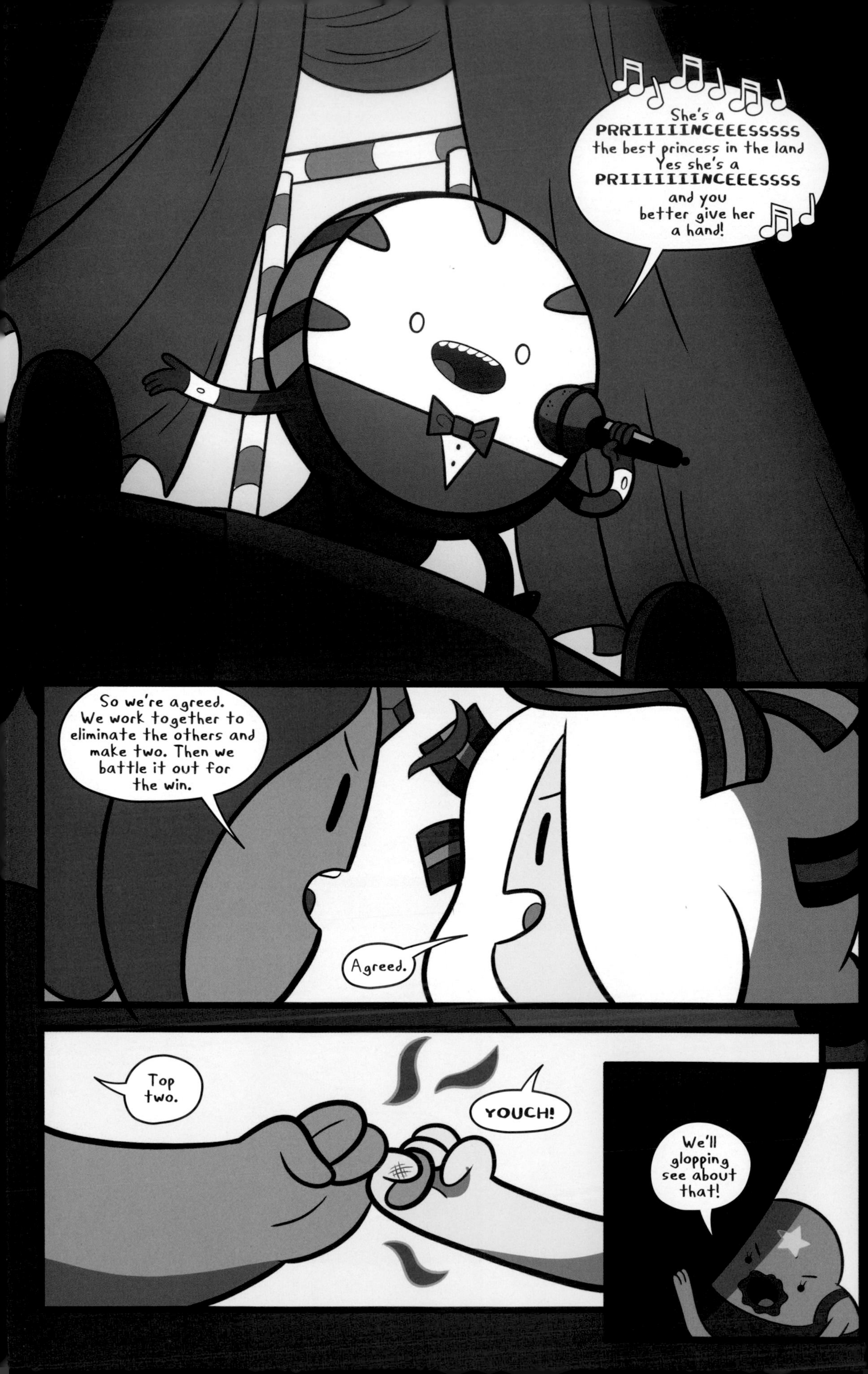
She's a PRRIIIIINCEEESSSSS the best princess in the land Yes she's a PRIIIIIIIINCEEESSSS and you better give her a hand!
So we're agreed. We work together to eliminate the others and make two. Then we battle it out for the win.
Agreed.
Top two.
YOUCH!
We'll glopping see about that!

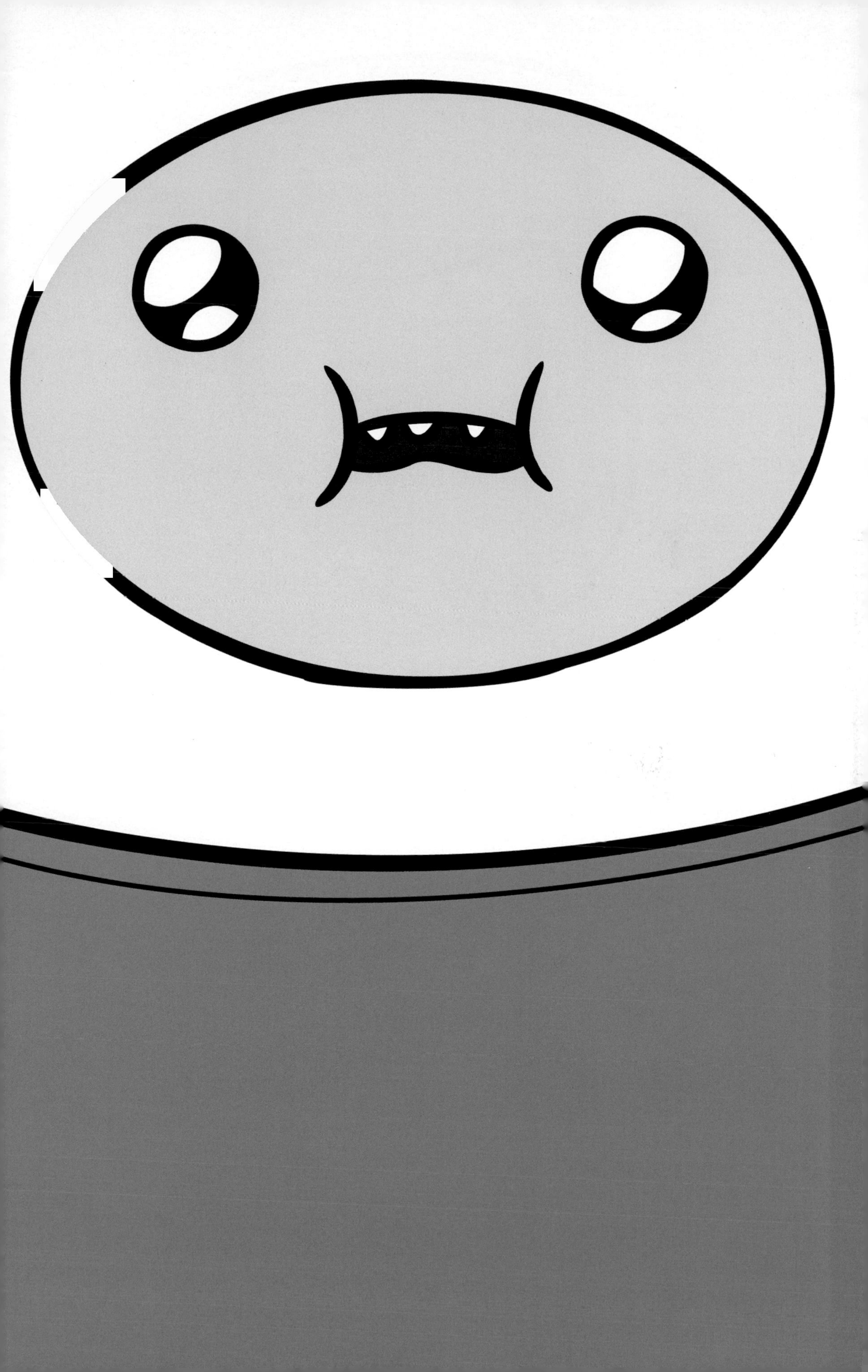

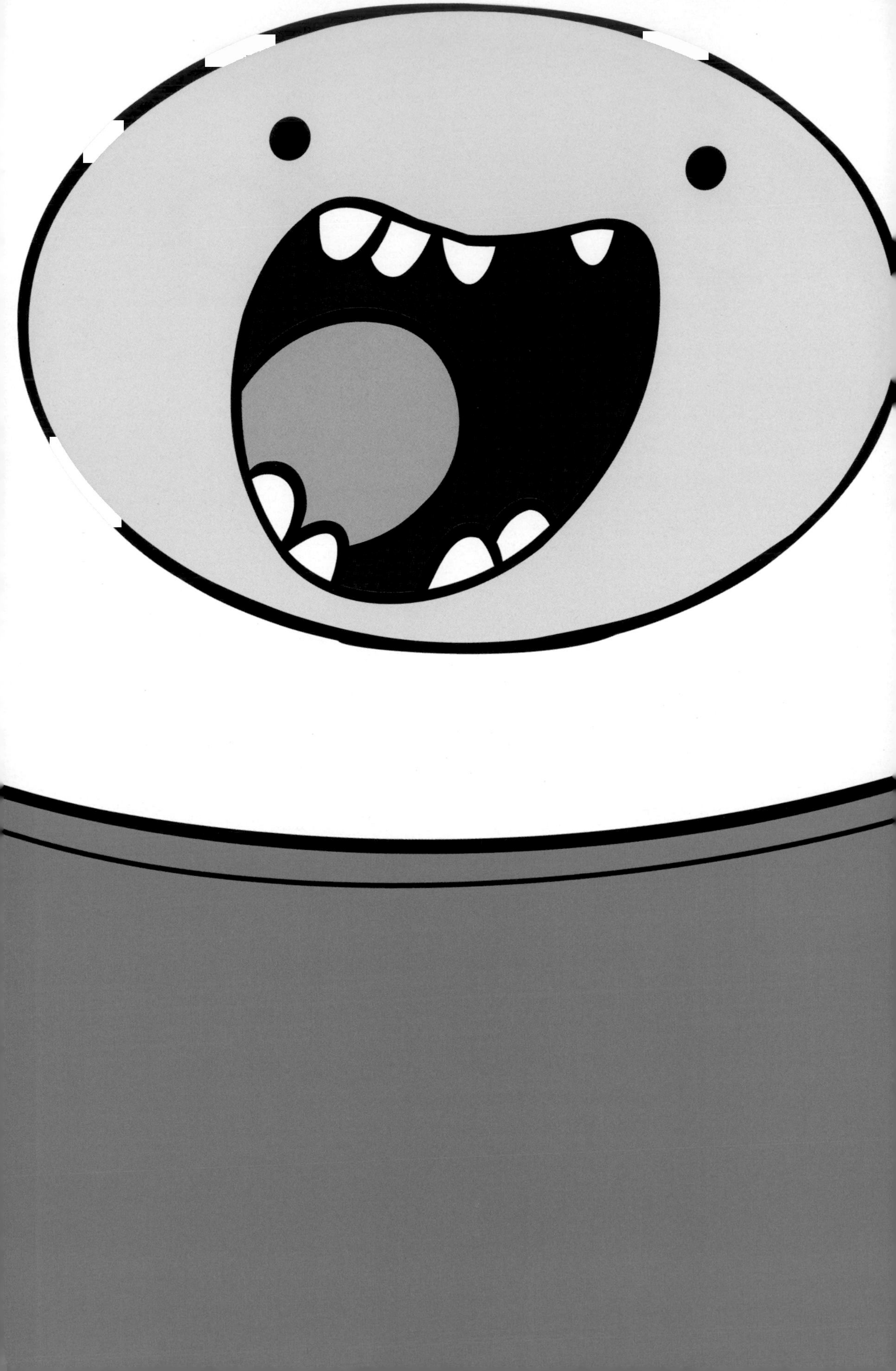

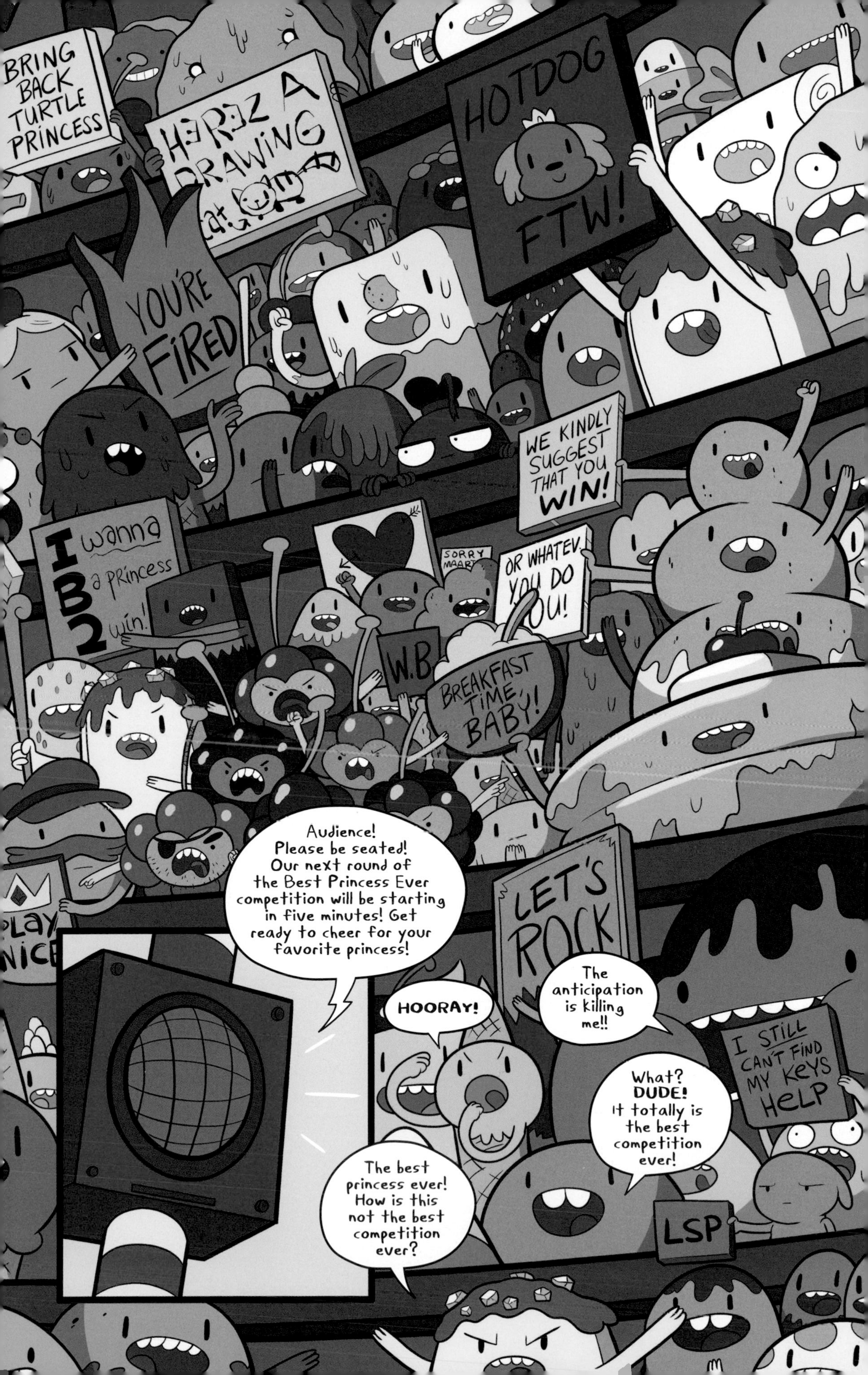
BRING BACK TURTLE PRINCESS
HERƎZ A DRAWING cat
HOTDOG FTW!
YOU'RE FIRED
WE KINDLY SUGGEST THAT YOU WIN!
I wanna B a princess 2 win!
OR WHATEV. YOU DO YOU!
W.B
BREAKFAST TIME, BABY!
Audience! Please be seated! Our next round of the Best Princess Ever competition will be starting in five minutes! Get ready to cheer for your favorite princess!
LET'S ROCK
HOORAY!
The anticipation is killing me!!
I STILL CAN'T FIND MY KEYS HELP
What? DUDE! It totally is the best competition ever!
The best princess ever! How is this not the best competition ever?
LSP

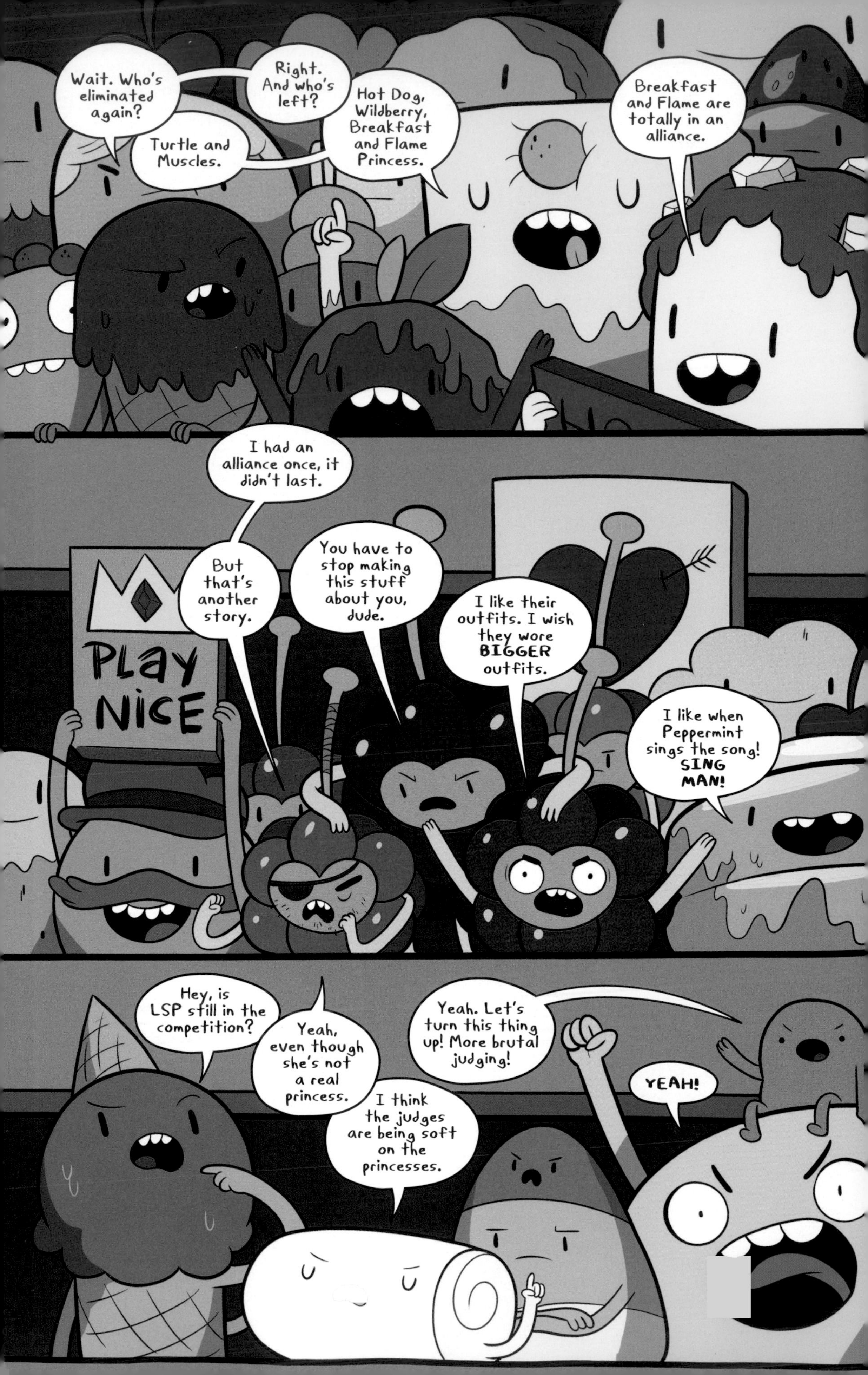
Wait. Who's eliminated again?
Turtle and Muscles.
Right. And who's left?
Hot Dog, Wildberry, Breakfast and Flame Princess.
Breakfast and Flame are totally in an alliance.
I had an alliance once, it didn't last.
But that's another story.
You have to stop making this stuff about you, dude.
I like their outfits. I wish they wore BIGGER outfits.
I like when Peppermint sings the song! SING MAN!
PLAY NICE
Hey, is LSP still in the competition?
Yeah, even though she's not a real princess.
I think the judges are being soft on the princesses.
Yeah. Let's turn this thing up! More brutal judging!
YEAH!

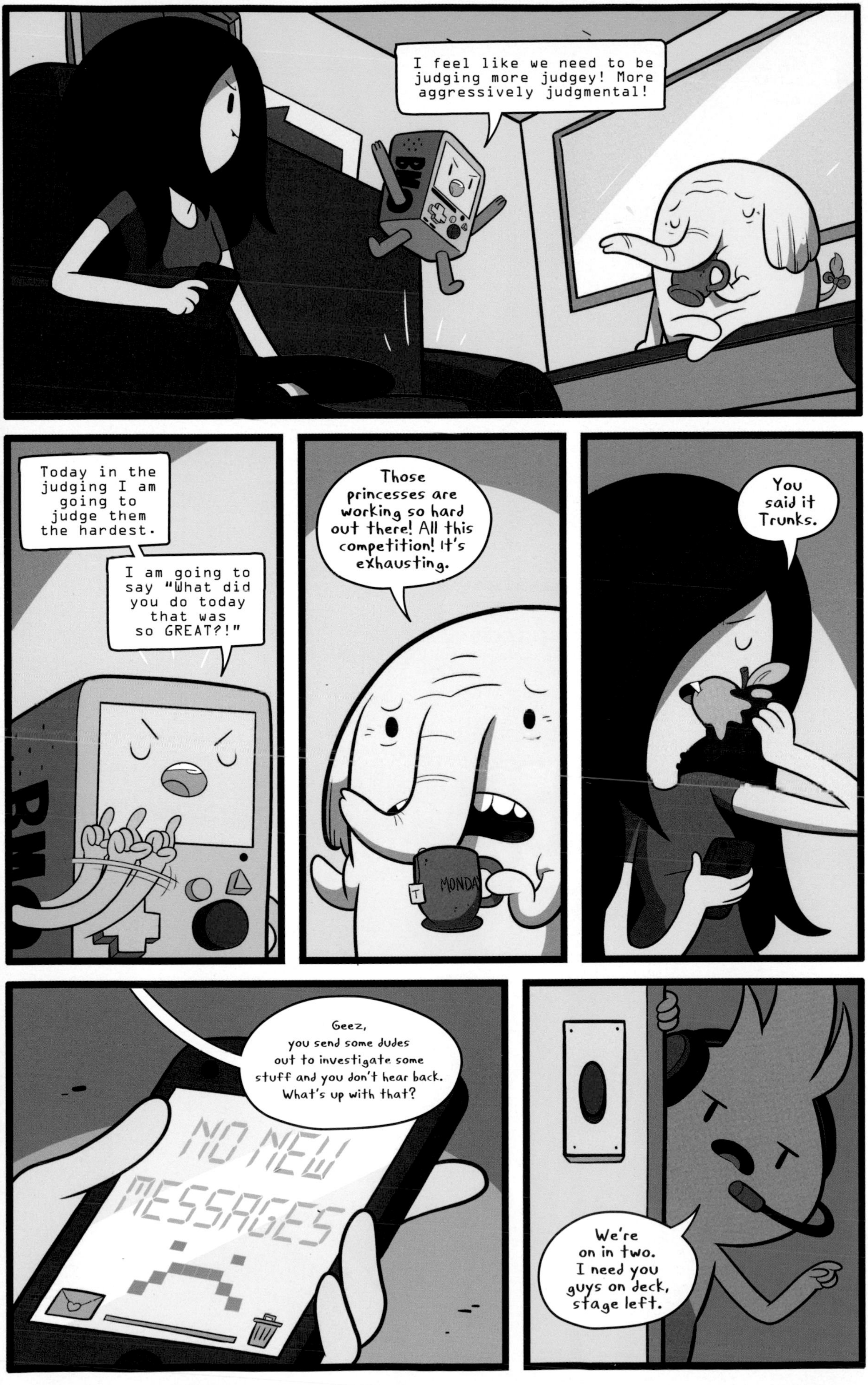
I feel like we need to be judging more judgey! More aggressively judgmental!
Today in the judging I am going to judge them the hardest.
I am going to say "What did you do today that was so GREAT?!"
Those princesses are working so hard out there! All this competition! It's exhausting.
MONDAY
You said it Trunks.
Geez, you send some dudes out to investigate some stuff and you don't hear back. What's up with that?
NO NEW MESSAGES
We're on in two. I need you guys on deck, stage left.

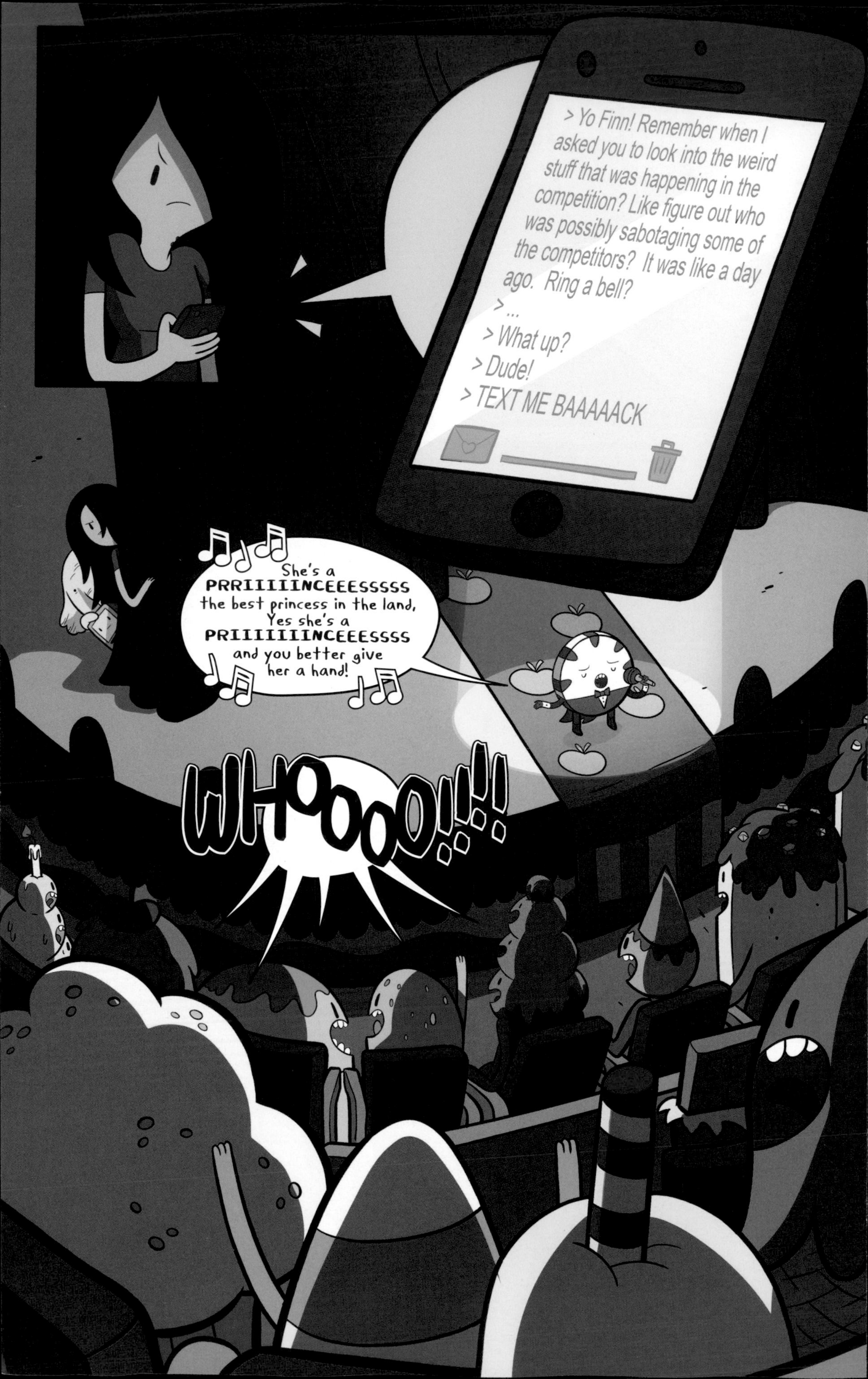
> Yo Finn! Remember when I asked you to look into the weird stuff that was happening in the competition? Like figure out who was possibly sabotaging some of the competitors? It was like a day ago. Ring a bell?
> ...
> What up?
> Dude!
> TEXT ME BAAAAACK
She's a PRRIIIIIINCEEEESSSSS the best princess in the land, Yes she's a PRIIIIIIINCEEEESSSS and you better give her a hand!
WHOOOO!!!!

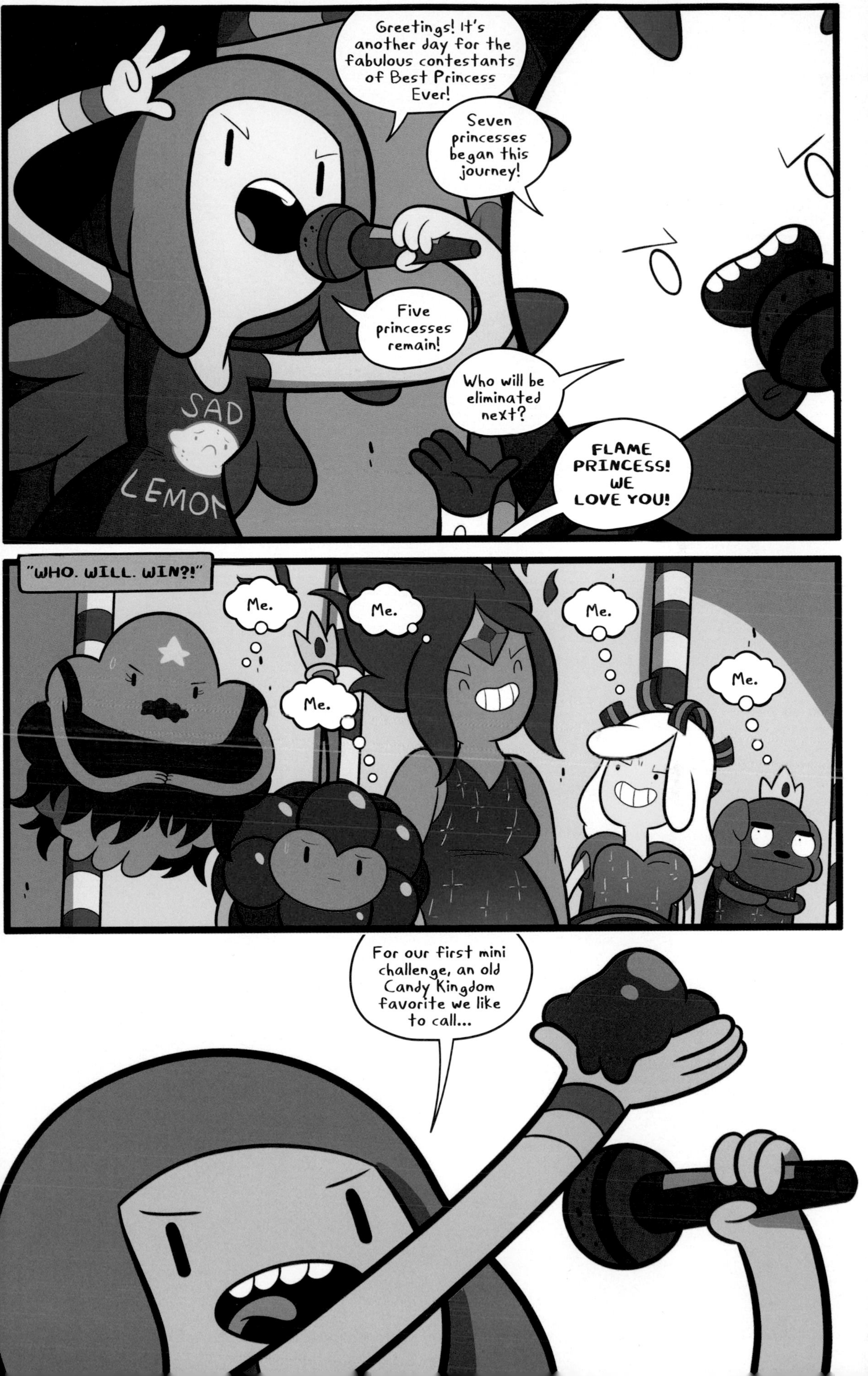
Greetings! It's another day for the fabulous contestants of Best Princess Ever!
Seven princesses began this journey!
Five princesses remain!
Who will be eliminated next?
FLAME PRINCESS! WE LOVE YOU!
SAD LEMON
"WHO. WILL. WIN?!"
Me.
Me.
Me.
Me.
Me.
For our first mini challenge, an old Candy Kingdom favorite we like to call...

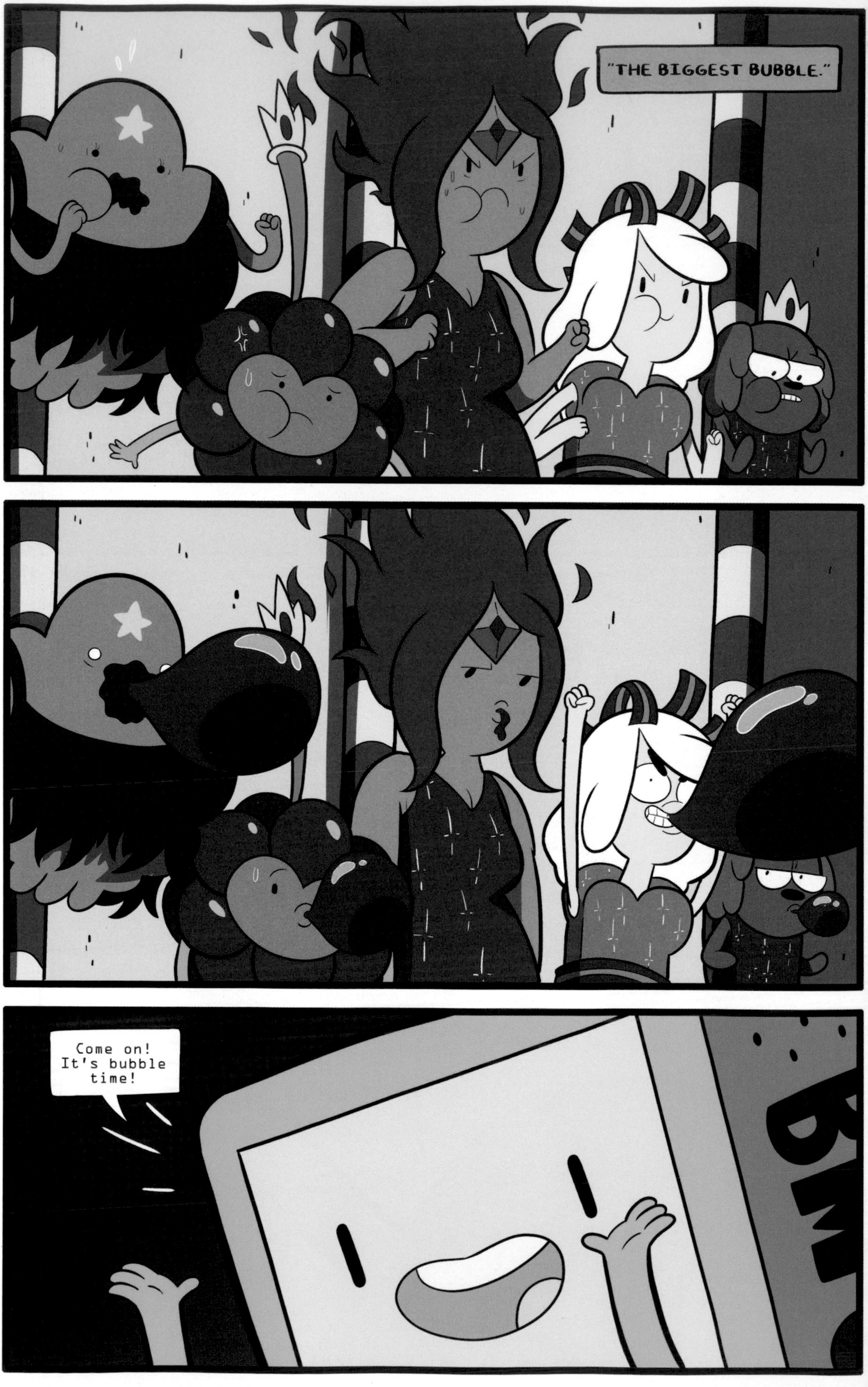
"THE BIGGEST BUBBLE."
Come on! It's bubble time!

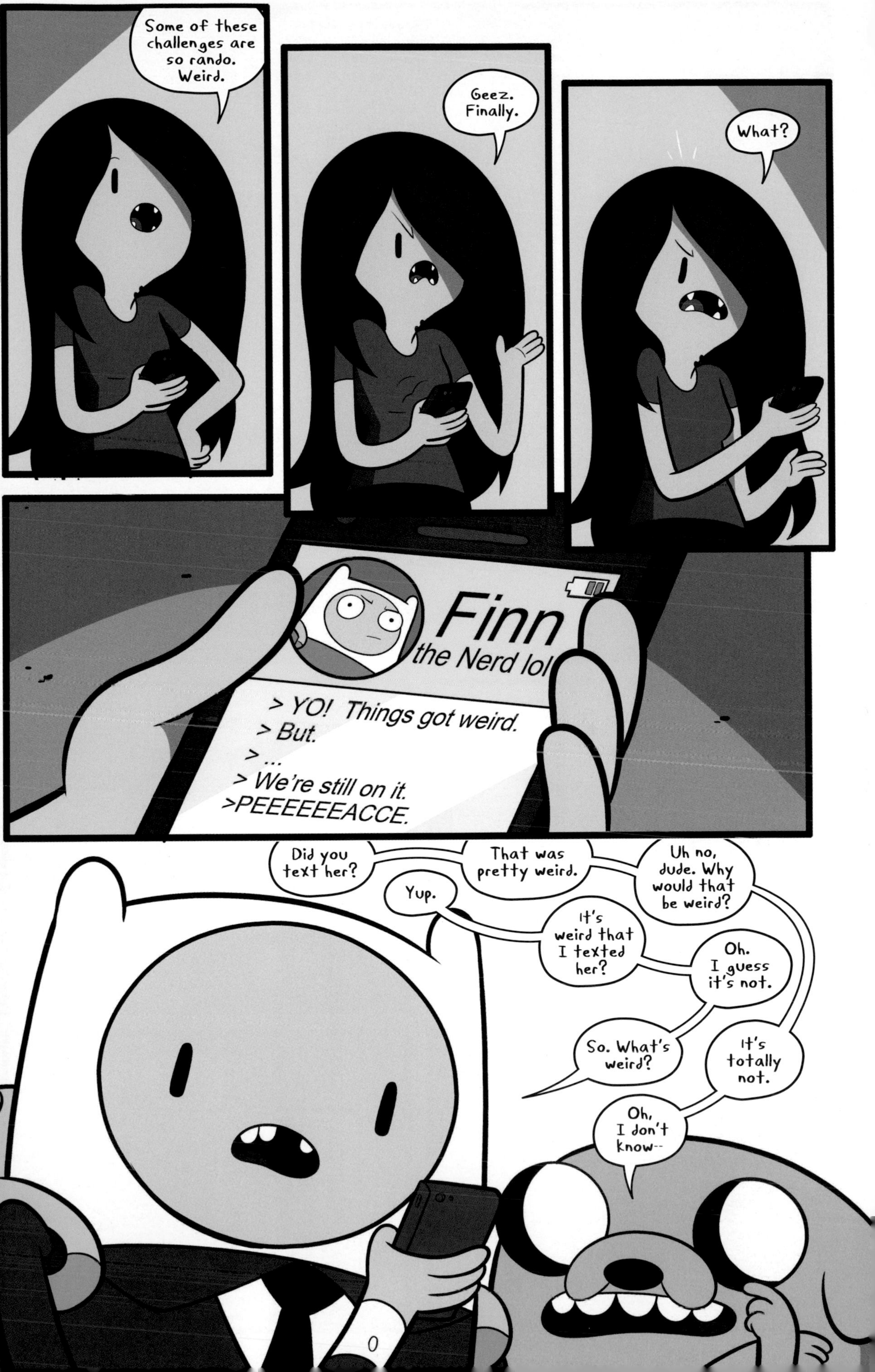
Some of these challenges are so rando. Weird.
Geez. Finally.
What?
Finn the Nerd lol
> YO! Things got weird.
> But.
> ...
> We're still on it.
>PEEEEEEACCE.
Did you text her?
Yup.
That was pretty weird.
It's weird that I texted her?
Uh no, dude. Why would that be weird?
Oh. I guess it's not.
So. What's weird?
It's totally not.
Oh, I don't know--

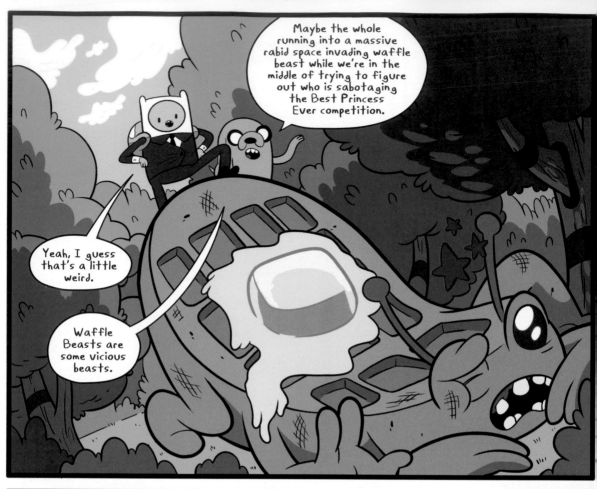

Maybe the whole running into a massive rabid space invading waffle beast while we're in the middle of trying to figure out who is sabotaging the Best Princess Ever competition.

Yeah, I guess that's a little weird.

Waffle Beasts are some vicious beasts.

Oh yeah, weren't we chasing a squirming bit of goo through the forest?

Oh yeah, where did that go?

Hey, you guys looking for goo?

Yeah!

All the goo is heading that way. Has been for days.

Thanks, man!

Back on the case!

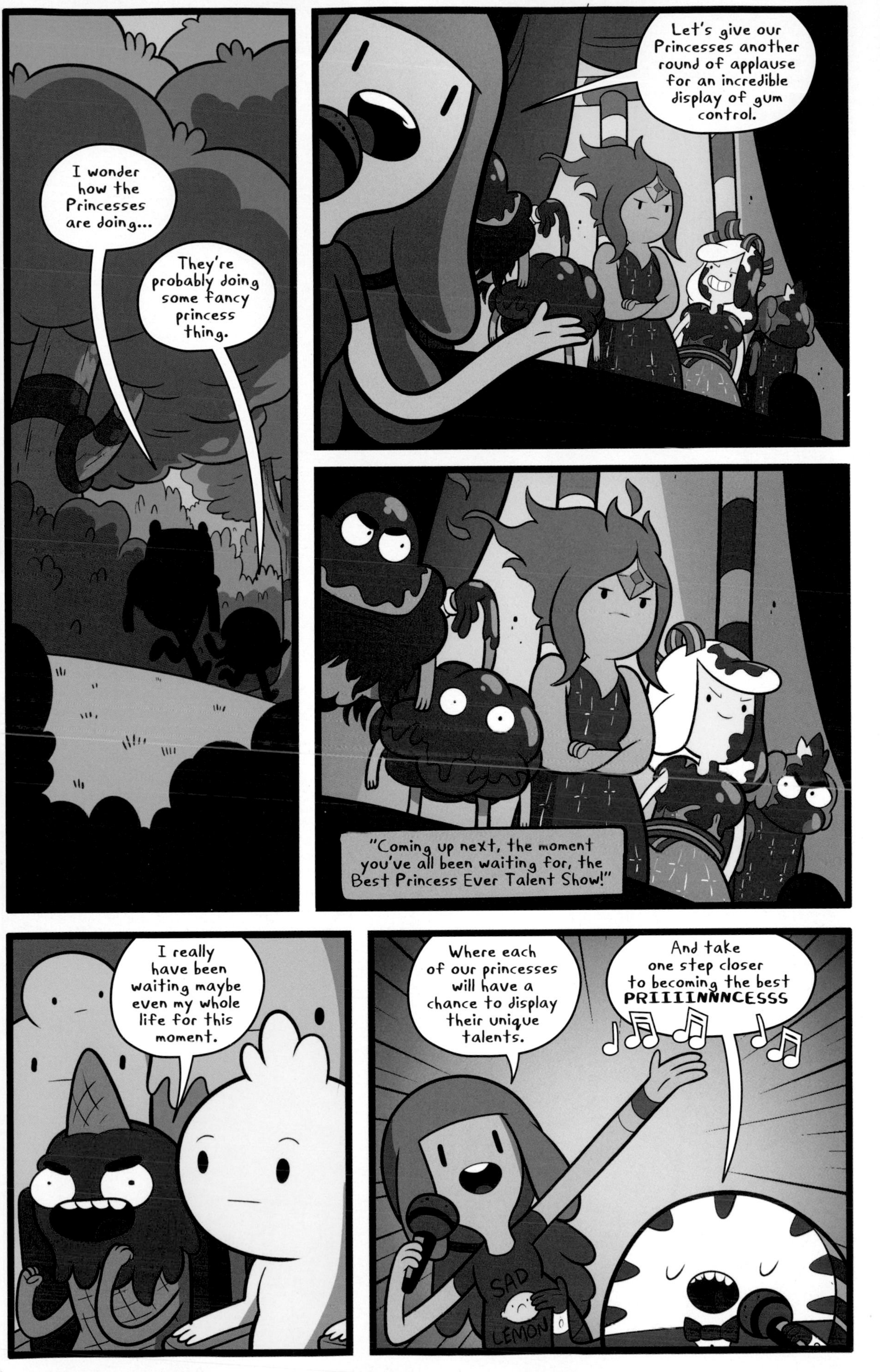
I wonder how the Princesses are doing...
They're probably doing some fancy princess thing.
Let's give our Princesses another round of applause for an incredible display of gum control.
"Coming up next, the moment you've all been waiting for, the Best Princess Ever Talent Show!"
I really have been waiting maybe even my whole life for this moment.
Where each of our princesses will have a chance to display their unique talents.
And take one step closer to becoming the best PRIIIINNNCESSS
SAD LEMON

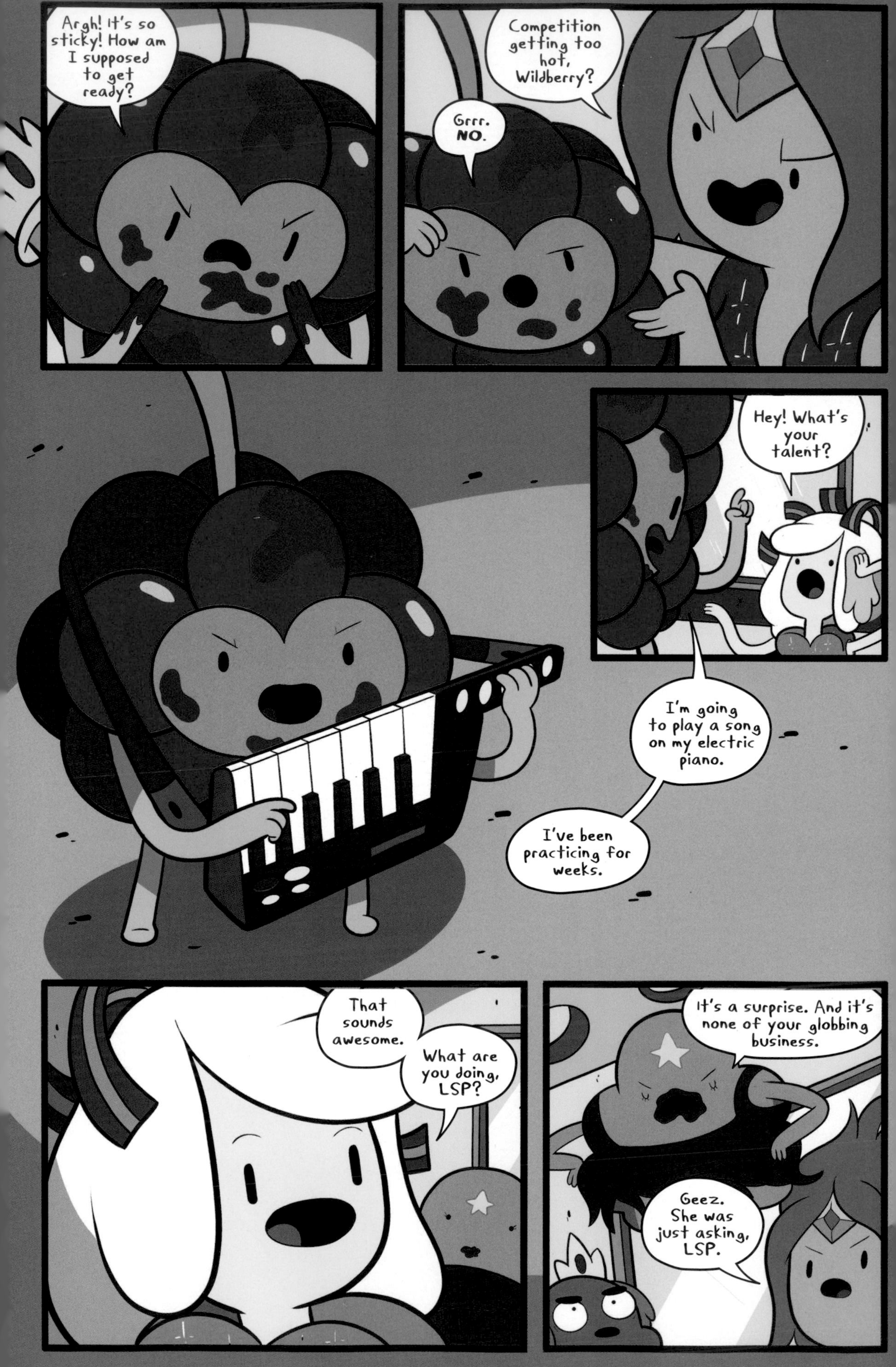
Argh! It's so sticky! How am I supposed to get ready?
Competition getting too hot, Wildberry?
Grrr. NO.
Hey! What's your talent?
I'm going to play a song on my electric piano.
I've been practicing for weeks.
That sounds awesome.
What are you doing, LSP?
It's a surprise. And it's none of your globbing business.
Geez. She was just asking, LSP.

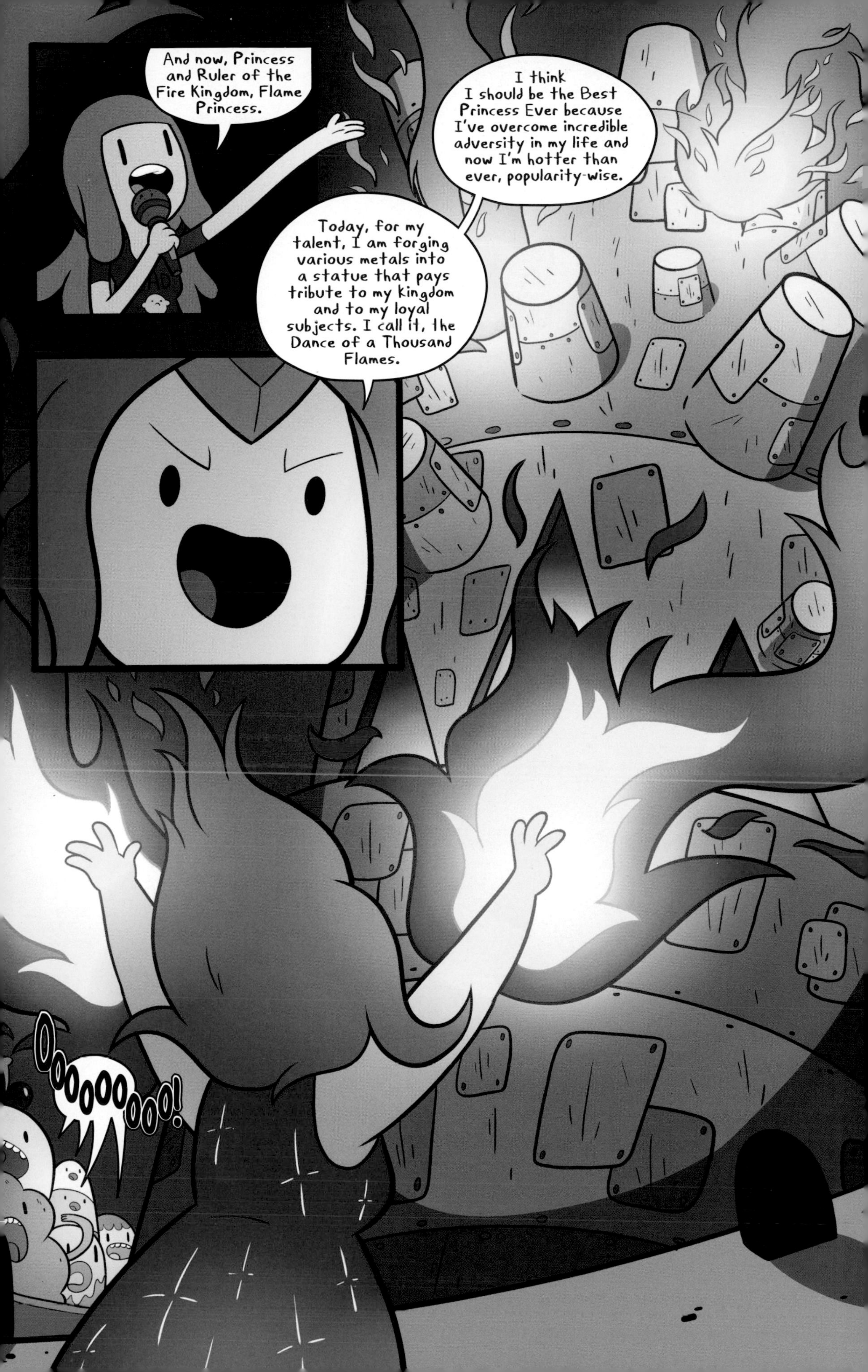
And now, Princess and Ruler of the Fire Kingdom, Flame Princess.
I think I should be the Best Princess Ever because I've overcome incredible adversity in my life and now I'm hotter than ever, popularity-wise.
Today, for my talent, I am forging various metals into a statue that pays tribute to my kingdom and to my loyal subjects. I call it, the Dance of a Thousand Flames.
OOOOOOOOOO!

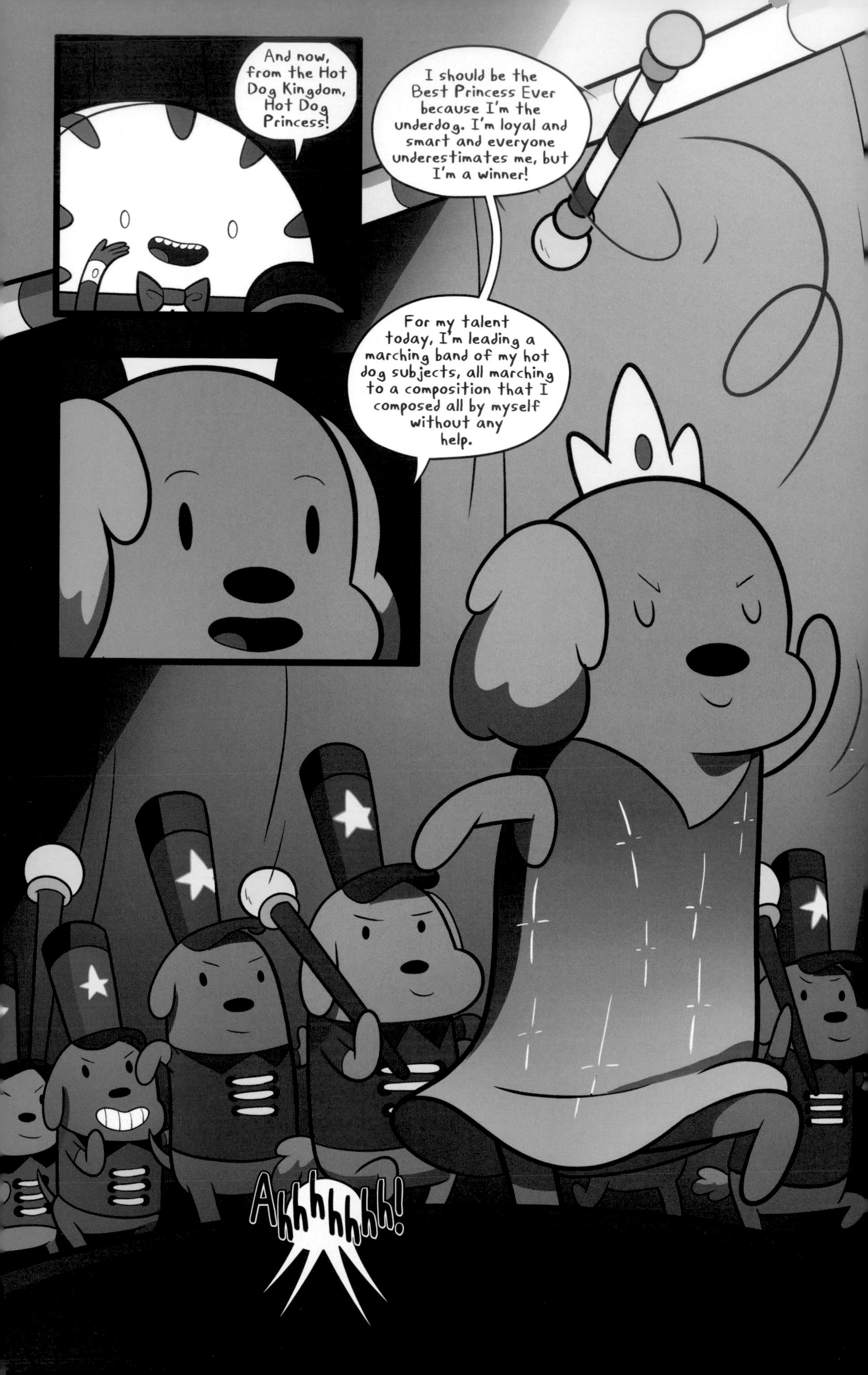
And now, from the Hot Dog Kingdom, Hot Dog Princess!
I should be the Best Princess Ever because I'm the underdog. I'm loyal and smart and everyone underestimates me, but I'm a winner!
For my talent today, I'm leading a marching band of my hot dog subjects, all marching to a composition that I composed all by myself without any help.
Ahhhhhhh!

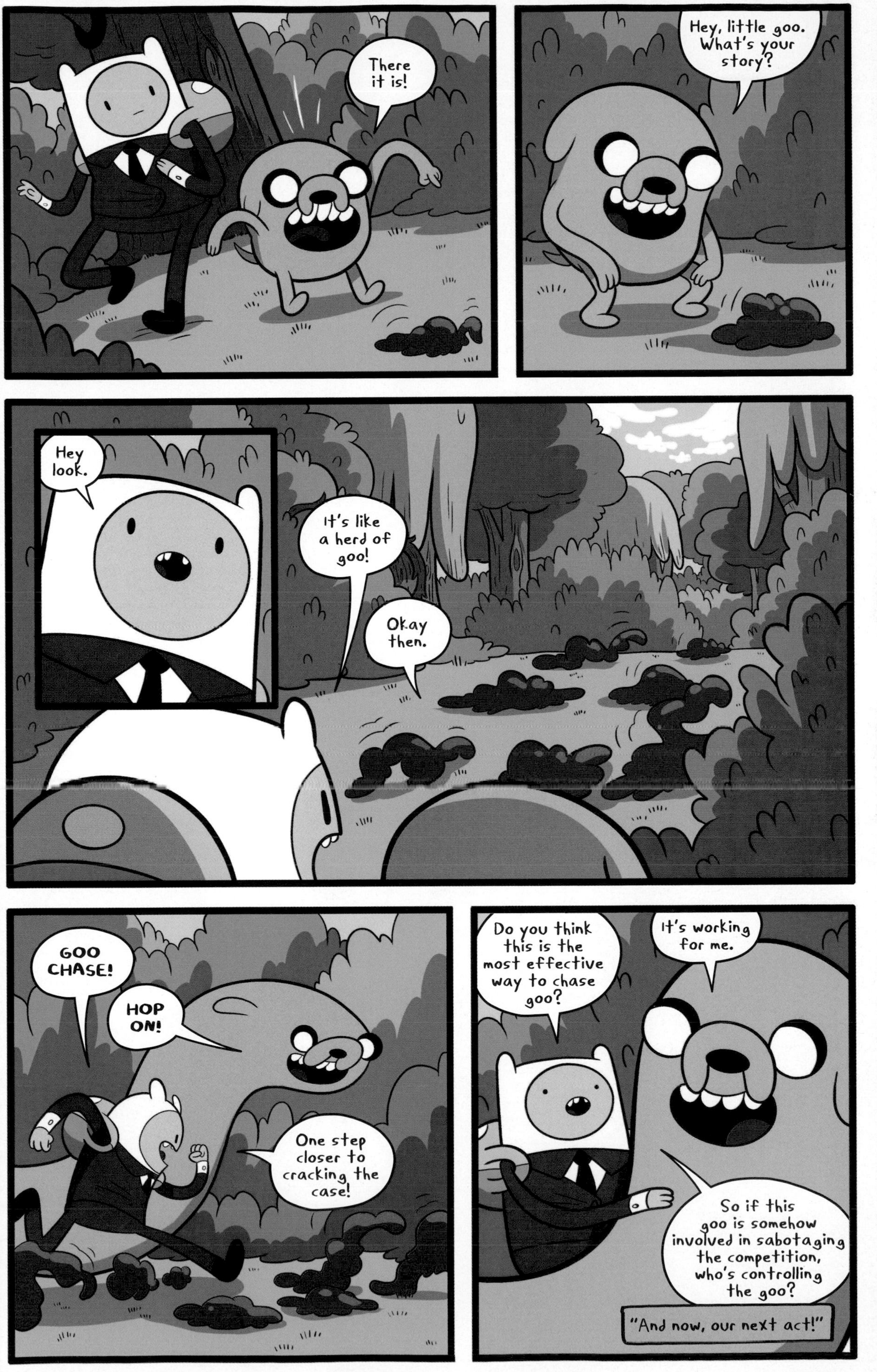
There it is!
Hey, little goo. What's your story?
Hey look.
It's like a herd of goo!
Okay then.
GOO CHASE!
HOP ON!
One step closer to cracking the case!
Do you think this is the most effective way to chase goo?
It's working for me.
So if this goo is somehow involved in sabotaging the competition, who's controlling the goo?
"And now, our next act!"

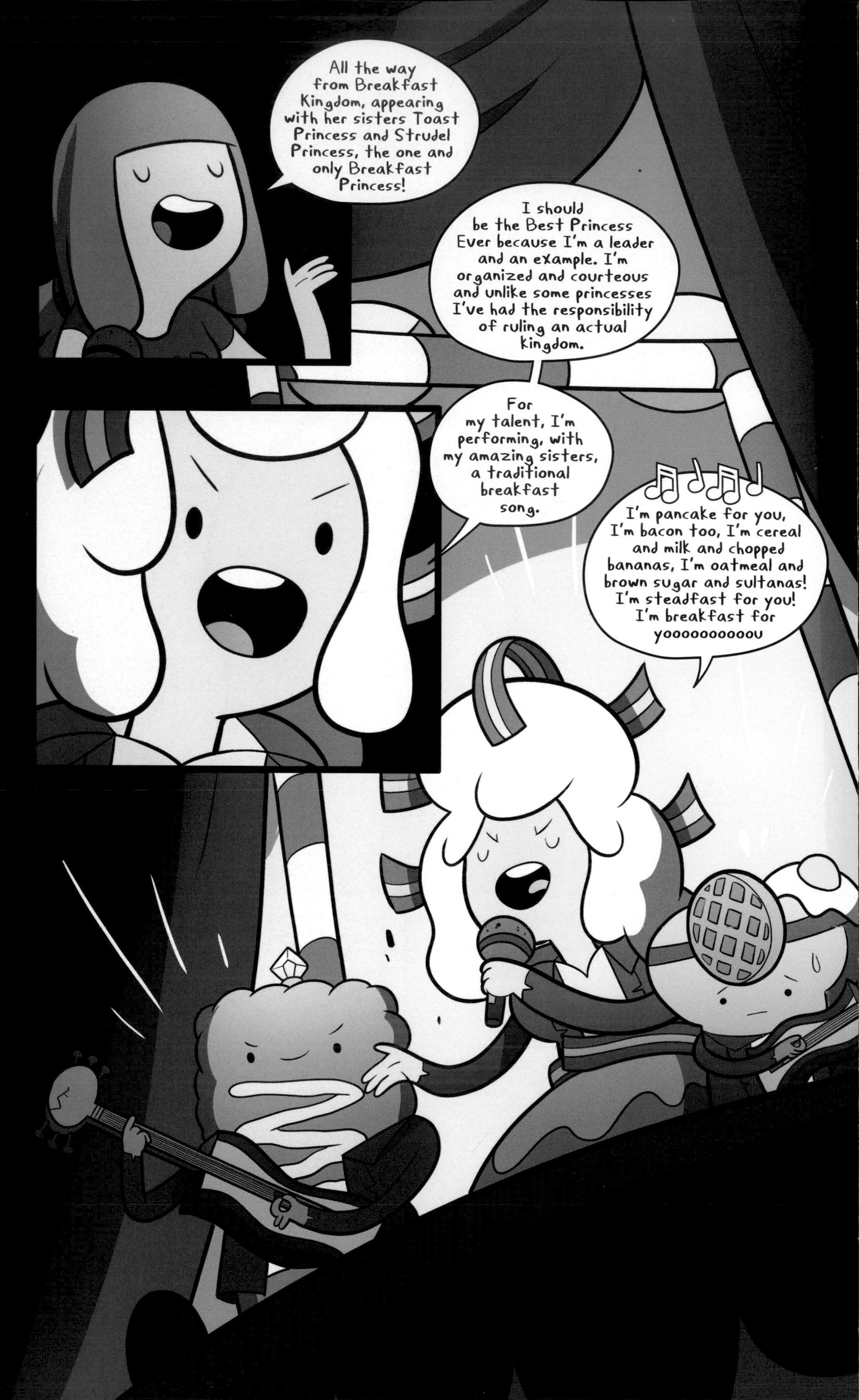
All the way from Breakfast Kingdom, appearing with her sisters Toast Princess and Strudel Princess, the one and only Breakfast Princess!
I should be the Best Princess Ever because I'm a leader and an example. I'm organized and courteous and unlike some princesses I've had the responsibility of ruling an actual kingdom.
For my talent, I'm performing, with my amazing sisters, a traditional breakfast song.
I'm pancake for you, I'm bacon too, I'm cereal and milk and chopped bananas, I'm oatmeal and brown sugar and sultanas! I'm steadfast for you! I'm breakfast for yoooooooooou

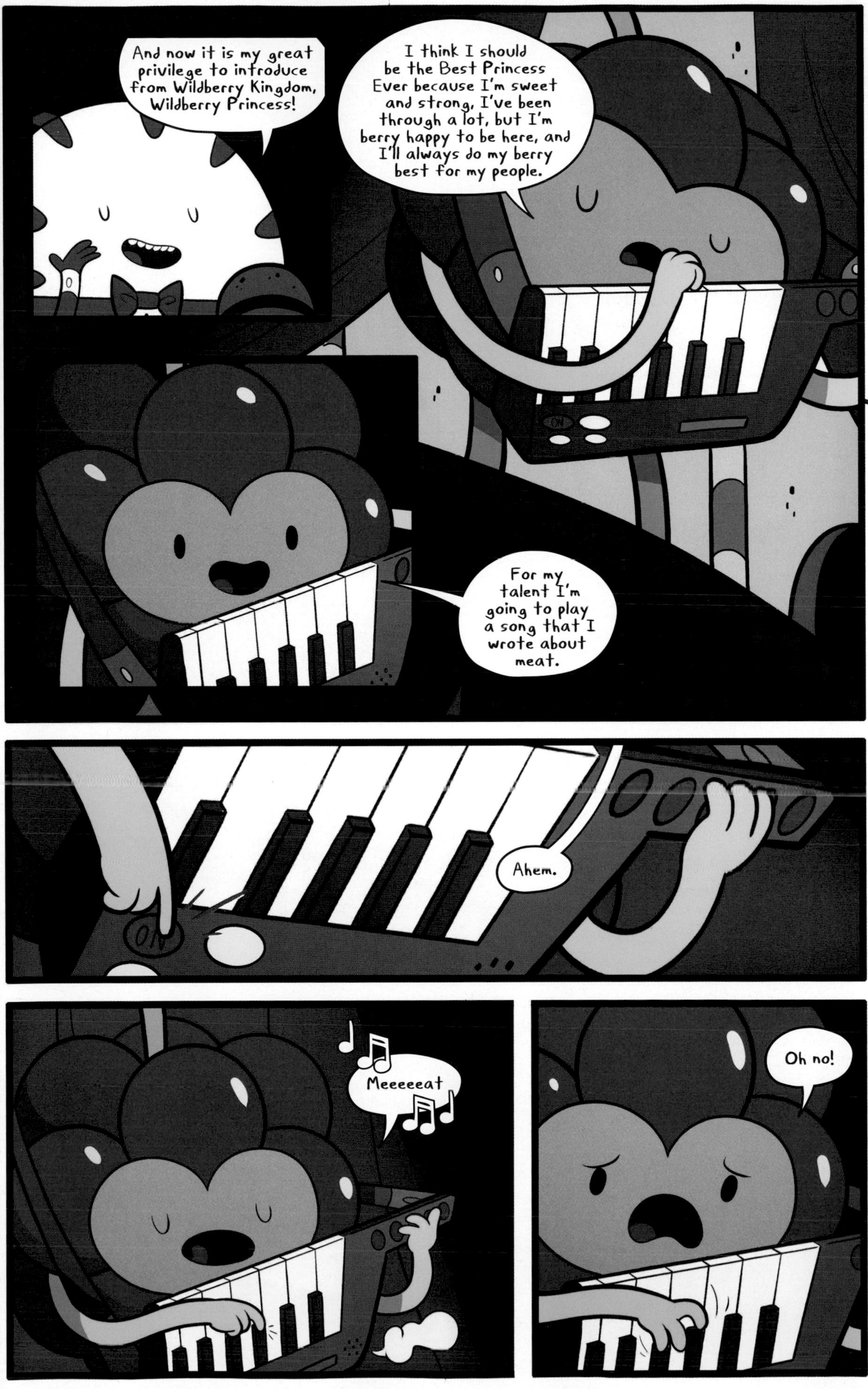
And now it is my great privilege to introduce from Wildberry Kingdom, Wildberry Princess!
I think I should be the Best Princess Ever because I'm sweet and strong, I've been through a lot, but I'm berry happy to be here, and I'll always do my berry best for my people.
For my talent I'm going to play a song that I wrote about meat.
Ahem.
Meeeeeat
Oh no!

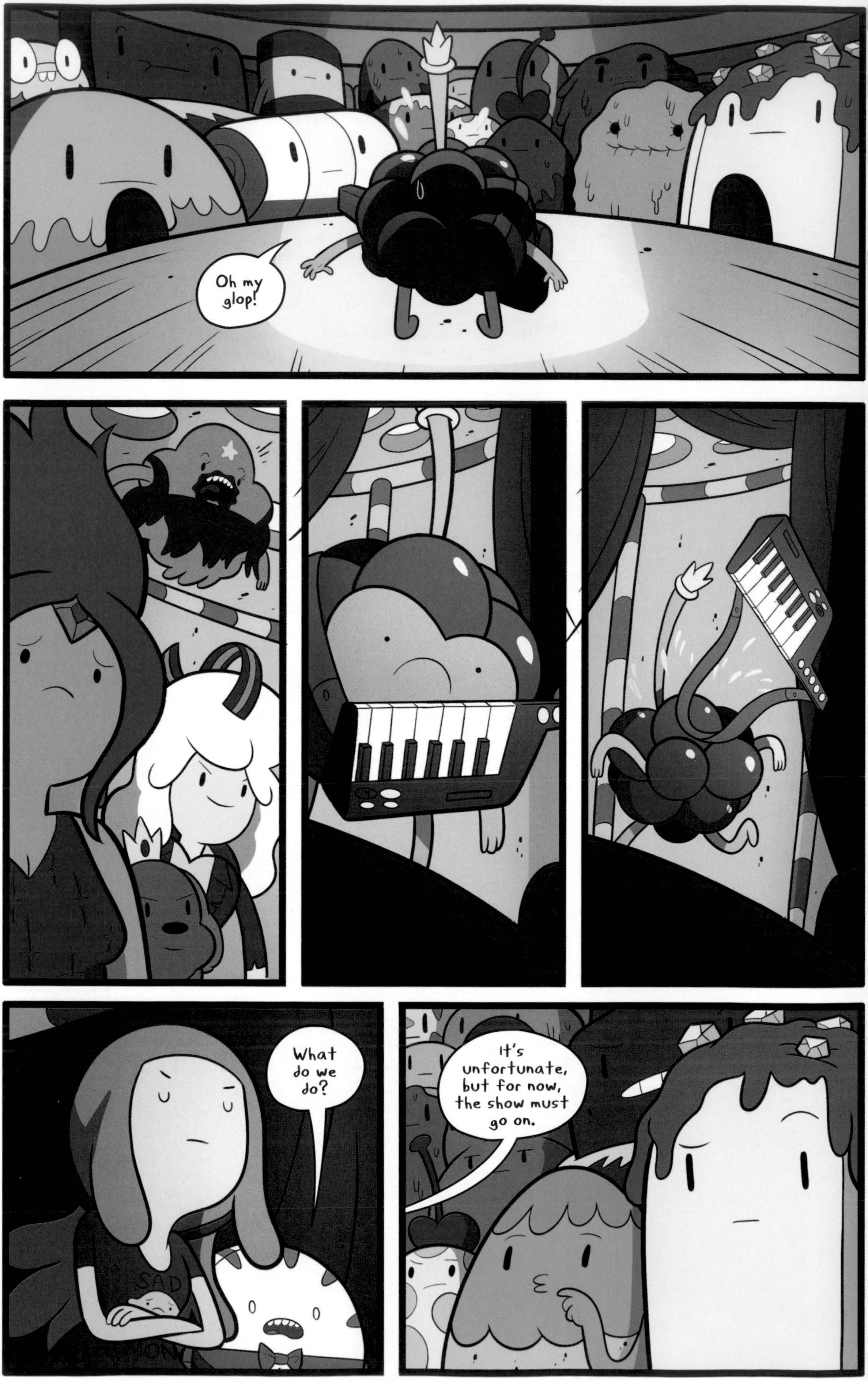
Oh my glop!
What do we do?
It's unfortunate, but for now, the show must go on.

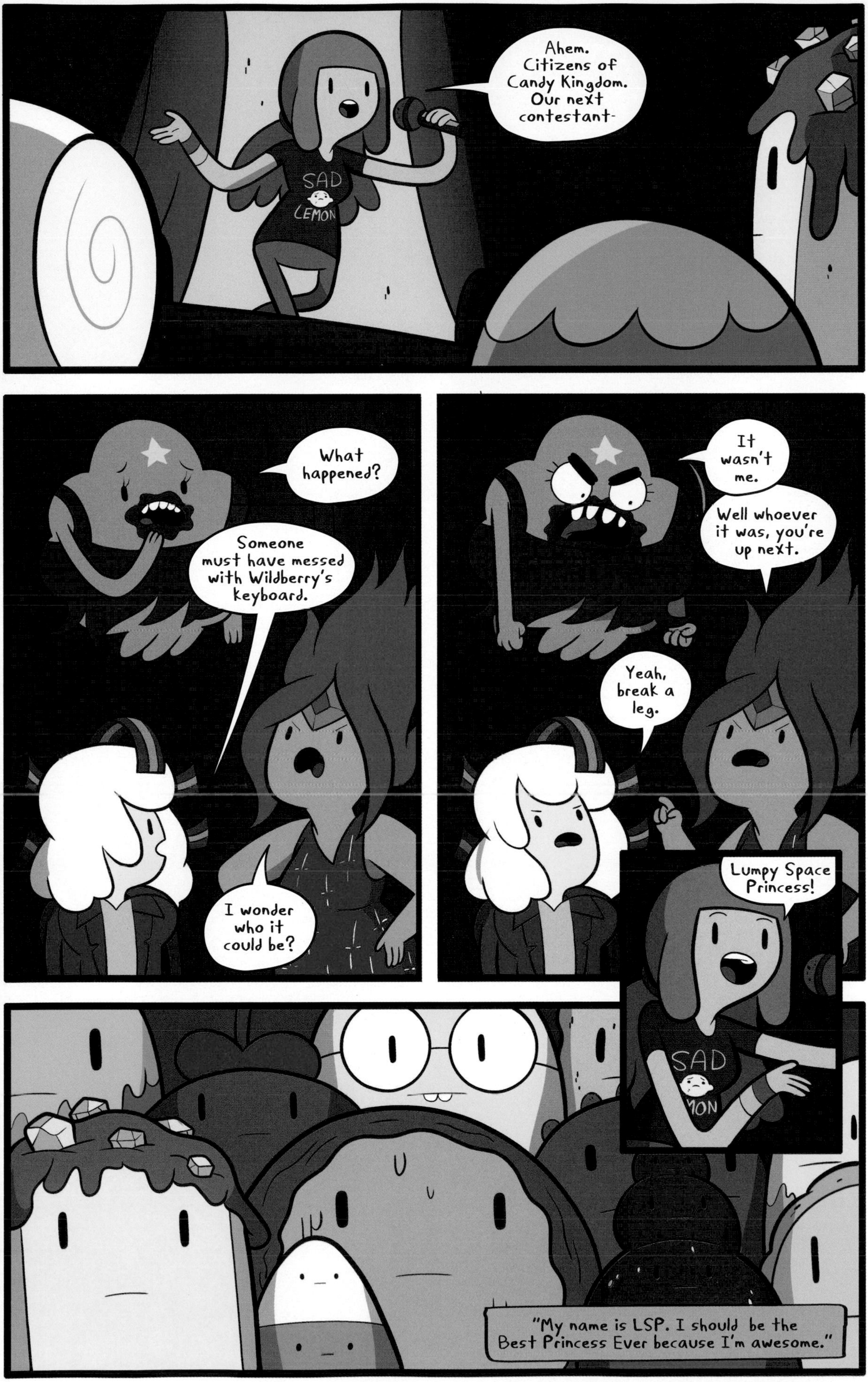
Ahem. Citizens of Candy Kingdom. Our next contestant-
SAD LEMON
What happened?
Someone must have messed with Wildberry's keyboard.
I wonder who it could be?
It wasn't me.
Well whoever it was, you're up next.
Yeah, break a leg.
Lumpy Space Princess!
SAD
"My name is LSP. I should be the Best Princess Ever because I'm awesome."

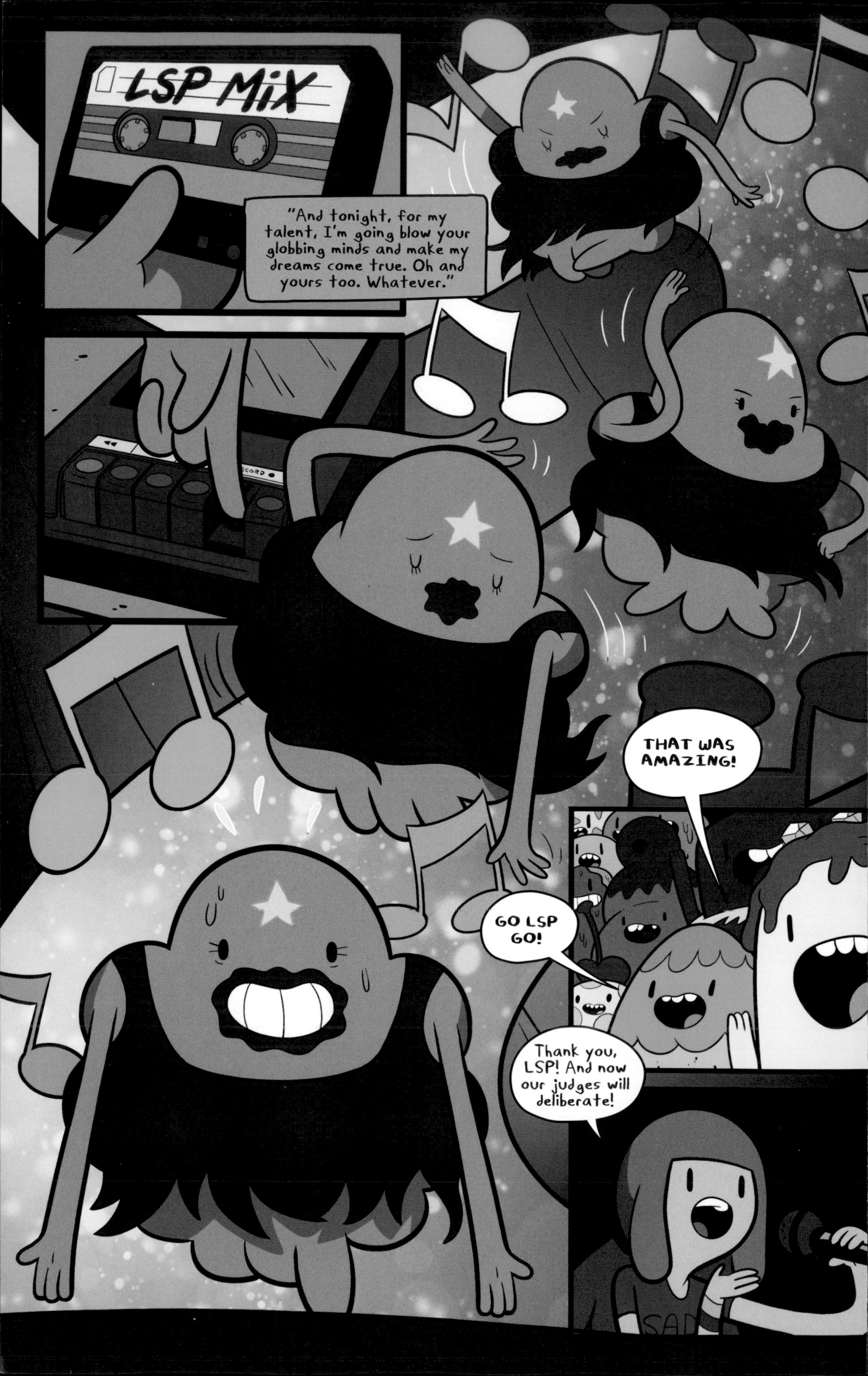
LSP MiX
"And tonight, for my talent, I'm going blow your globbing minds and make my dreams come true. Oh and yours too. Whatever."
RECORD
THAT WAS AMAZING!
GO LSP GO!
Thank you, LSP! And now our judges will deliberate!

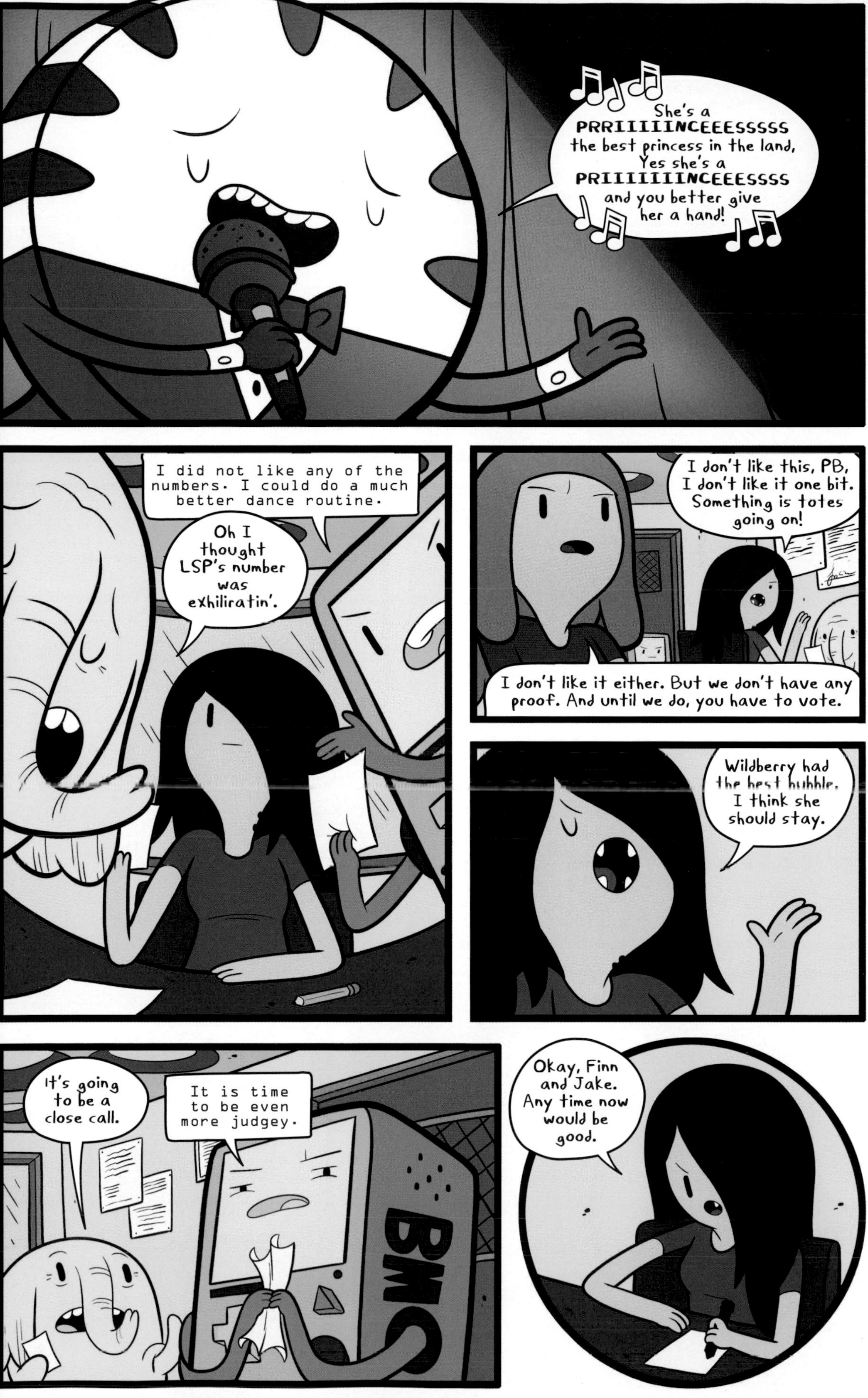

She's a PRRIIIIINCEEESSSSS the best princess in the land, Yes she's a PRIIIIIIINCEEESSSS and you better give her a hand!
I did not like any of the numbers. I could do a much better dance routine.
Oh I thought LSP's number was exhiliratin'.
I don't like this, PB, I don't like it one bit. Something is totes going on!
I don't like it either. But we don't have any proof. And until we do, you have to vote.
Wildberry had the best bubble. I think she should stay.
It's going to be a close call.
It is time to be even more judgey.
BMO
Okay, Finn and Jake. Any time now would be good.

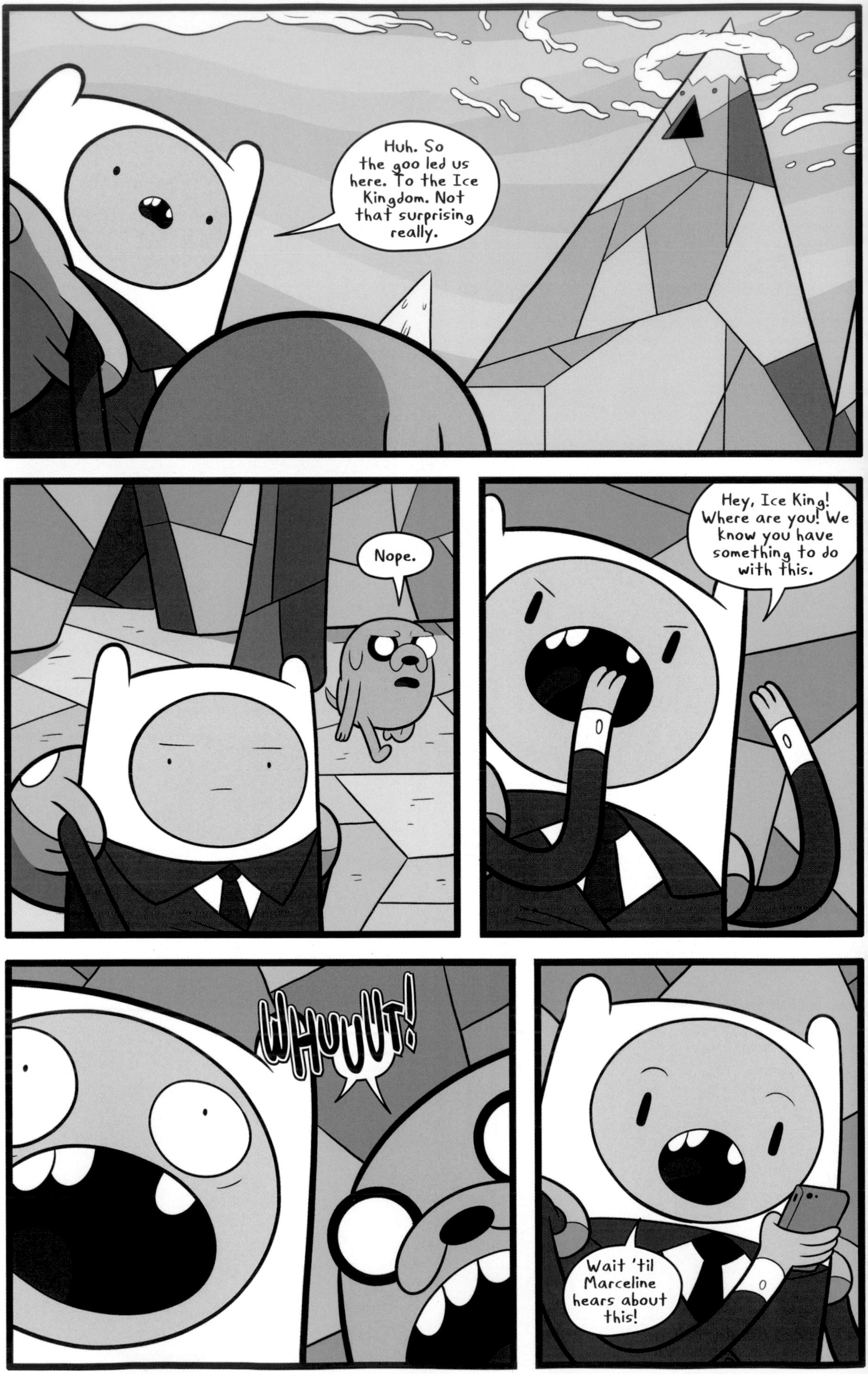
Huh. So the goo led us here. To the Ice Kingdom. Not that surprising really.
Nope.
Hey, Ice King! Where are you! We know you have something to do with this.
WHUUUT!
Wait 'til Marceline hears about this!

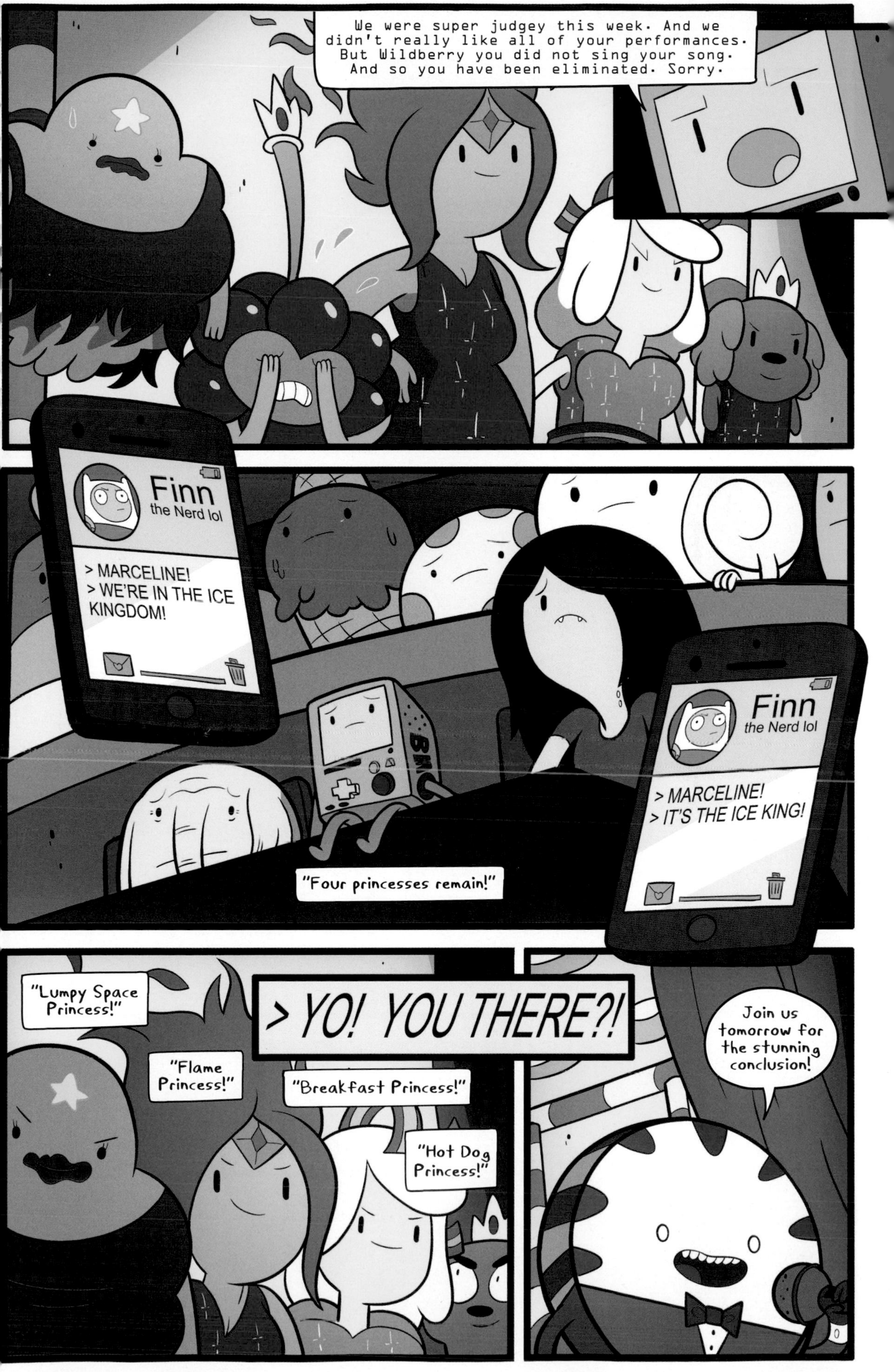
We were super judgey this week. And we didn't really like all of your performances. But Wildberry you did not sing your song. And so you have been eliminated. Sorry.
Finn
the Nerd lol
> MARCELINE!
> WE'RE IN THE ICE KINGDOM!
Finn
the Nerd lol
> MARCELINE!
> IT'S THE ICE KING!
"Four princesses remain!"
"Lumpy Space Princess!"
> YO! YOU THERE?!
"Flame Princess!"
"Breakfast Princess!"
"Hot Dog Princess!"
Join us tomorrow for the stunning conclusion!

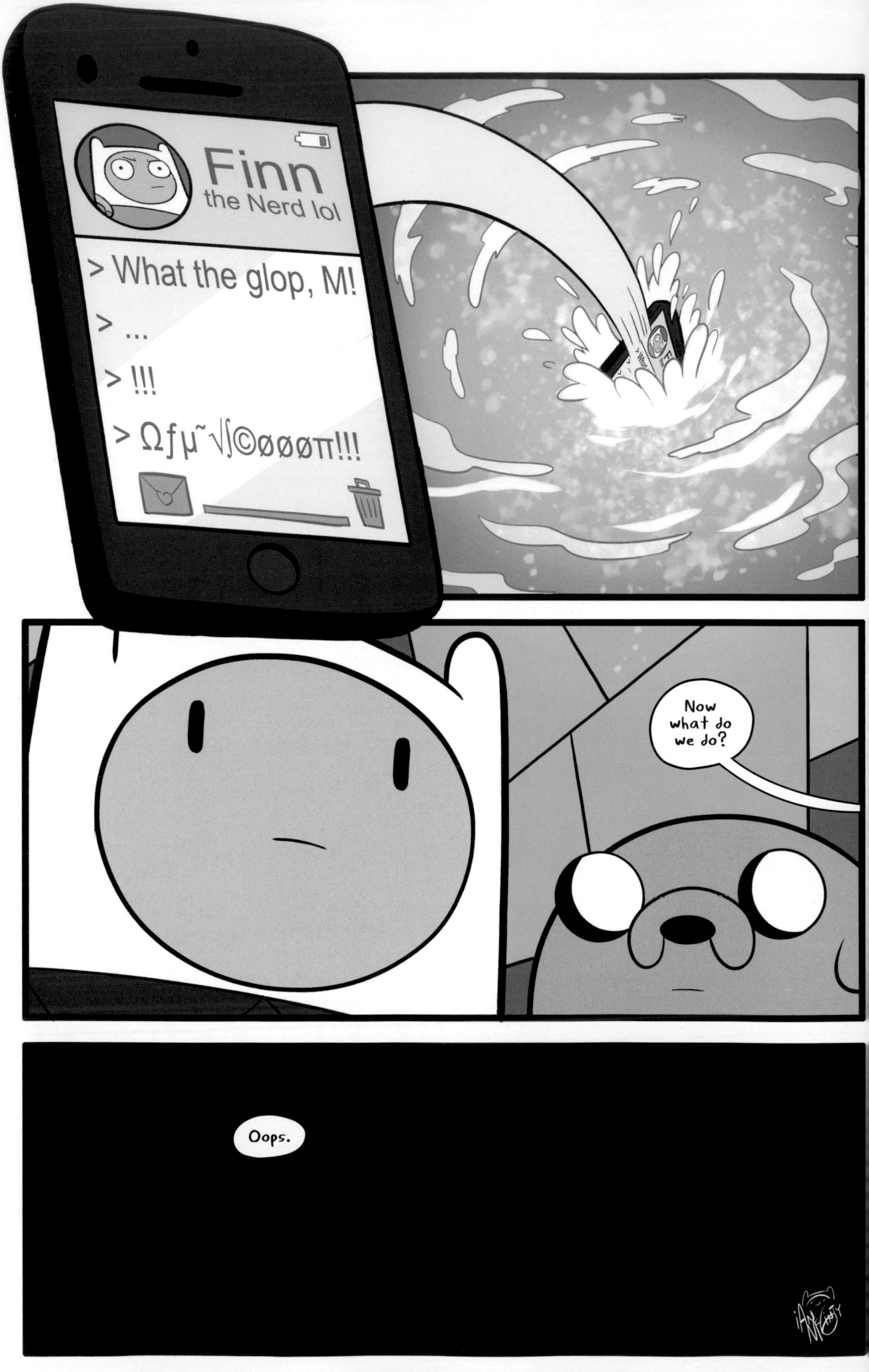
Finn
the Nerd lol
> What the glop, M!
> ...
> !!!
> Ωƒµ˜√∫©øøøπ!!!
Now what do we do?
Oops.

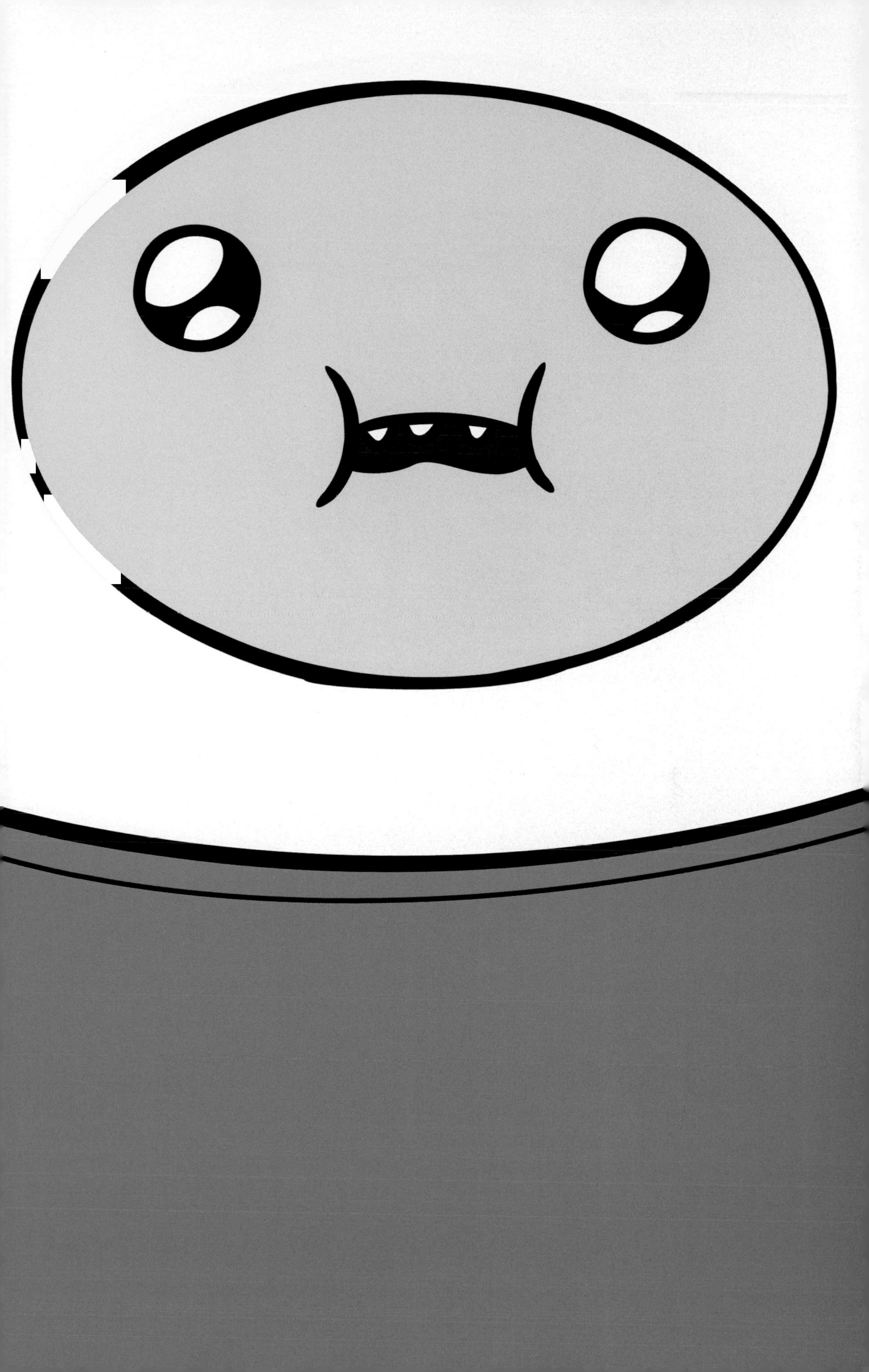

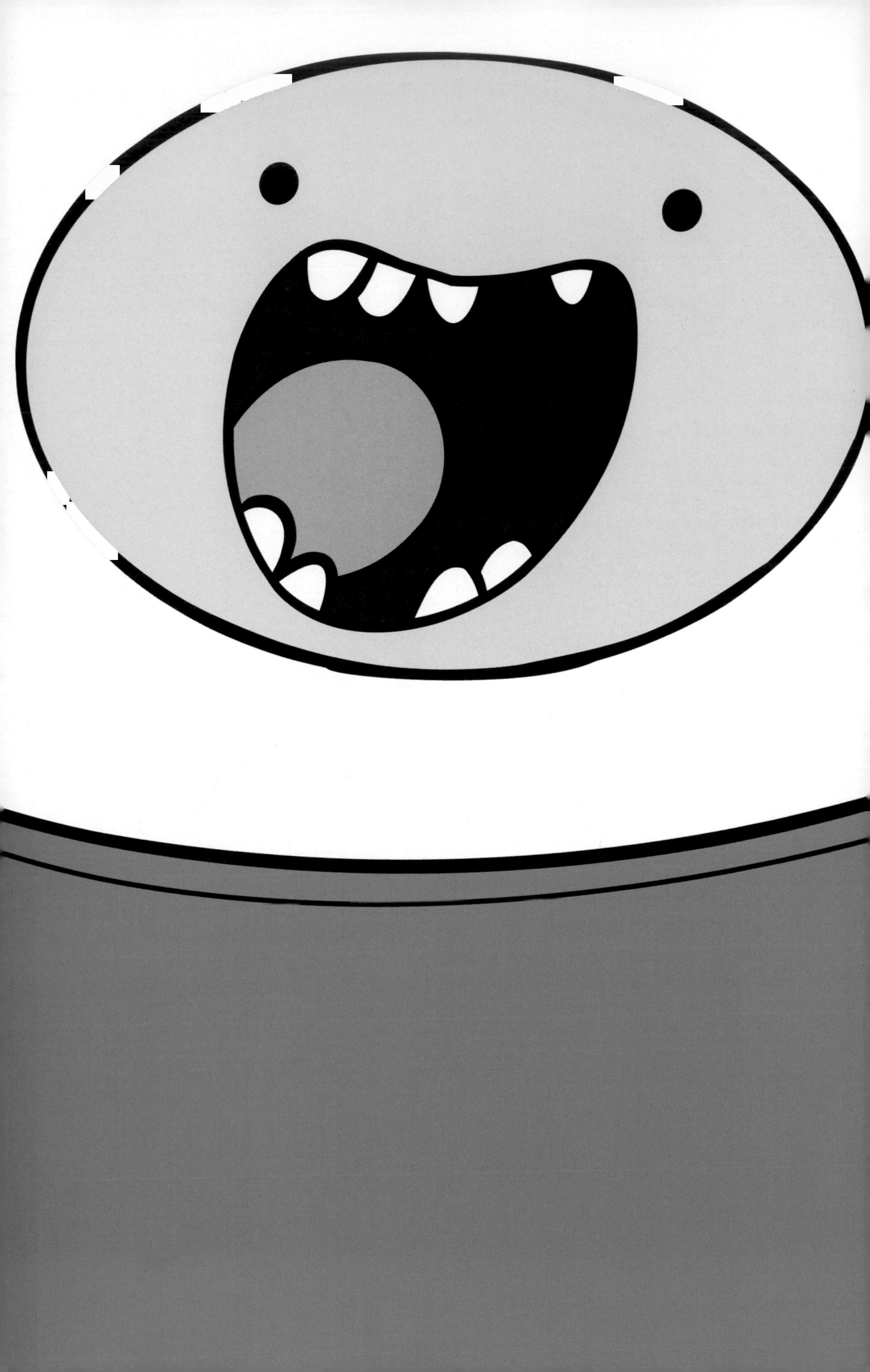

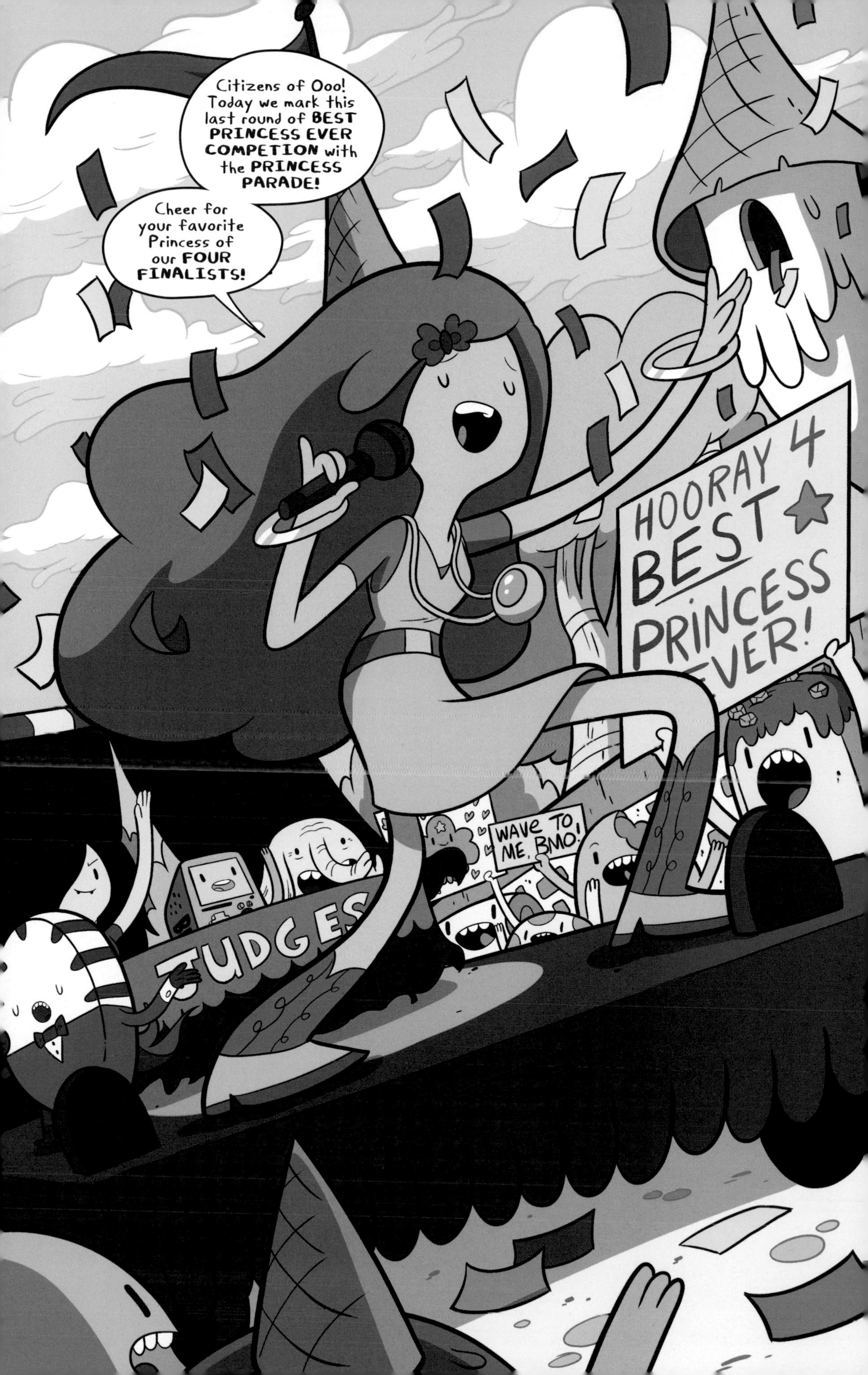
Citizens of Ooo! Today we mark this last round of BEST PRINCESS EVER COMPETION with the PRINCESS PARADE!
Cheer for your favorite Princess of our FOUR FINALISTS!
HOORAY 4 BEST PRINCESS EVER!
WAVE TO ME, BMO!
JUDGES

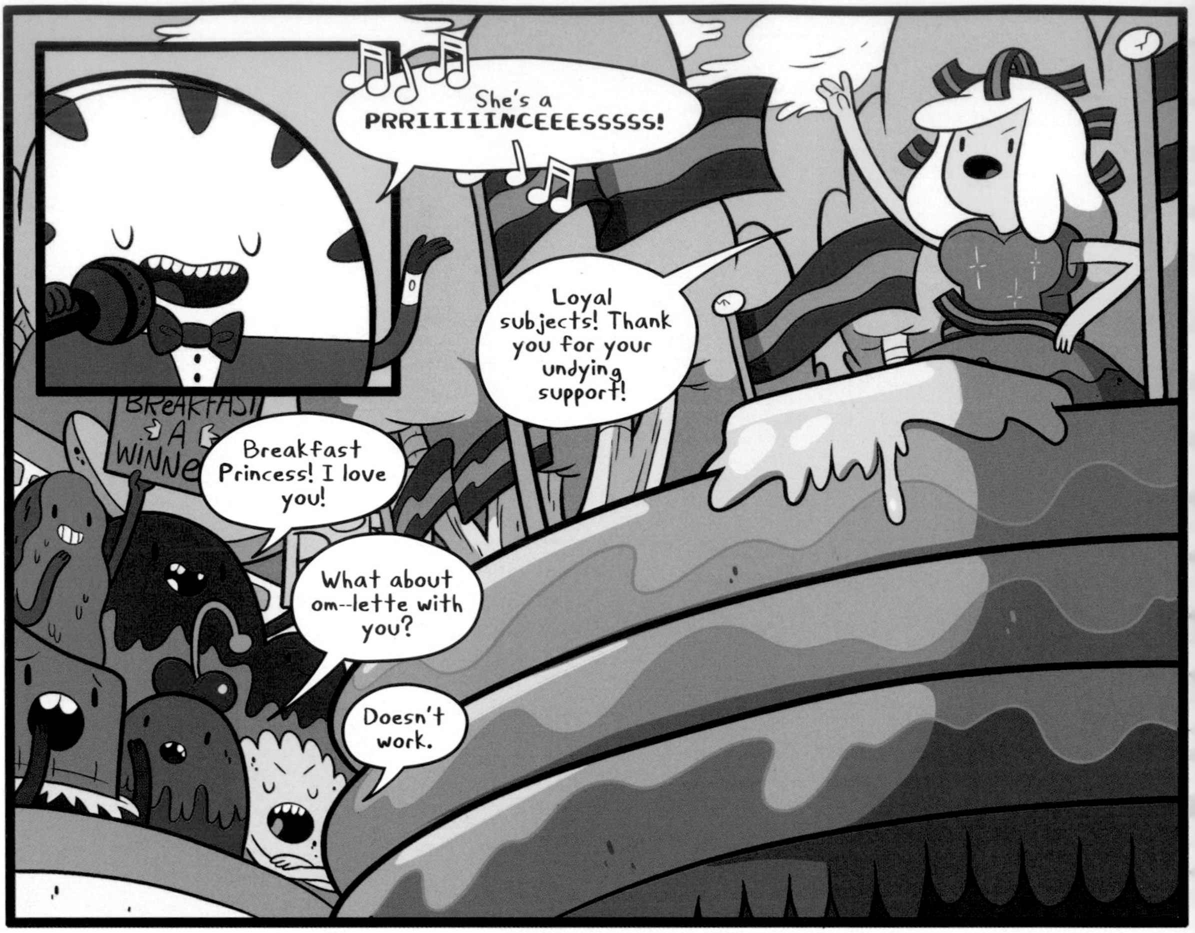
She's a PRRIIIIIINCEEEESSSSS!
Loyal subjects! Thank you for your undying support!
BREAKFAST A WINNE
Breakfast Princess! I love you!
What about om--lette with you?
Doesn't work.

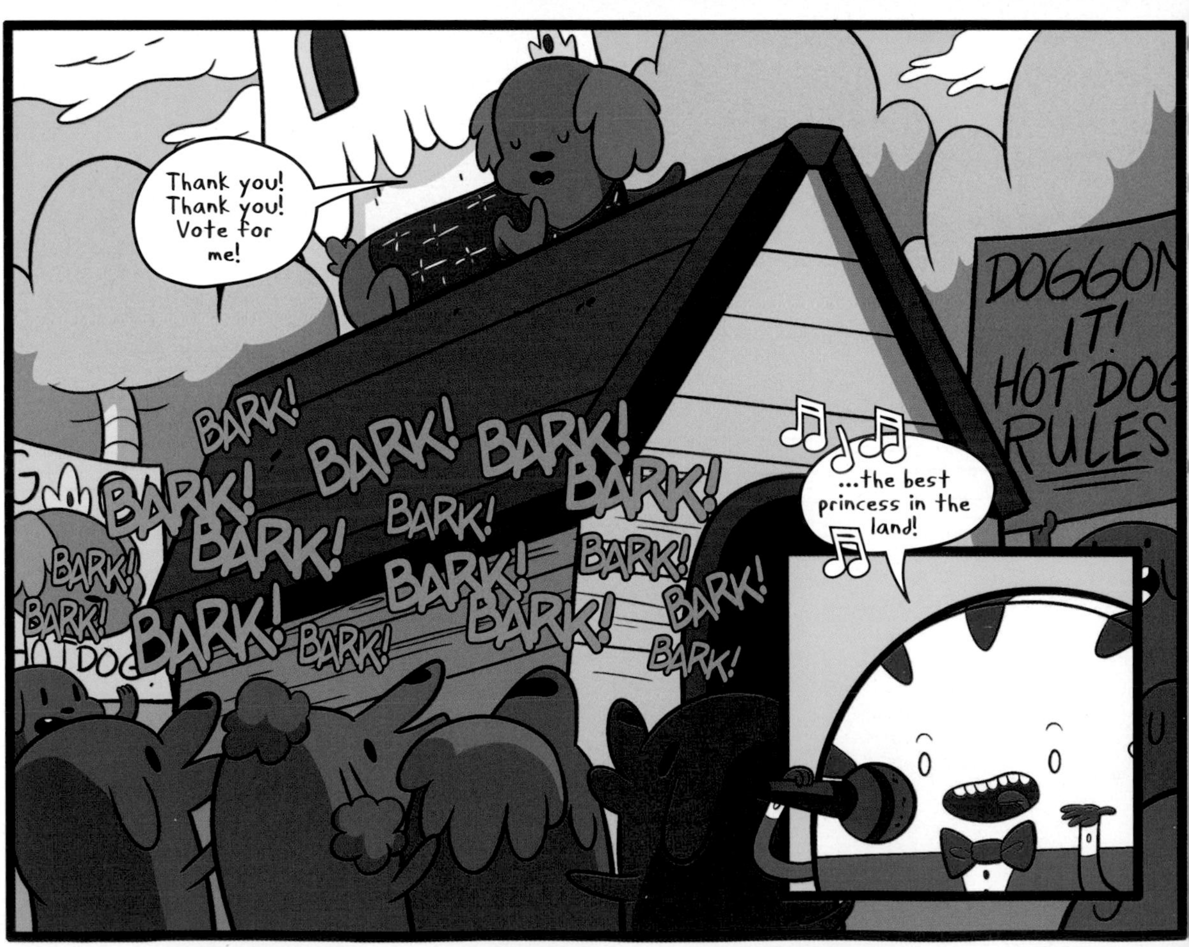
Thank you! Thank you! Vote for me!
DOGGON IT! HOT DOG RULES
BARK! BARK! BARK! BARK! BARK! BARK! BARK! BARK! BARK! BARK! BARK! BARK! BARK! BARK! BARK! BARK!
...the best princess in the land!

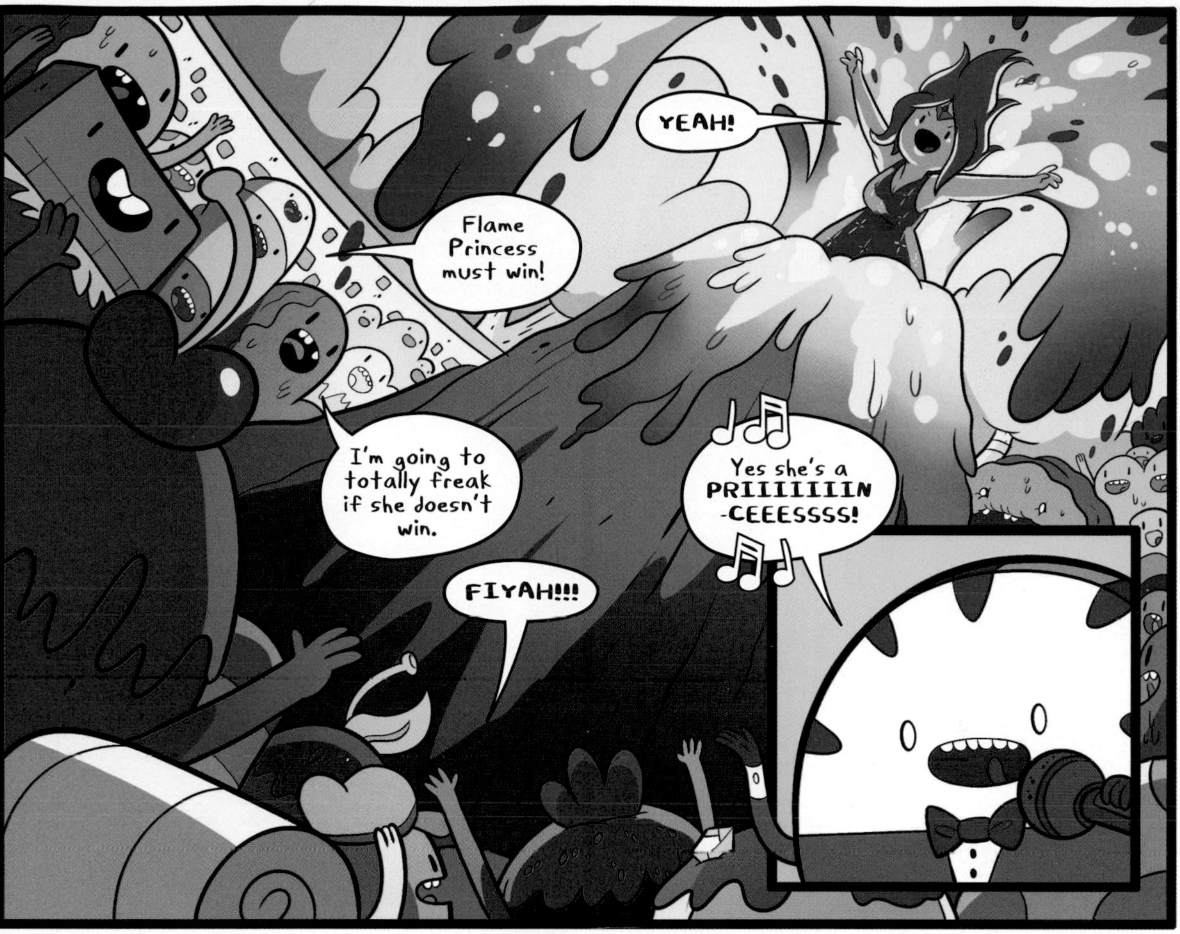
YEAH!
Flame Princess must win!
I'm going to totally freak if she doesn't win.
FIYAH!!!
Yes she's a PRIIIIIIIN-CEEESSSS!

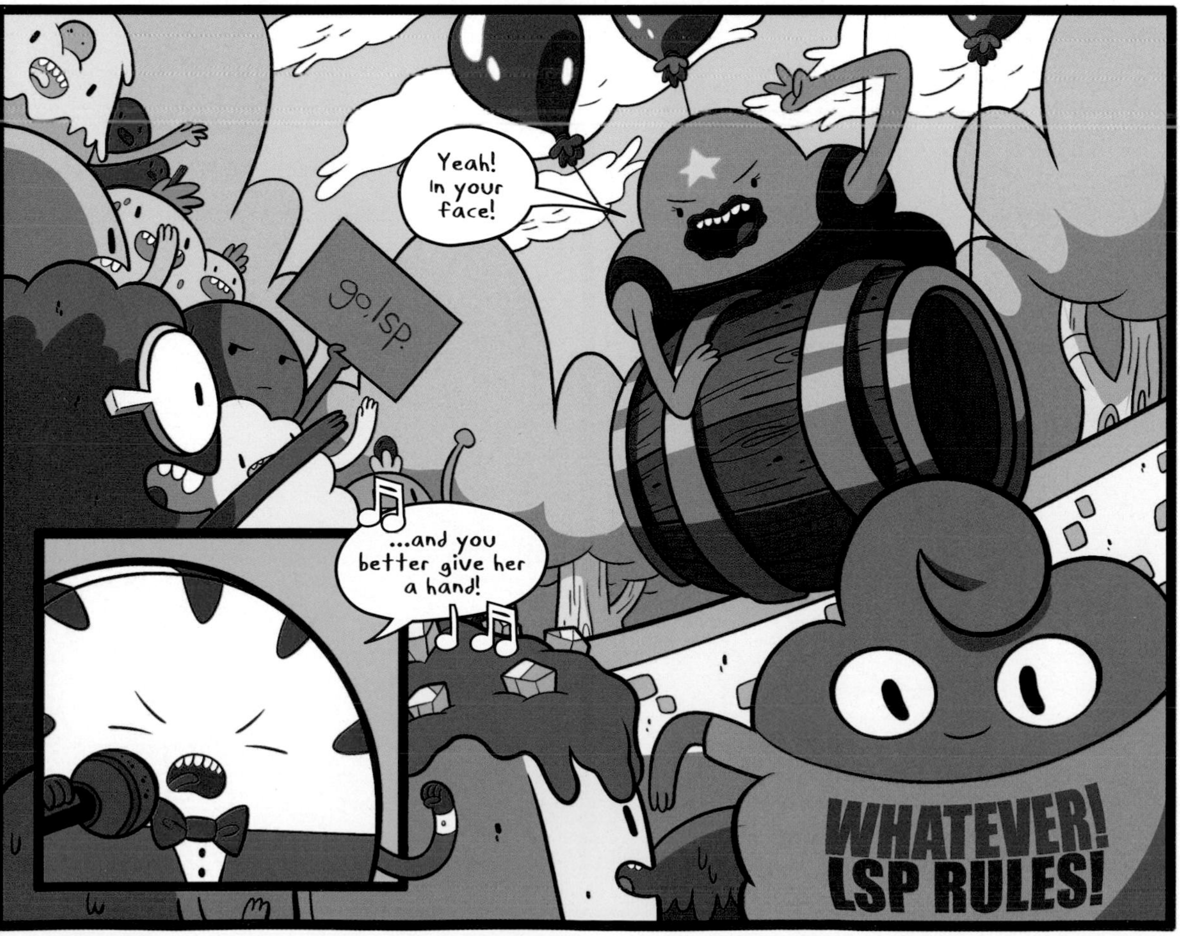
Yeah! In your face!
go lsp
...and you better give her a hand!
WHATEVER! LSP RULES!

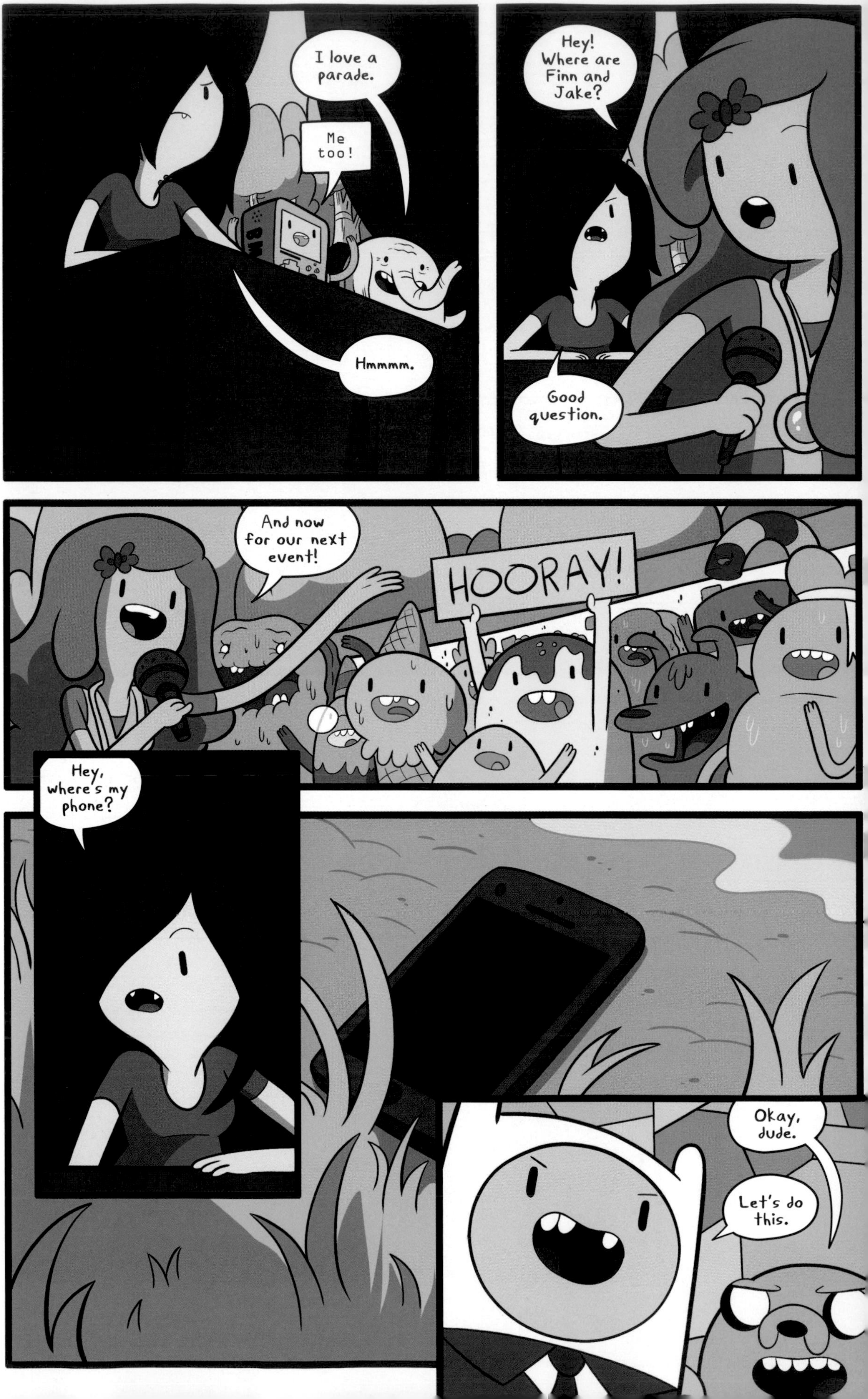
I love a parade.
Me too!
Hmmmm.
Hey! Where are Finn and Jake?
Good question.
And now for our next event!
HOORAY!
Hey, where's my phone?
Okay, dude.
Let's do this.

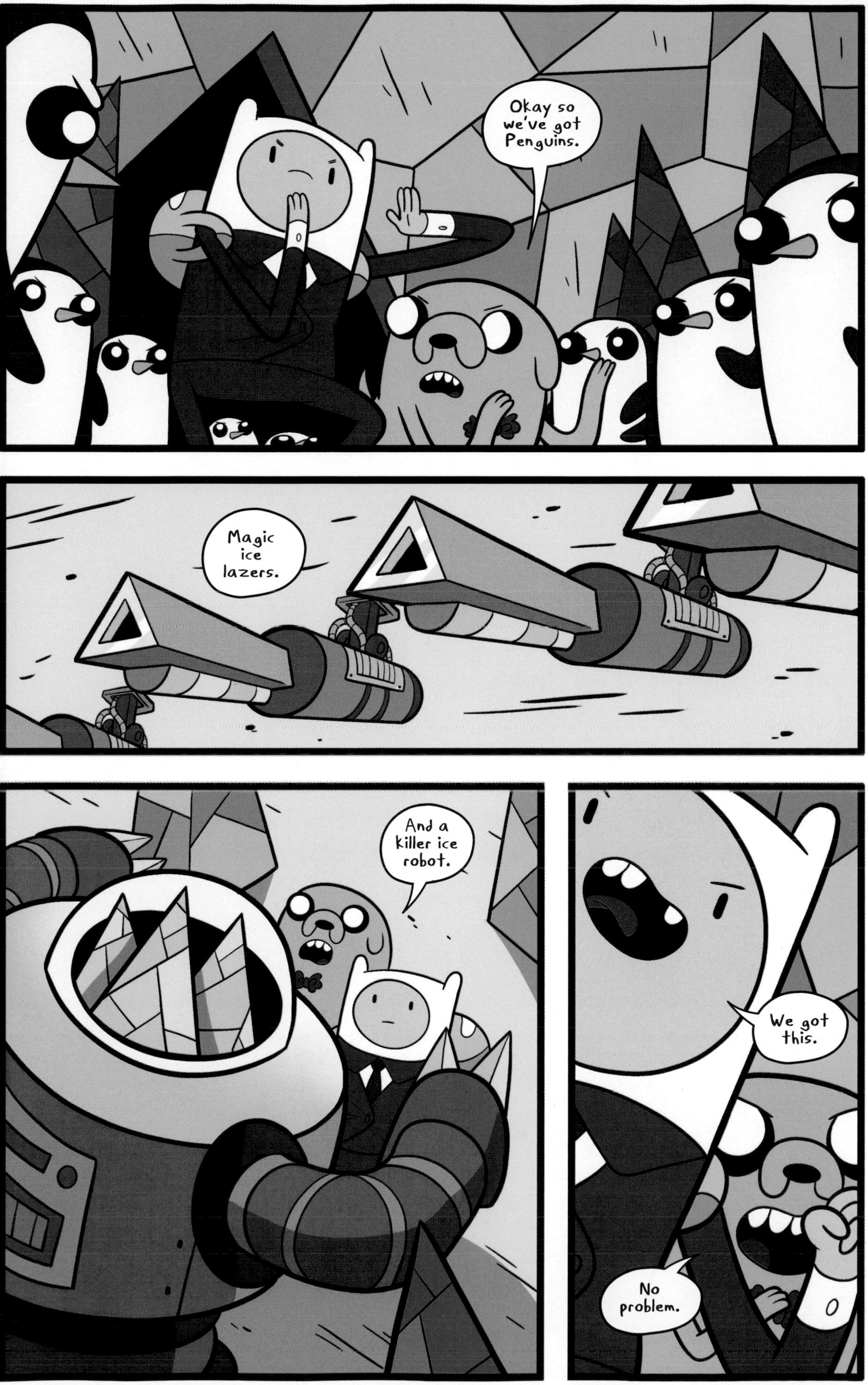
Okay so we've got Penguins.
Magic ice lazers.
And a killer ice robot.
We got this.
No problem.

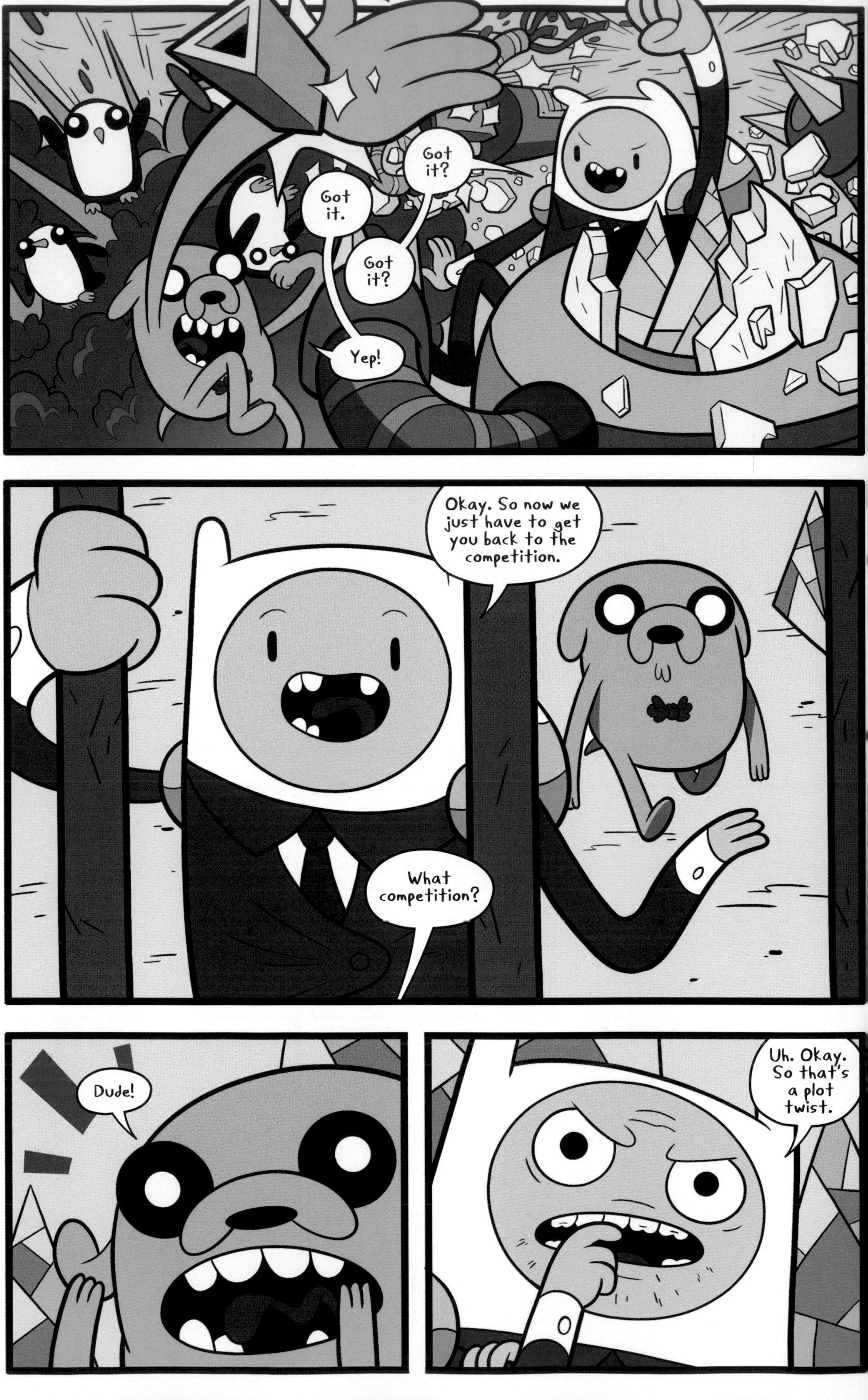
Got it?
Got it.
Got it?
Yep!
Okay. So now we just have to get you back to the competition.
What competition?
Dude!
Uh. Okay. So that's a plot twist.

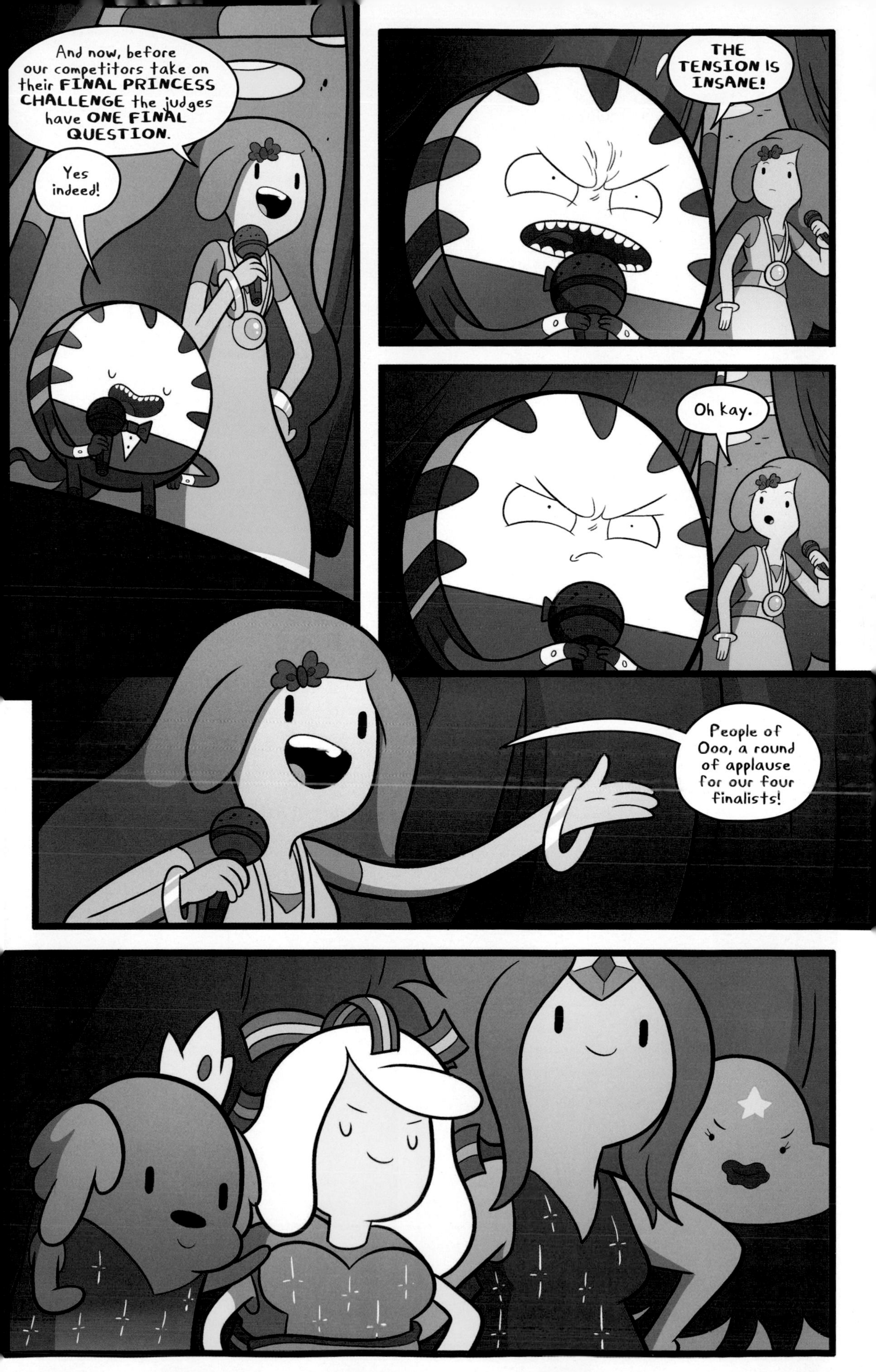
And now, before our competitors take on their **FINAL PRINCESS CHALLENGE** the judges have **ONE FINAL QUESTION.**
Yes indeed!
THE TENSION IS INSANE!
Oh kay.
People of Ooo, a round of applause for our four finalists!

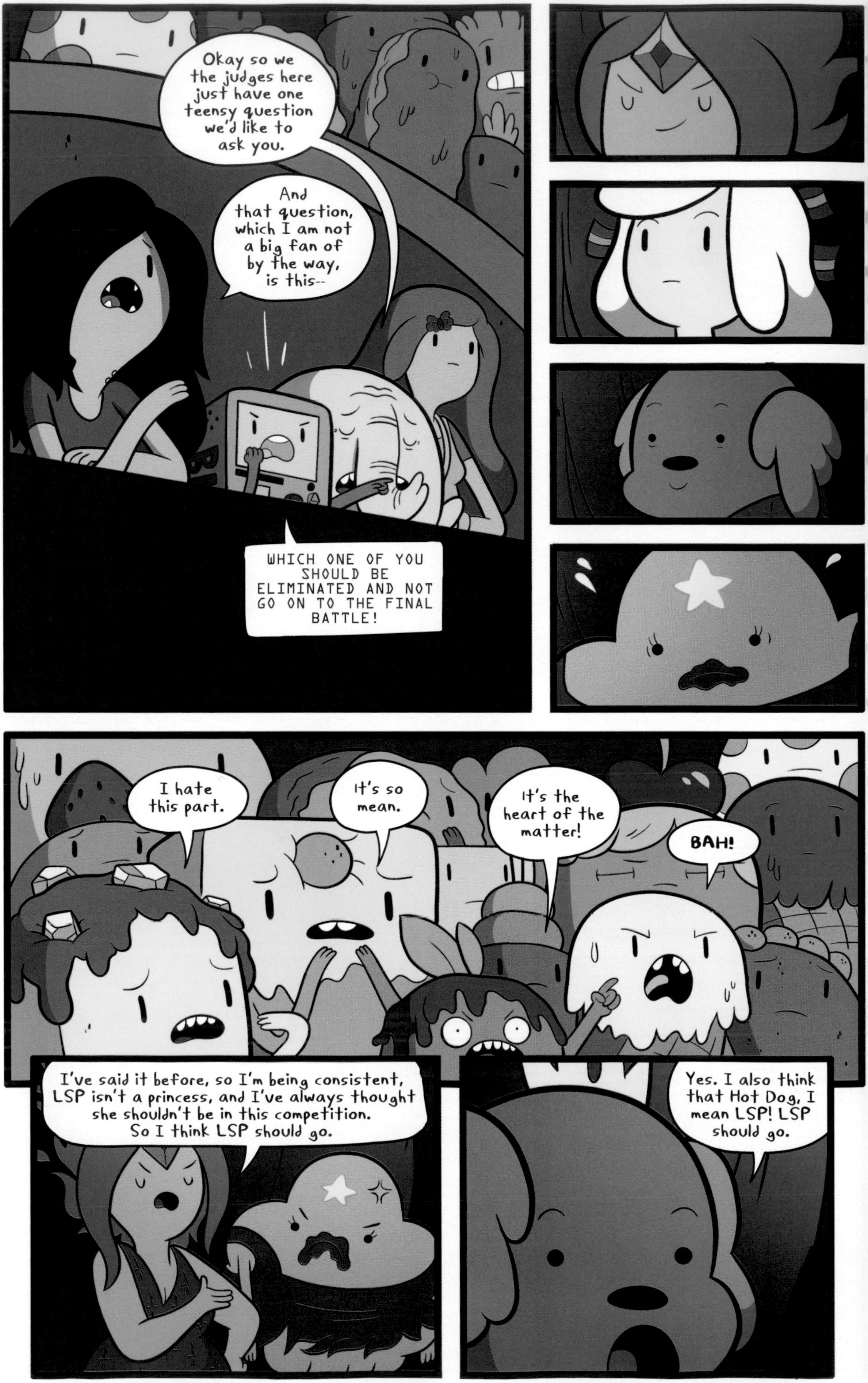

Okay so we the judges here just have one teensy question we'd like to ask you.
And that question, which I am not a big fan of by the way, is this--
WHICH ONE OF YOU SHOULD BE ELIMINATED AND NOT GO ON TO THE FINAL BATTLE!
I hate this part.
It's so mean.
It's the heart of the matter!
BAH!
I've said it before, so I'm being consistent, LSP isn't a princess, and I've always thought she shouldn't be in this competition. So I think LSP should go.
Yes. I also think that Hot Dog, I mean LSP! LSP should go.

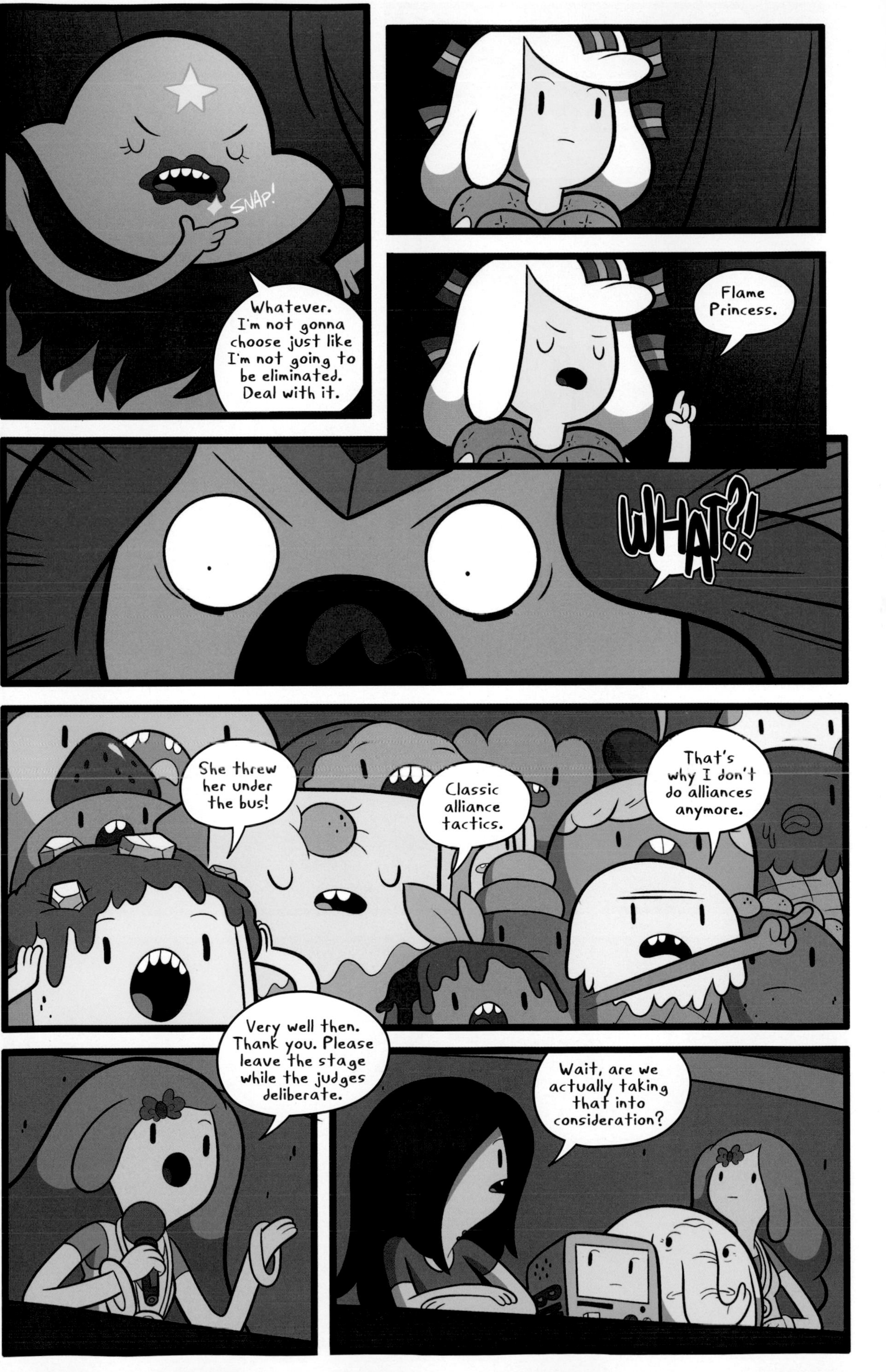
SNAP!
Whatever. I'm not gonna choose just like I'm not going to be eliminated. Deal with it.
Flame Princess.
WHAT?!
She threw her under the bus!
Classic alliance tactics.
That's why I don't do alliances anymore.
Very well then. Thank you. Please leave the stage while the judges deliberate.
Wait, are we actually taking that into consideration?

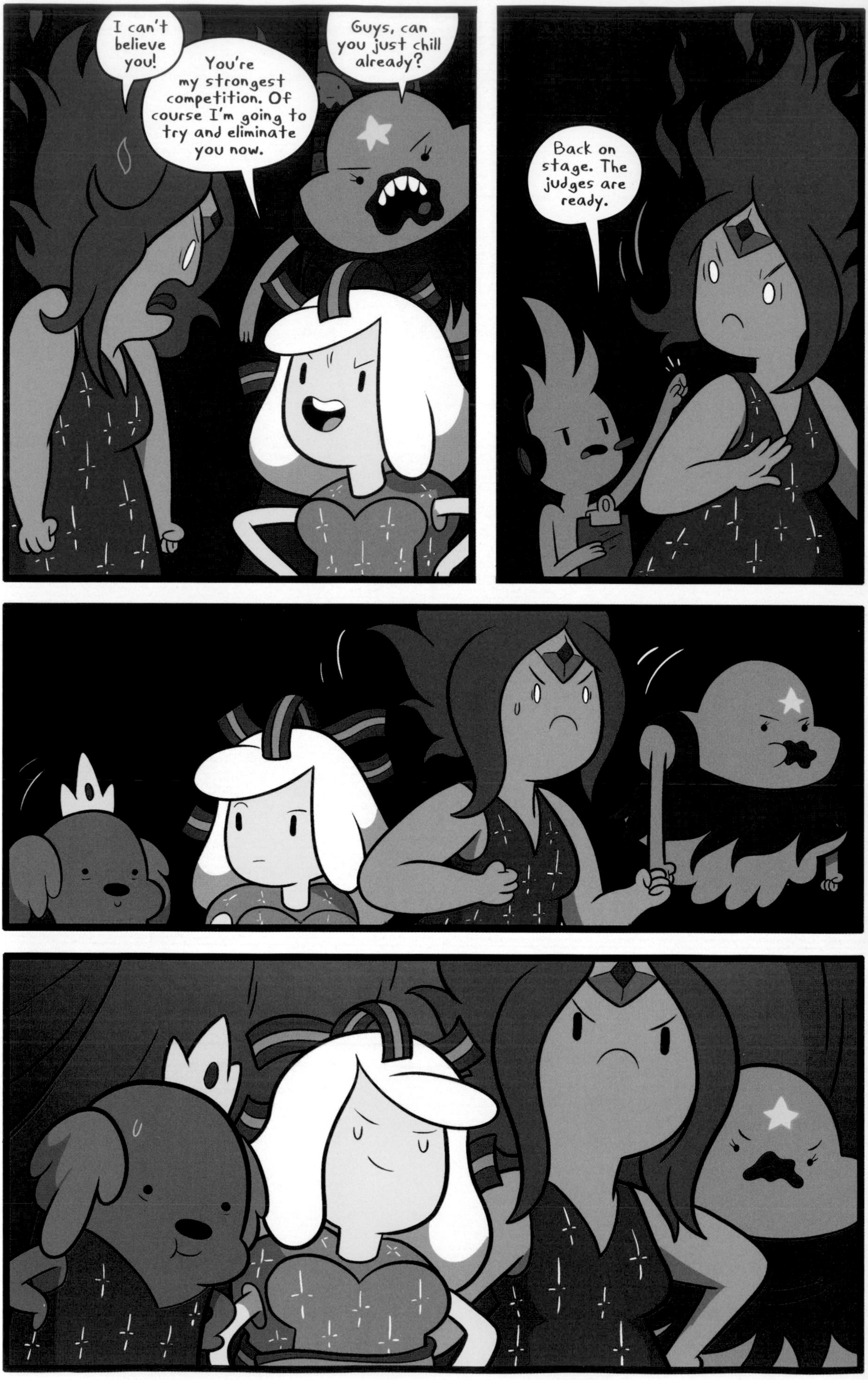

I can't believe you!
You're my strongest competition. Of course I'm going to try and eliminate you now.
Guys, can you just chill already?
Back on stage. The judges are ready.

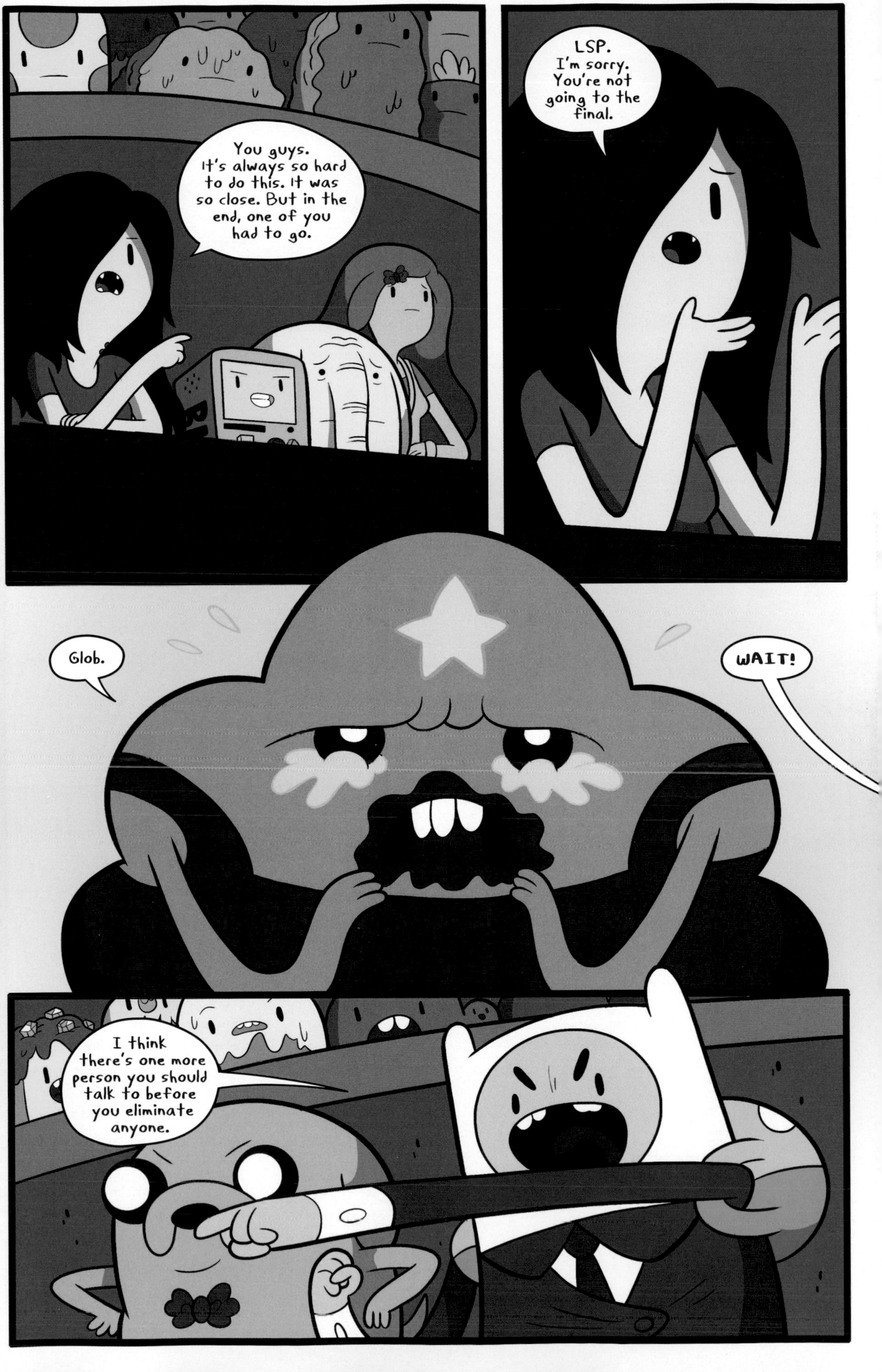
You guys. It's always so hard to do this. It was so close. But in the end, one of you had to go.
LSP. I'm sorry. You're not going to the final.
Glob.
WAIT!
I think there's one more person you should talk to before you eliminate anyone.

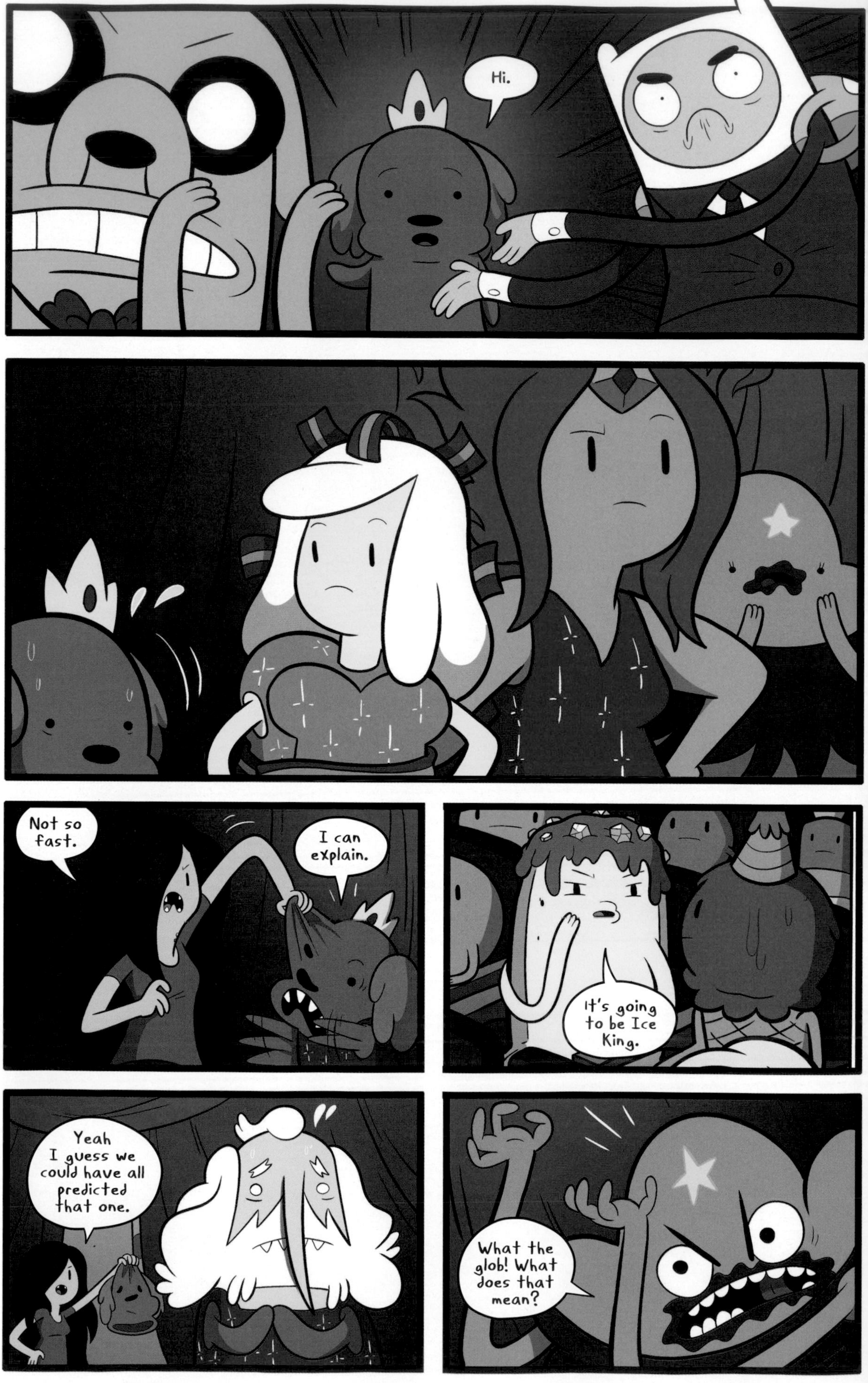
Hi.
Not so fast.
I can explain.
It's going to be Ice King.
Yeah I guess we could have all predicted that one.
What the glob! What does that mean?

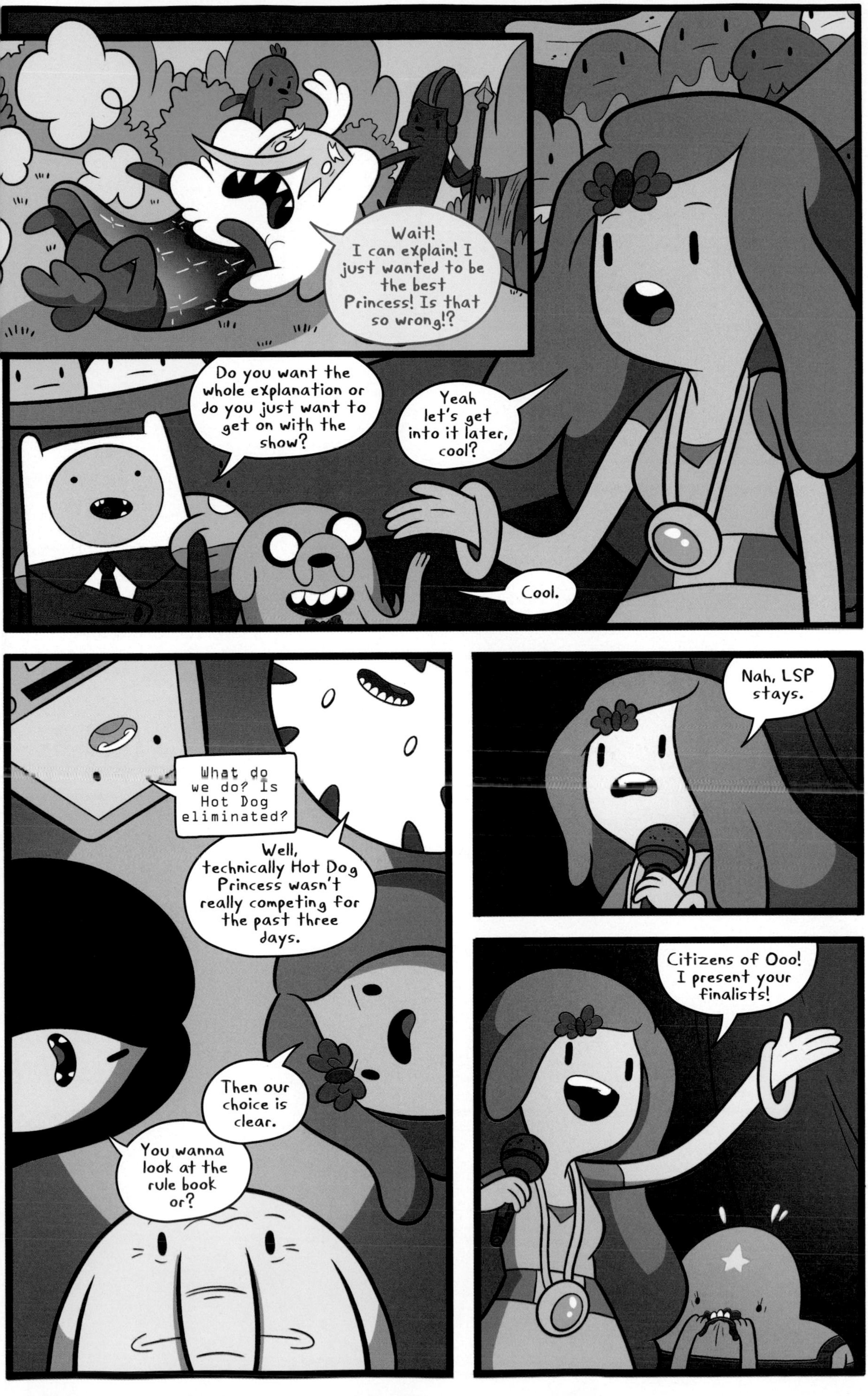

Wait! I can explain! I just wanted to be the best Princess! Is that so wrong!?
Do you want the whole explanation or do you just want to get on with the show?
Yeah let's get into it later, cool?
Cool.
What do we do? Is Hot Dog eliminated?
Well, technically Hot Dog Princess wasn't really competing for the past three days.
Then our choice is clear.
You wanna look at the rule book or?
Nah, LSP stays.
Citizens of Ooo! I present your finalists!

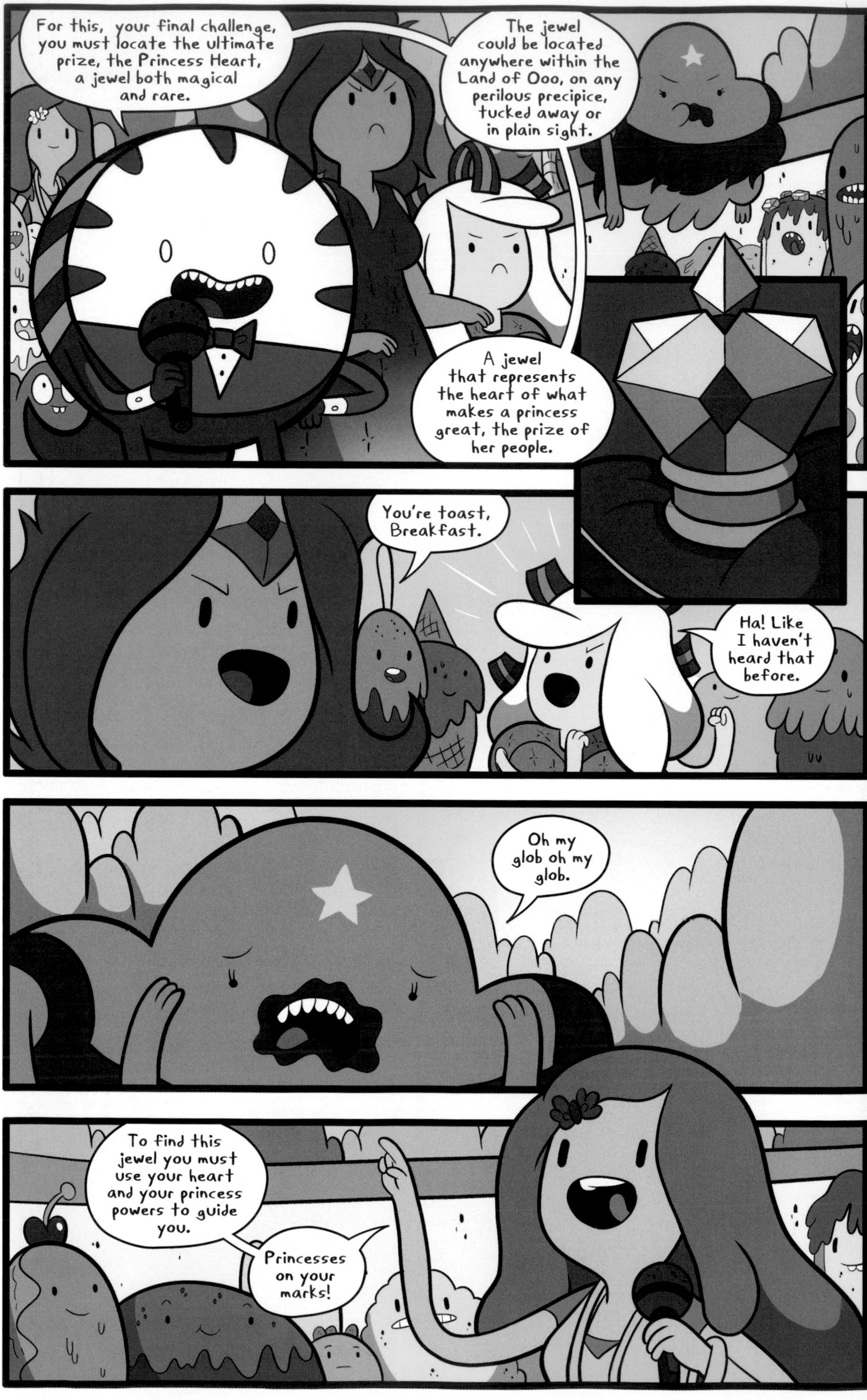
For this, your final challenge, you must locate the ultimate prize, the Princess Heart, a jewel both magical and rare.
The jewel could be located anywhere within the Land of Ooo, on any perilous precipice, tucked away or in plain sight.
A jewel that represents the heart of what makes a princess great, the prize of her people.
You're toast, Breakfast.
Ha! Like I haven't heard that before.
Oh my glob oh my glob.
To find this jewel you must use your heart and your princess powers to guide you.
Princesses on your marks!

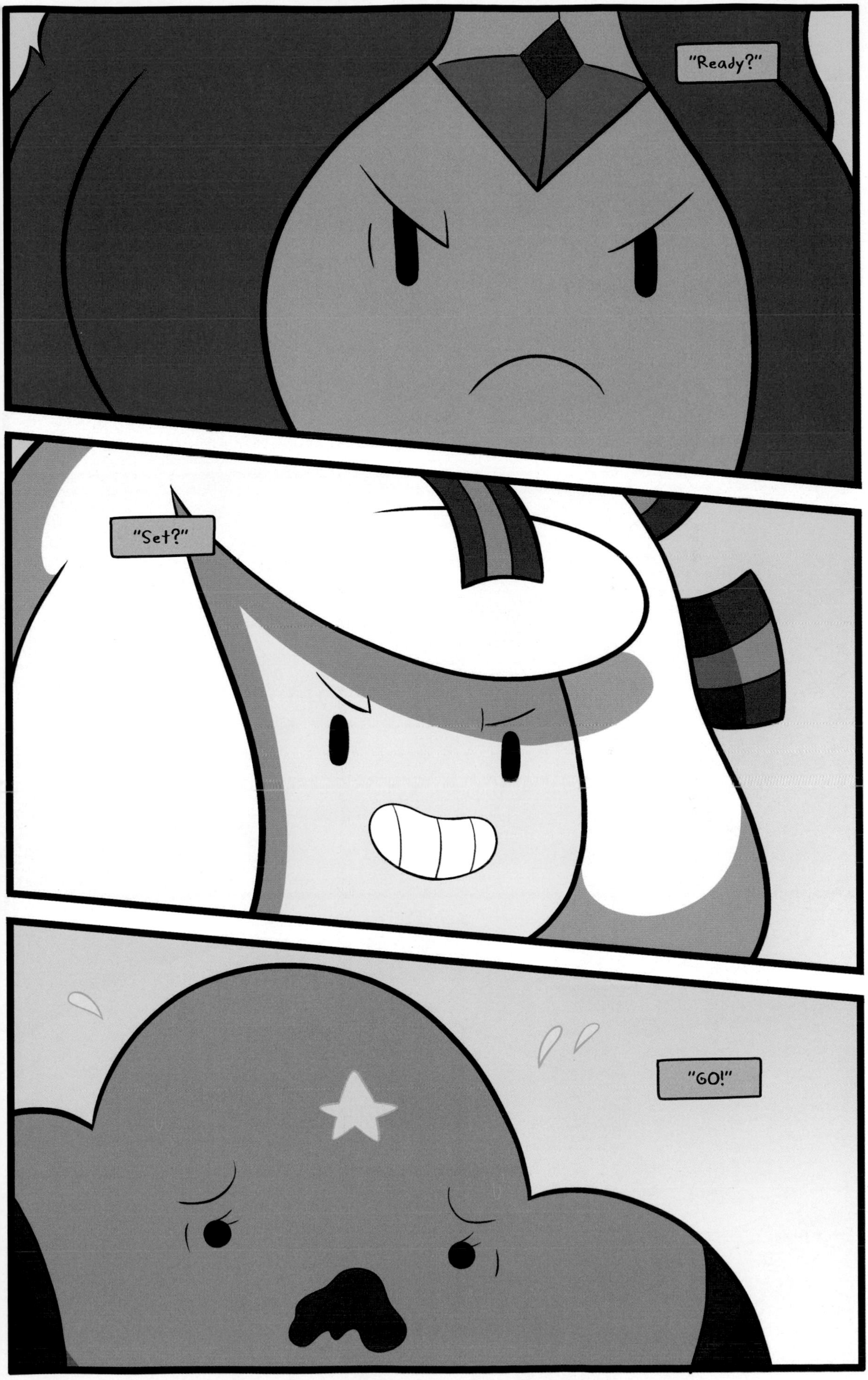
"Ready?"
"Set?"
"GO!"

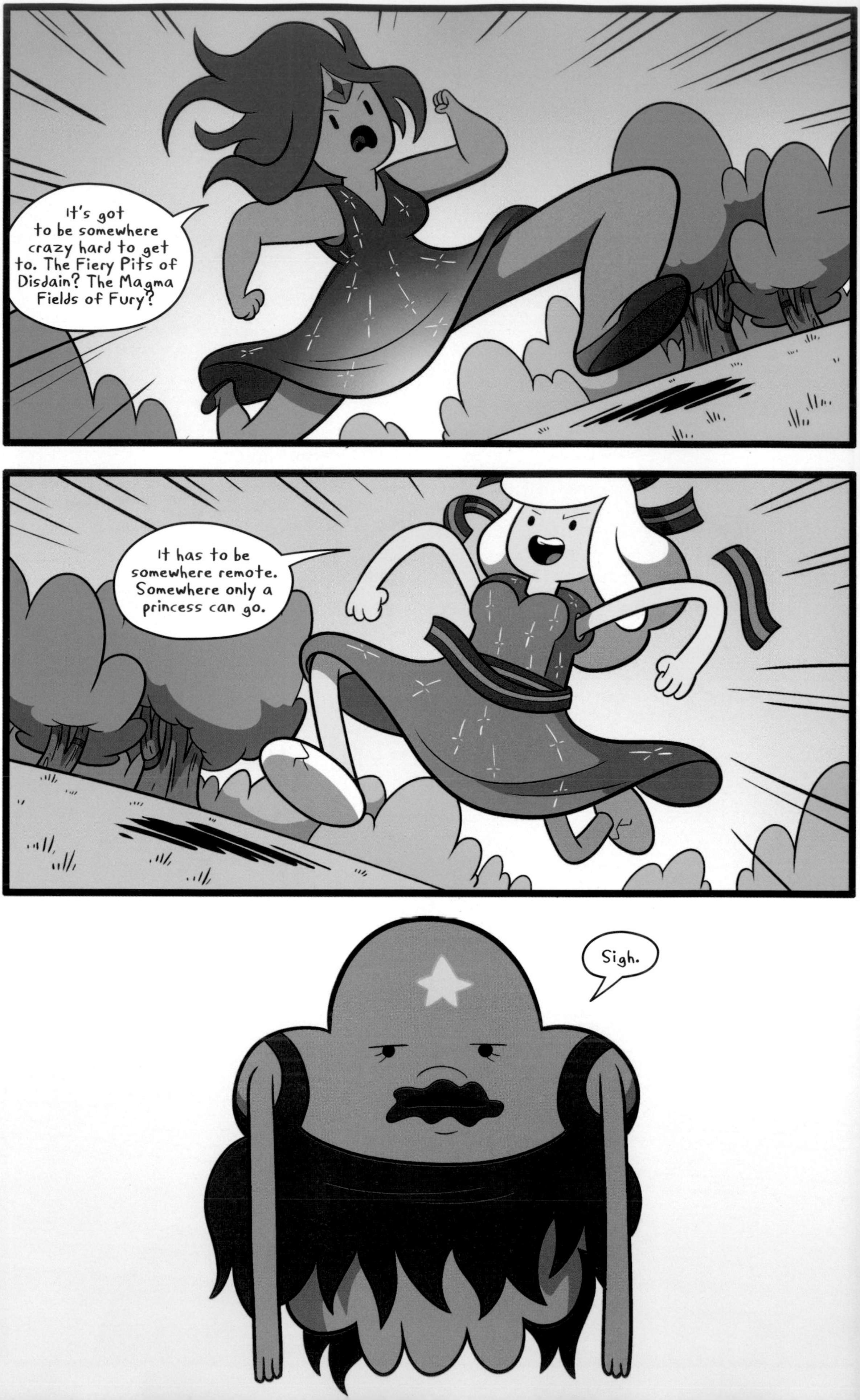

It's got to be somewhere crazy hard to get to. The Fiery Pits of Disdain? The Magma Fields of Fury?
It has to be somewhere remote. Somewhere only a princess can go.
Sigh.

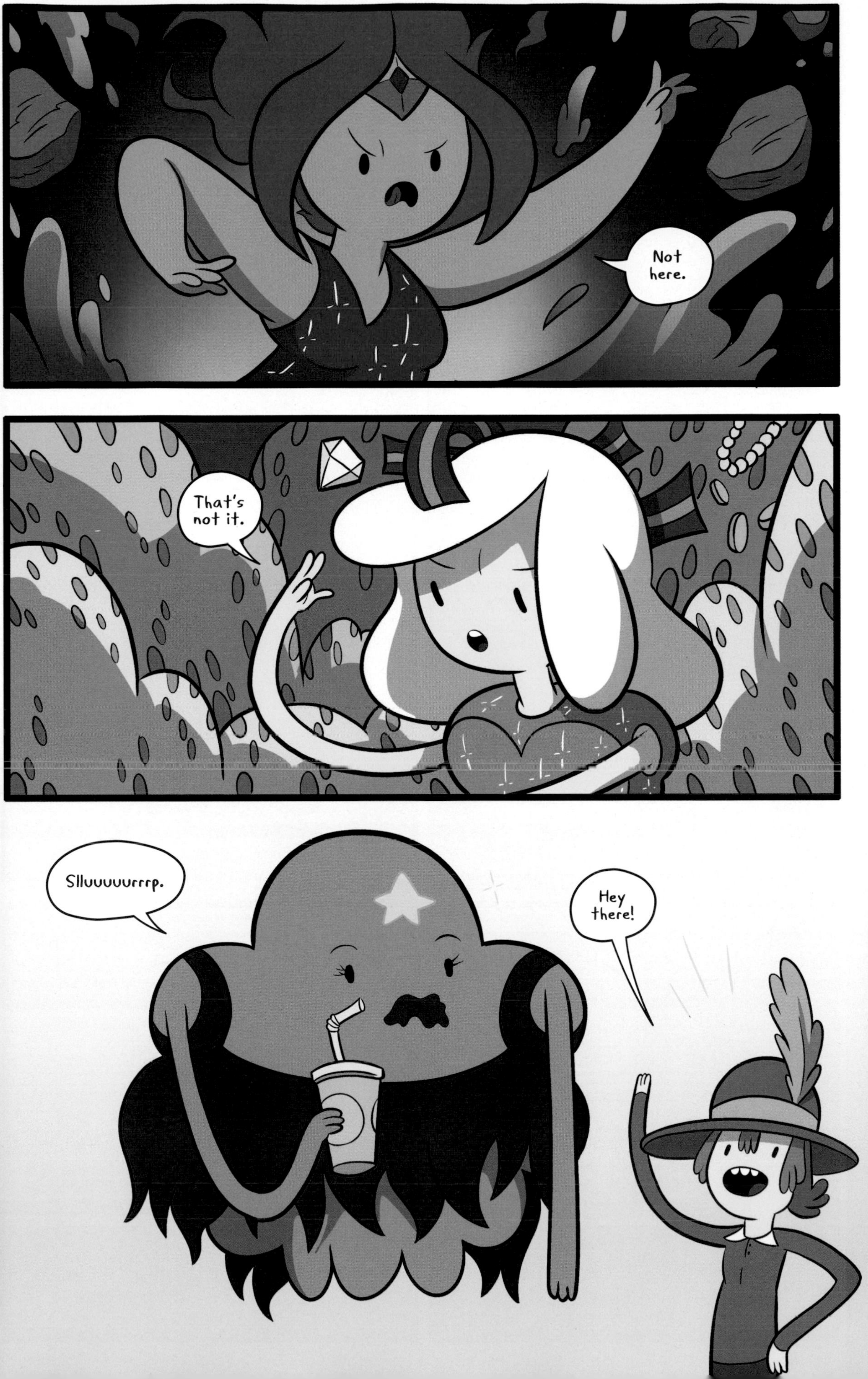
Not here.
That's not it.
Slluuuuurrrp.
Hey there!

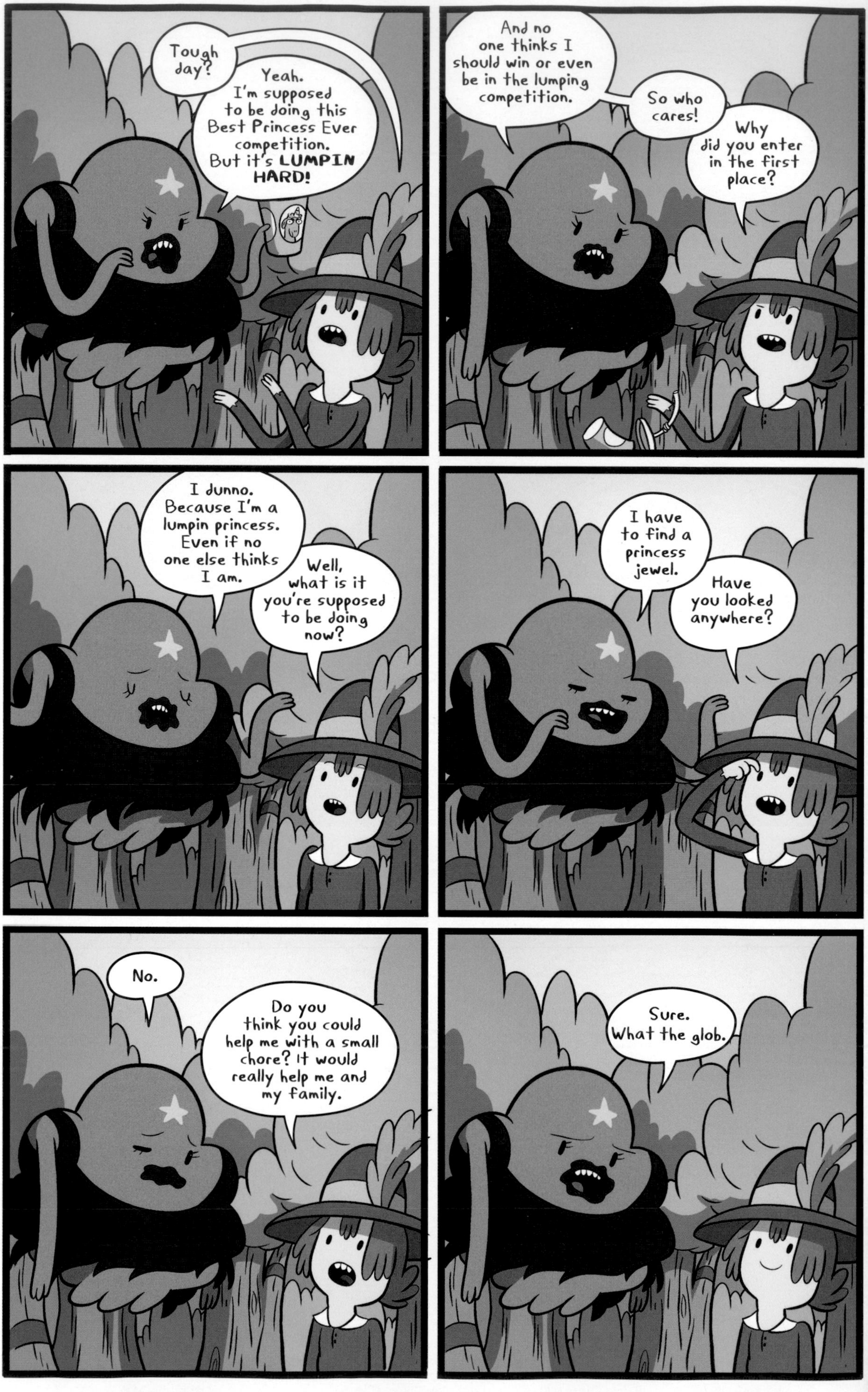
Tough day?
Yeah. I'm supposed to be doing this Best Princess Ever competition. But it's LUMPIN HARD!
And no one thinks I should win or even be in the lumping competition.
So who cares!
Why did you enter in the first place?
I dunno. Because I'm a lumpin princess. Even if no one else thinks I am.
Well, what is it you're supposed to be doing now?
I have to find a princess jewel.
Have you looked anywhere?
No.
Do you think you could help me with a small chore? It would really help me and my family.
Sure. What the glob.

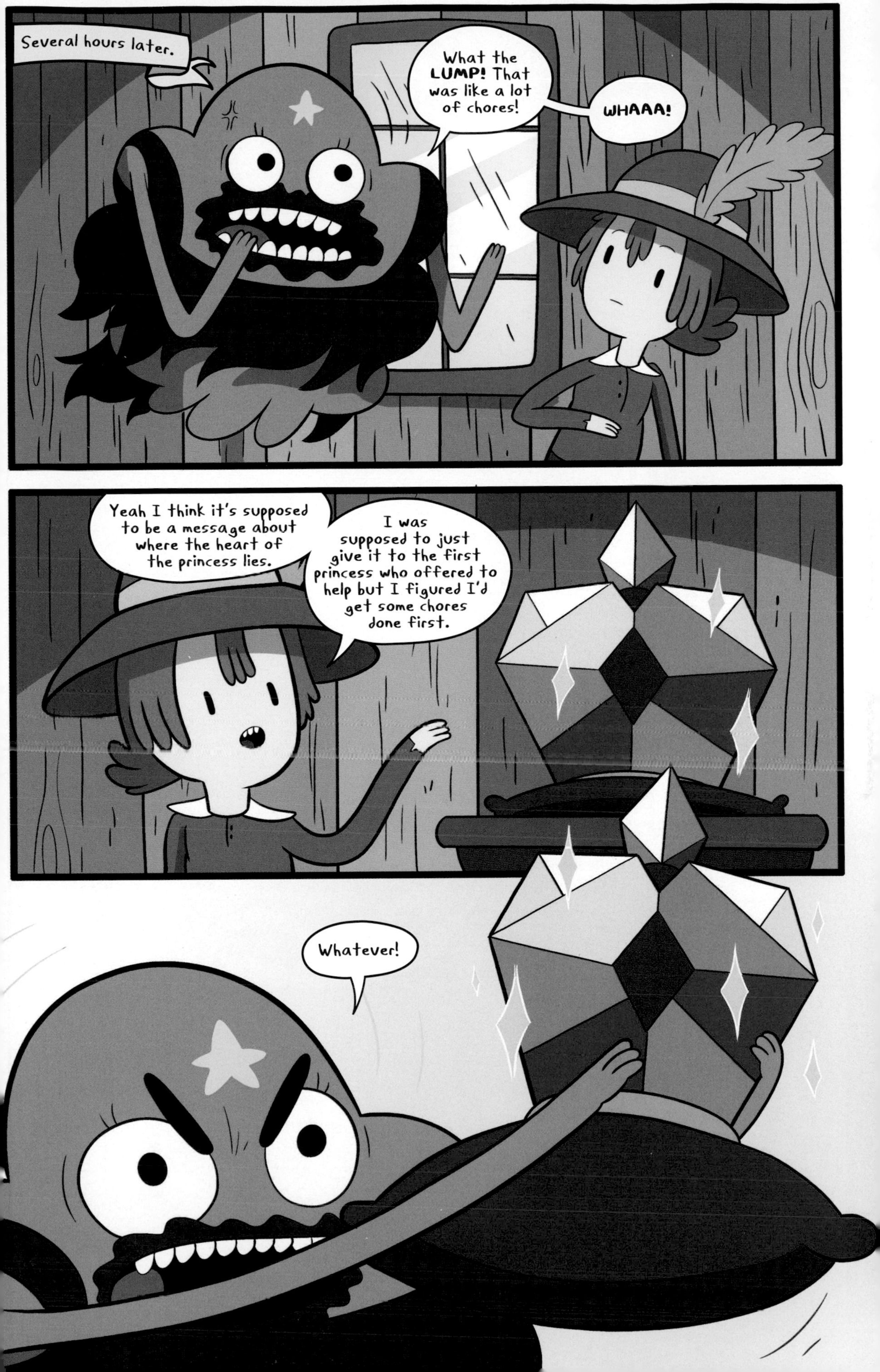
Several hours later.
What the LUMP! That was like a lot of chores!
WHAAA!
Yeah I think it's supposed to be a message about where the heart of the princess lies.
I was supposed to just give it to the first princess who offered to help but I figured I'd get some chores done first.
Whatever!

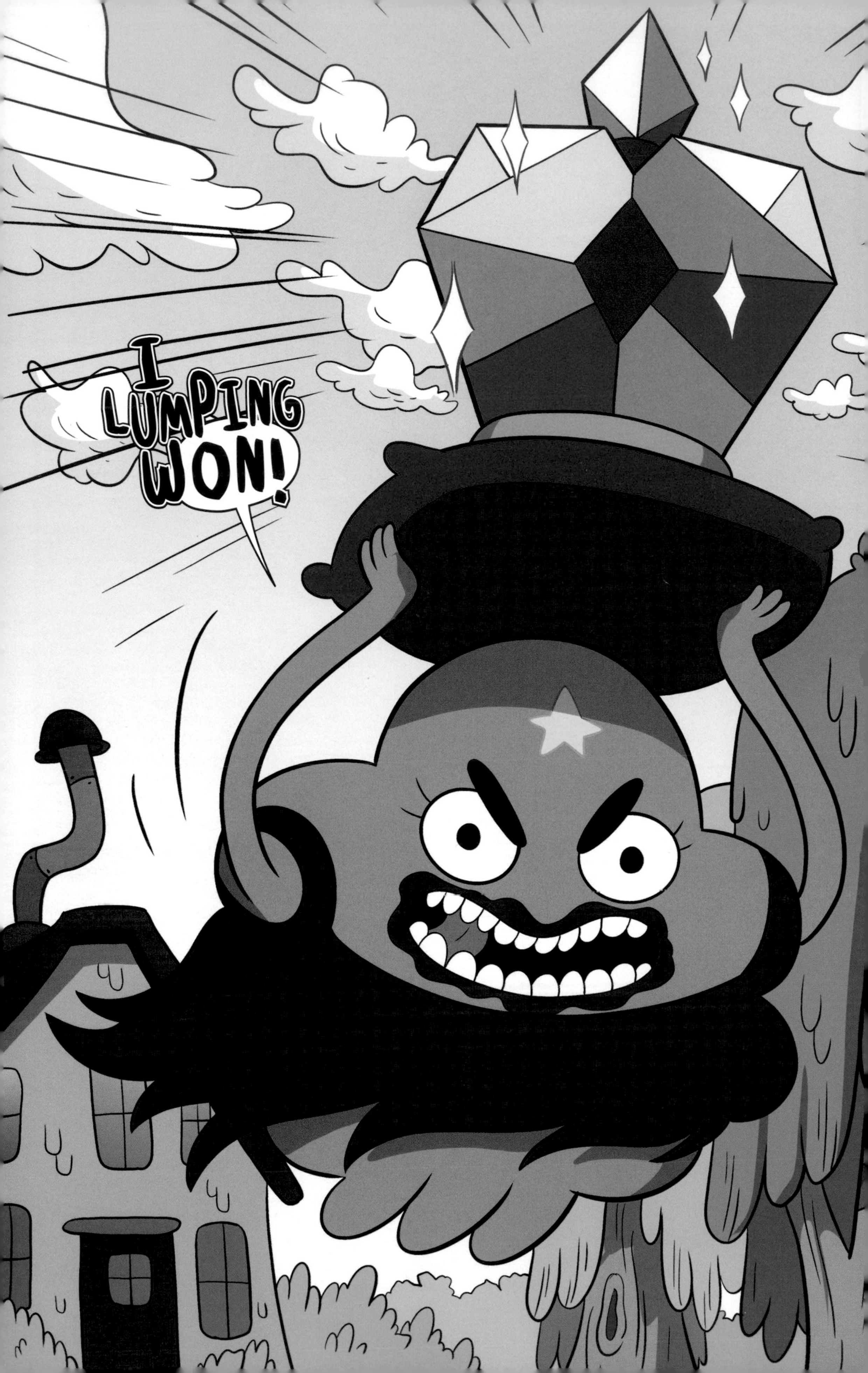
I LUMPING WON!

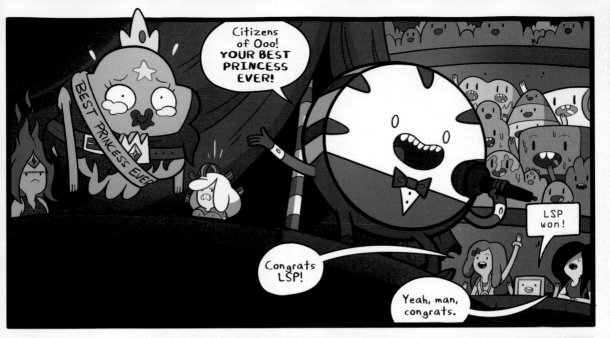

Citizens of Ooo! YOUR BEST PRINCESS EVER!

Congrats LSP!

LSP won!

Yeah, man, congrats.

WOOOOO!

What an underdog story!

YAY LSP!

Well that was something. Who would have thought, huh?

It seems a bit predictably unpredictable if you ask me.

I wonder how the Ice King's doing?

C'mon guys, can't anyone take a joke?!

Hey, what's this?

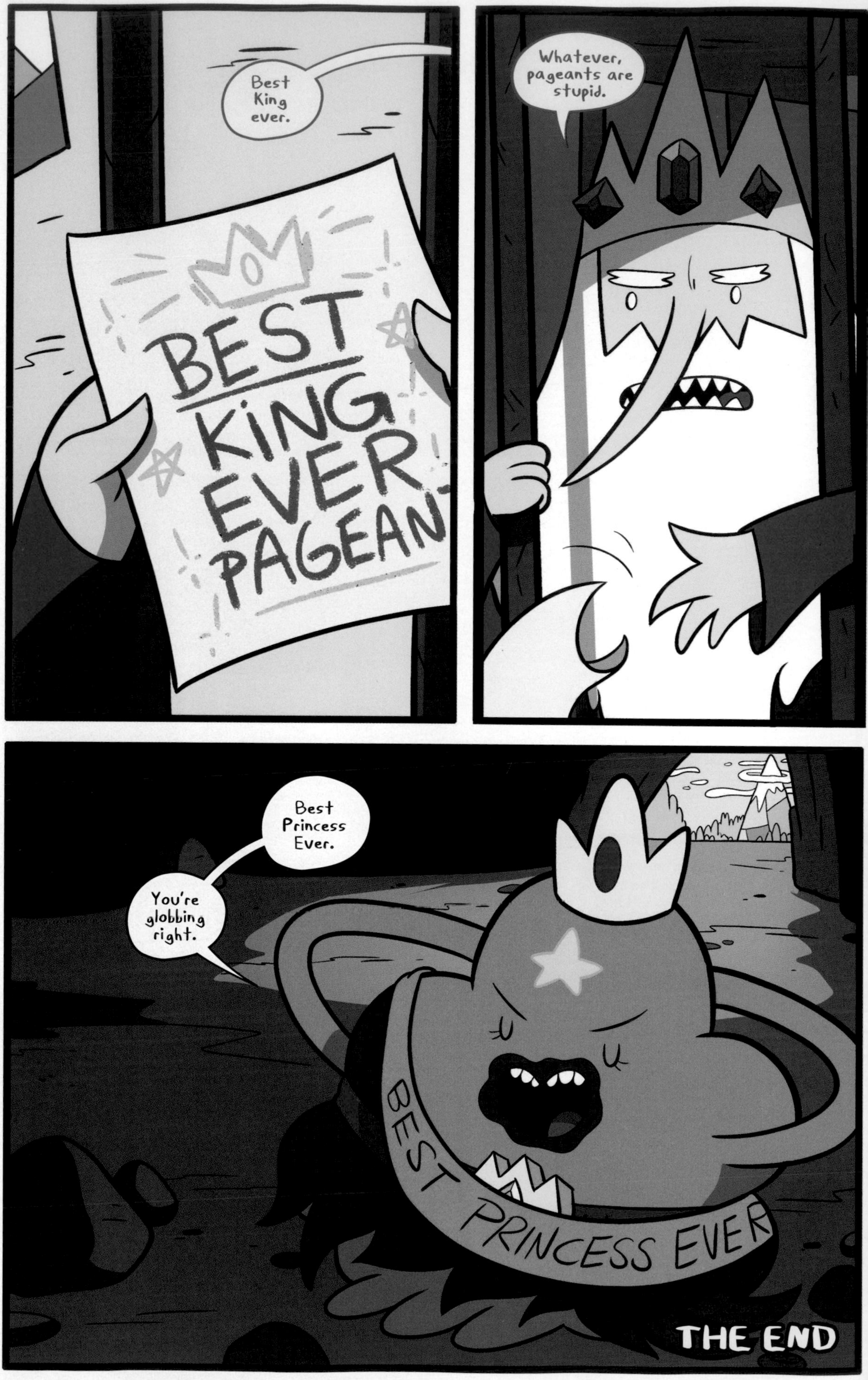
Best
King
ever.
BEST
KiNG
EVER
PAGEAN
Whatever,
pageants are
stupid.
Best
Princess
Ever.
You're
globbing
right.
BEST PRINCESS EVER
THE END

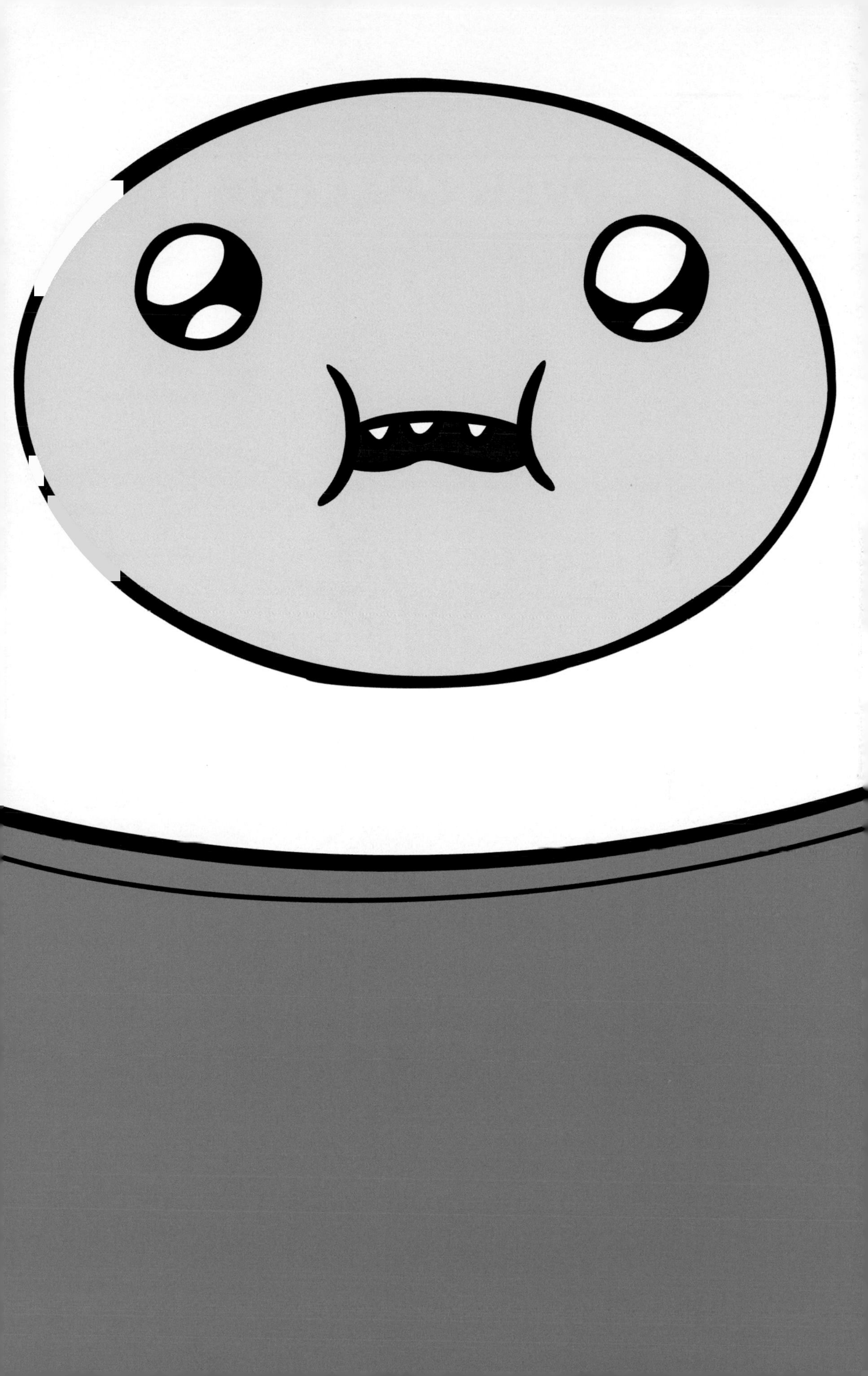

COVER GALLERY

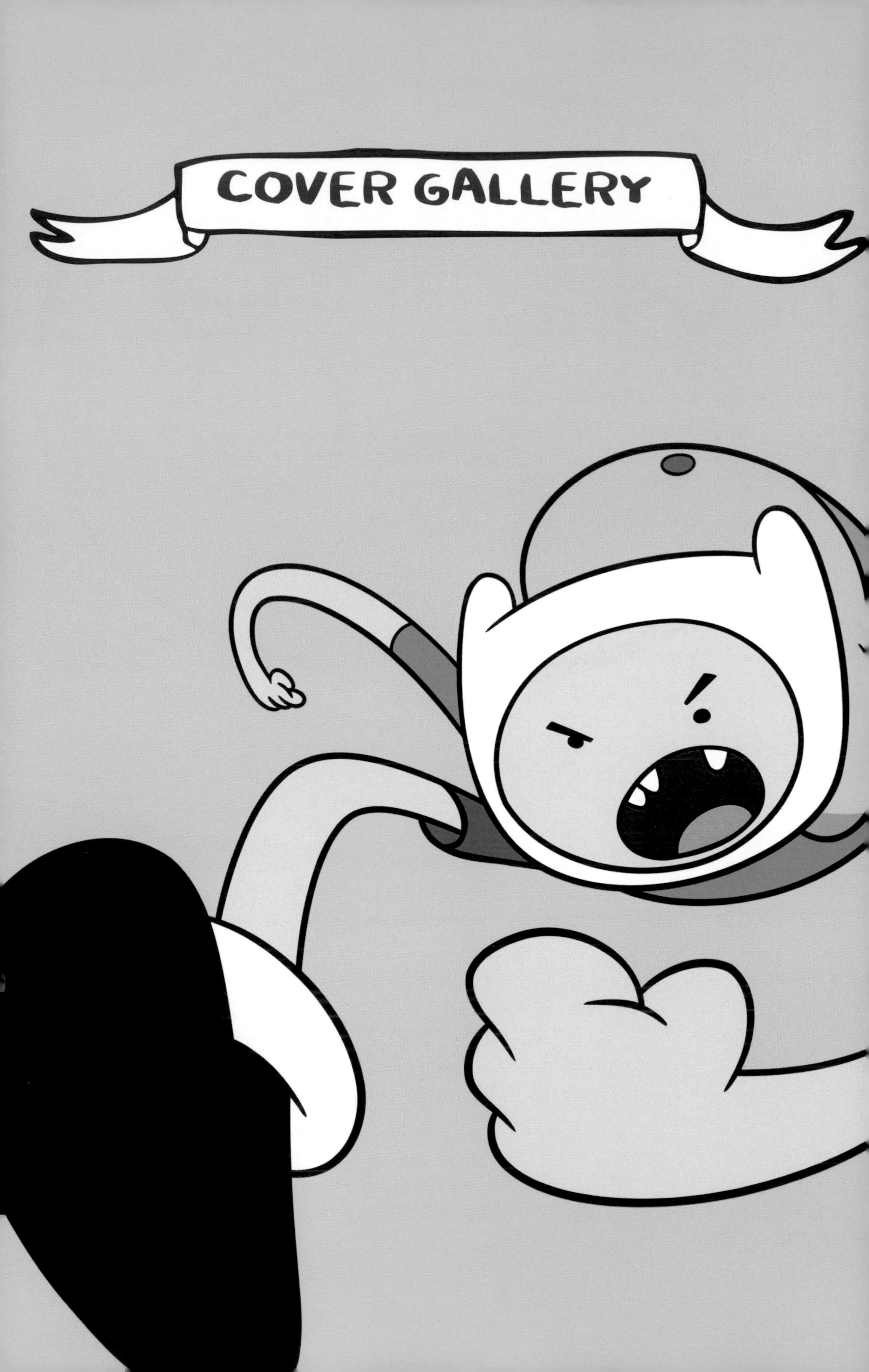

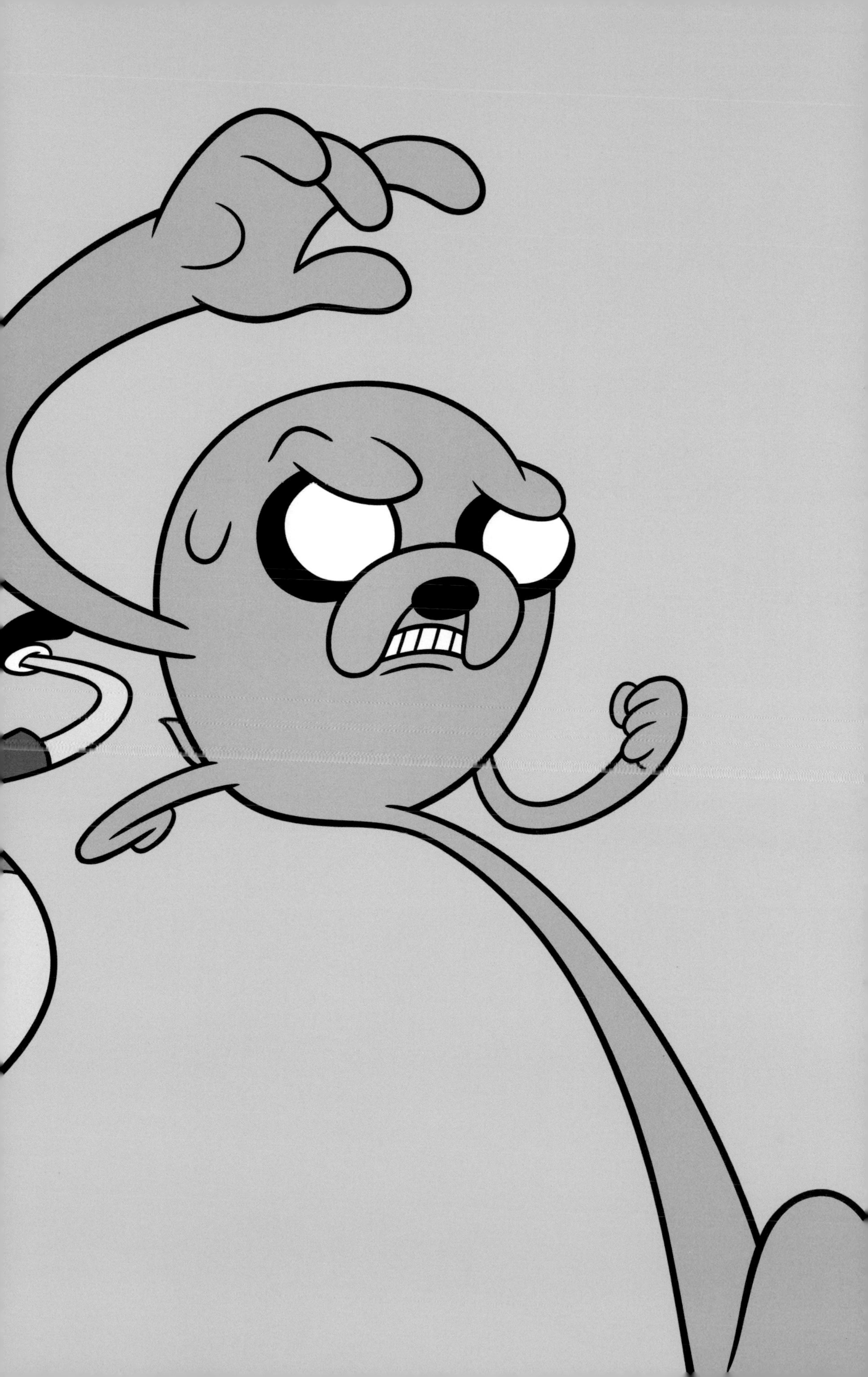

Issue 62 Cover:
Shelli Paroline & Braden Lamb

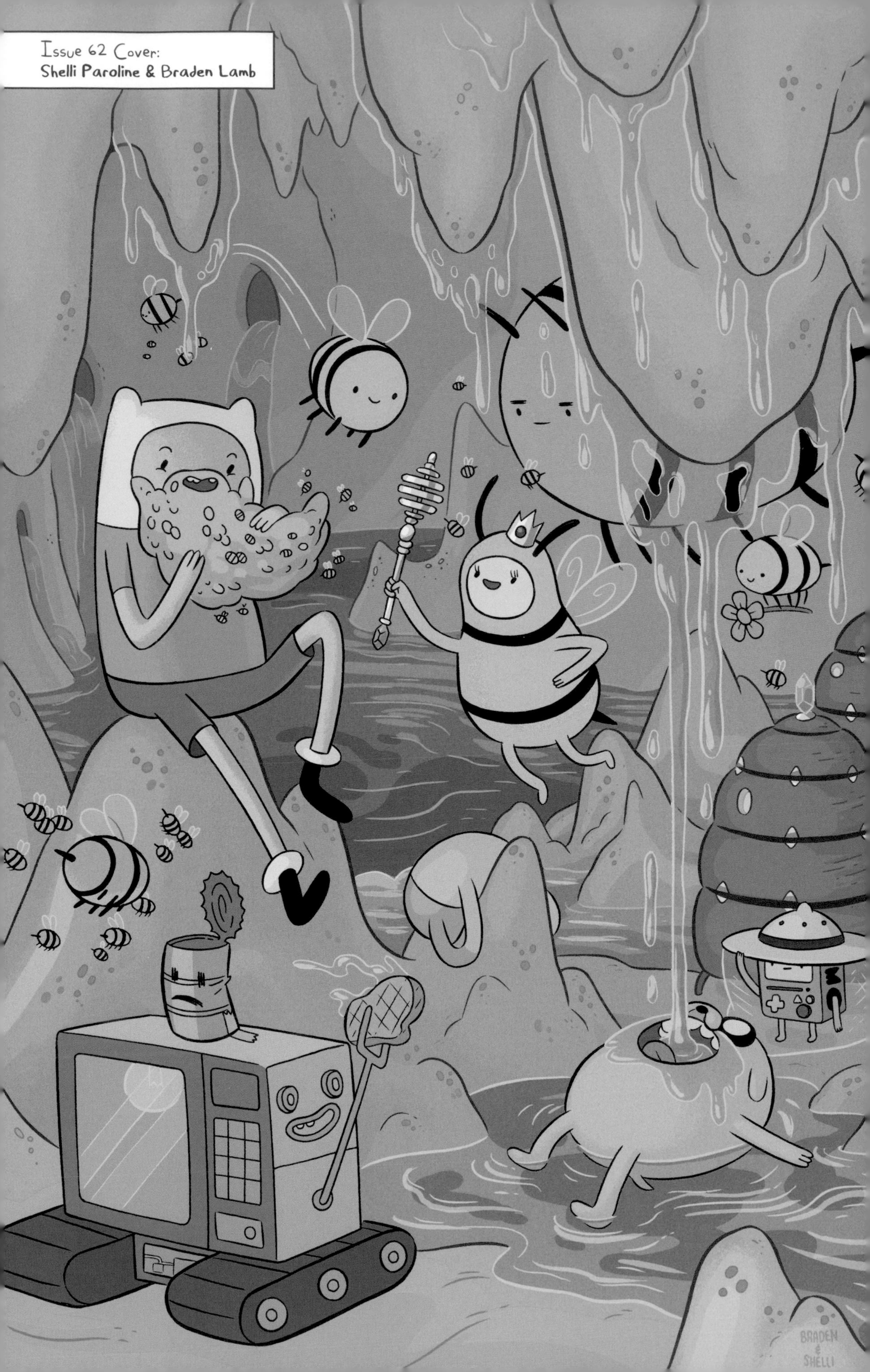
BRADEN & SHELLI

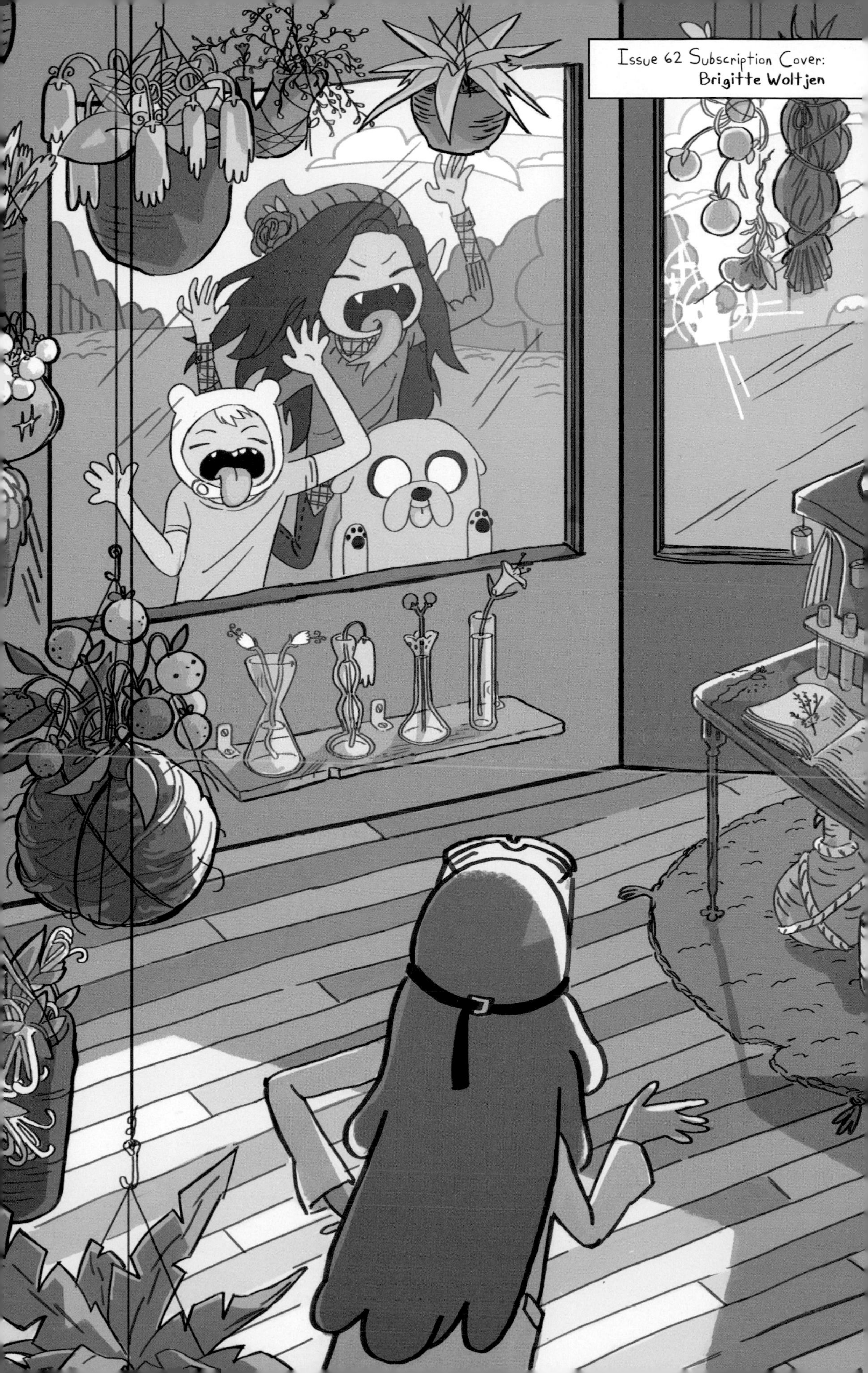
Issue 62 Subscription Cover:
Brigitte Woltjen

Issue 63 Cover:
Shelli Paroline & Braden Lamb

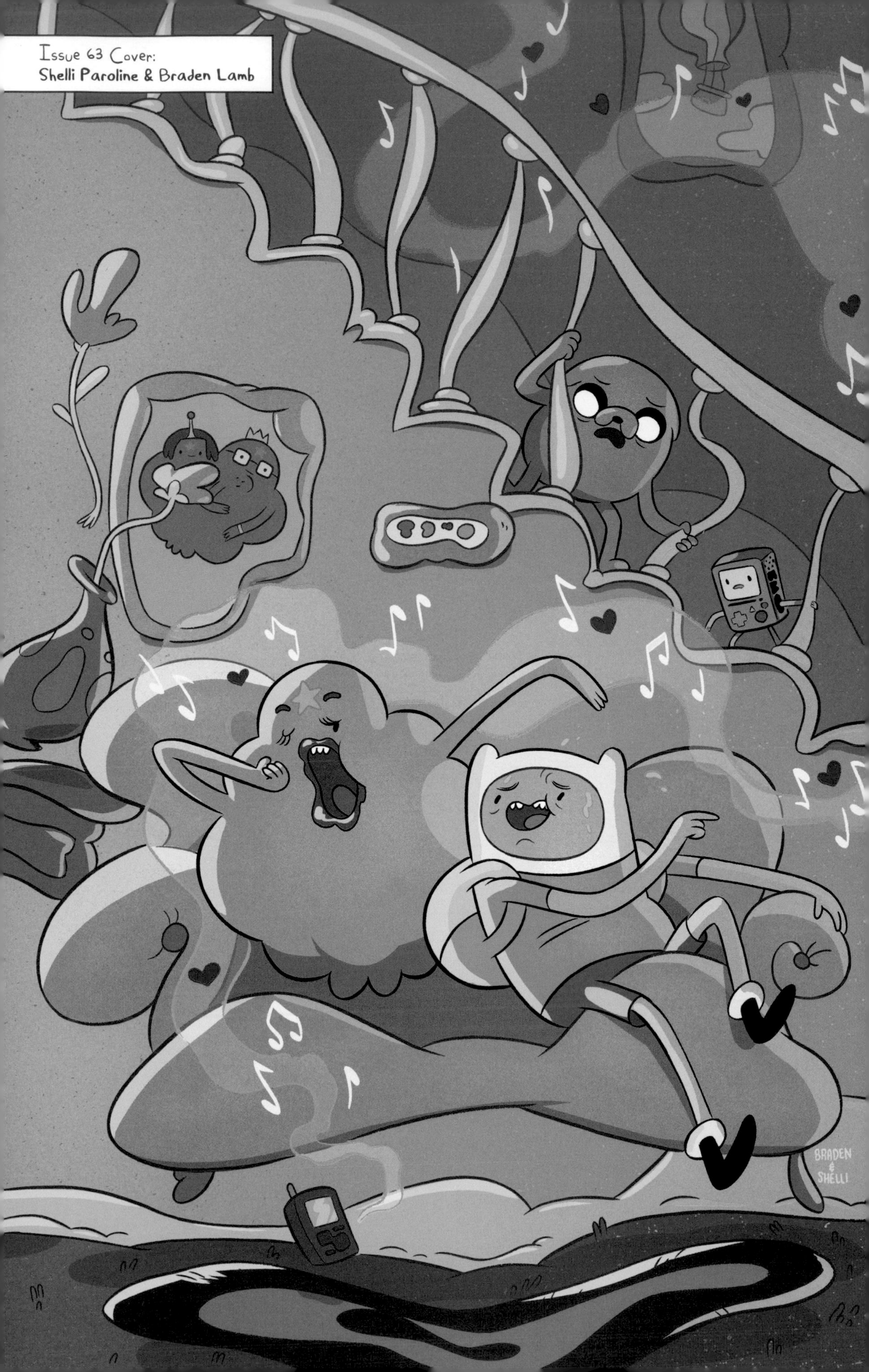
BRADEN & SHELLI

Issue 63 Subscription Cover:
Pranas Naujokaitis

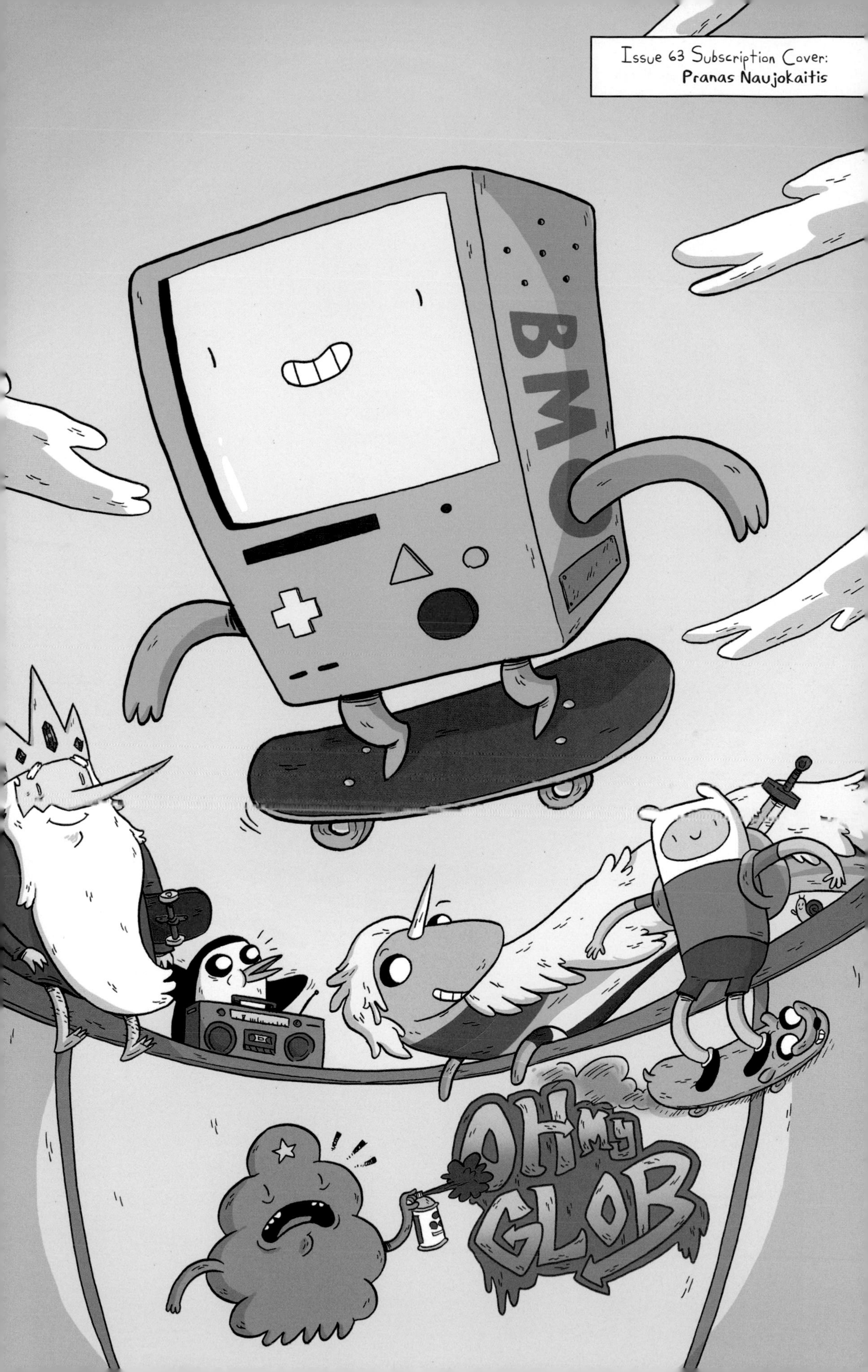

Issue 64 Cover:
Shelli Paroline & Braden Lamb

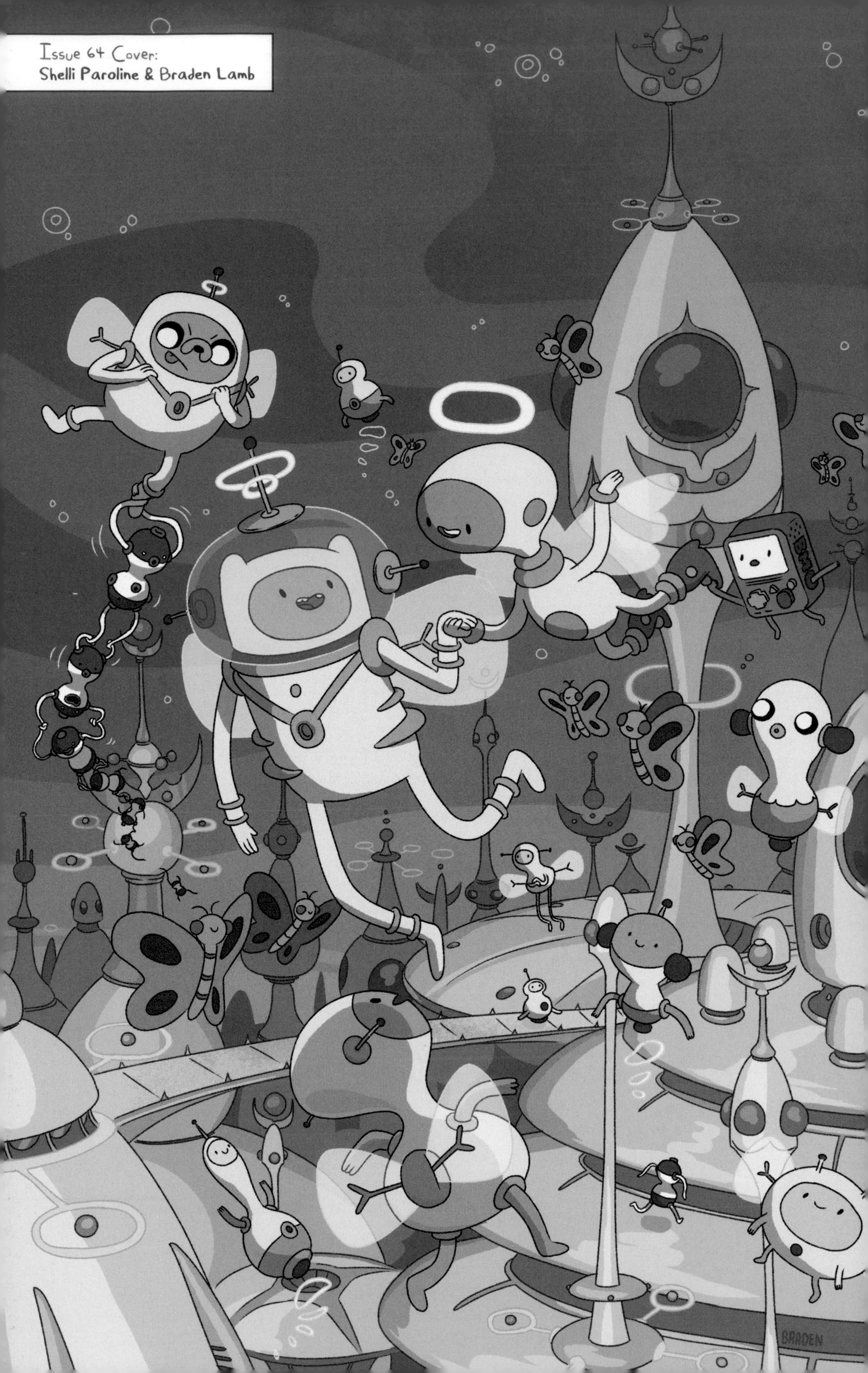
BRADEN

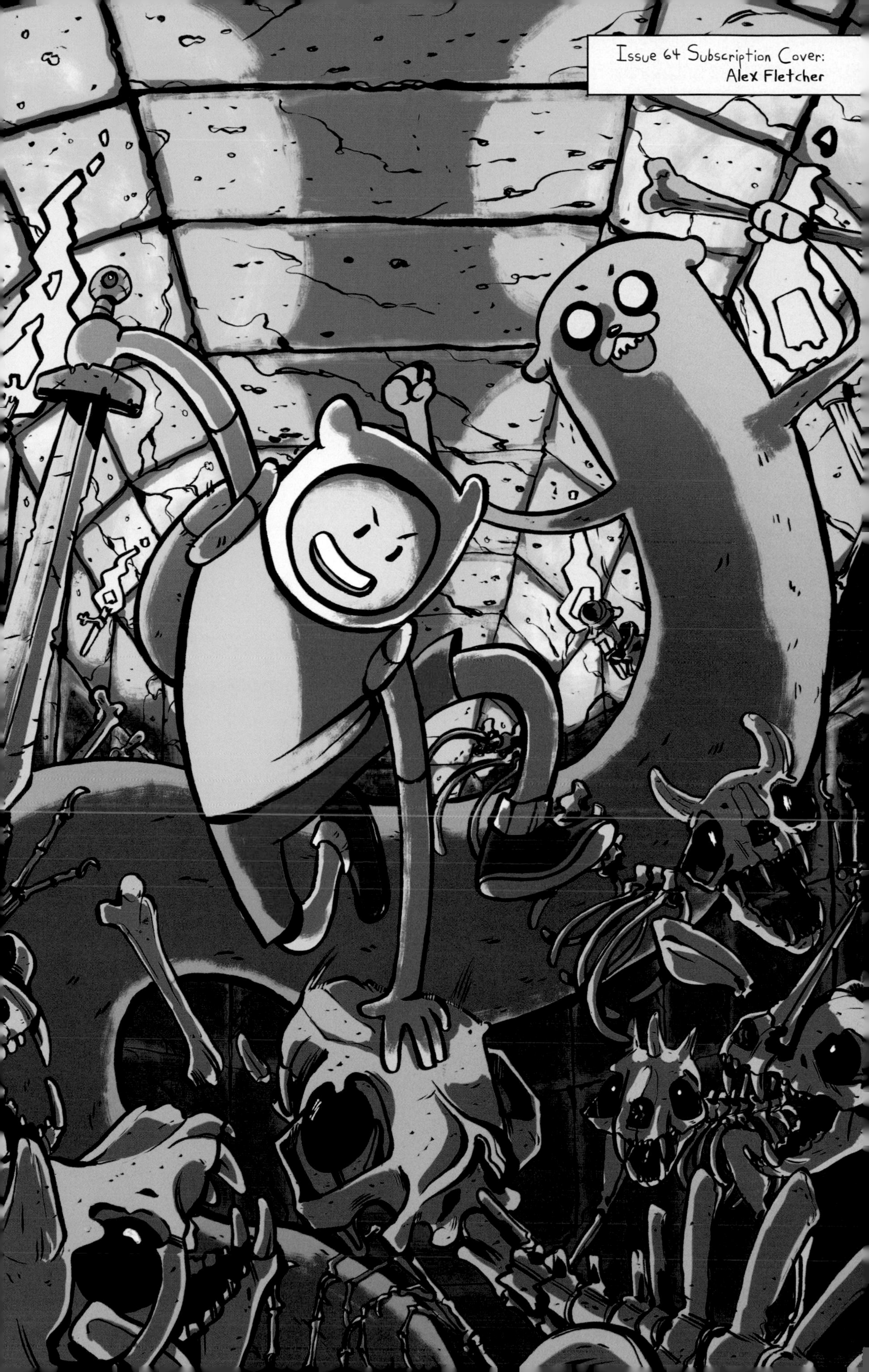

Issue 64 Subscription Cover:
Alex Fletcher

Issue 65 Cover:
Shelli Paroline & Braden Lamb

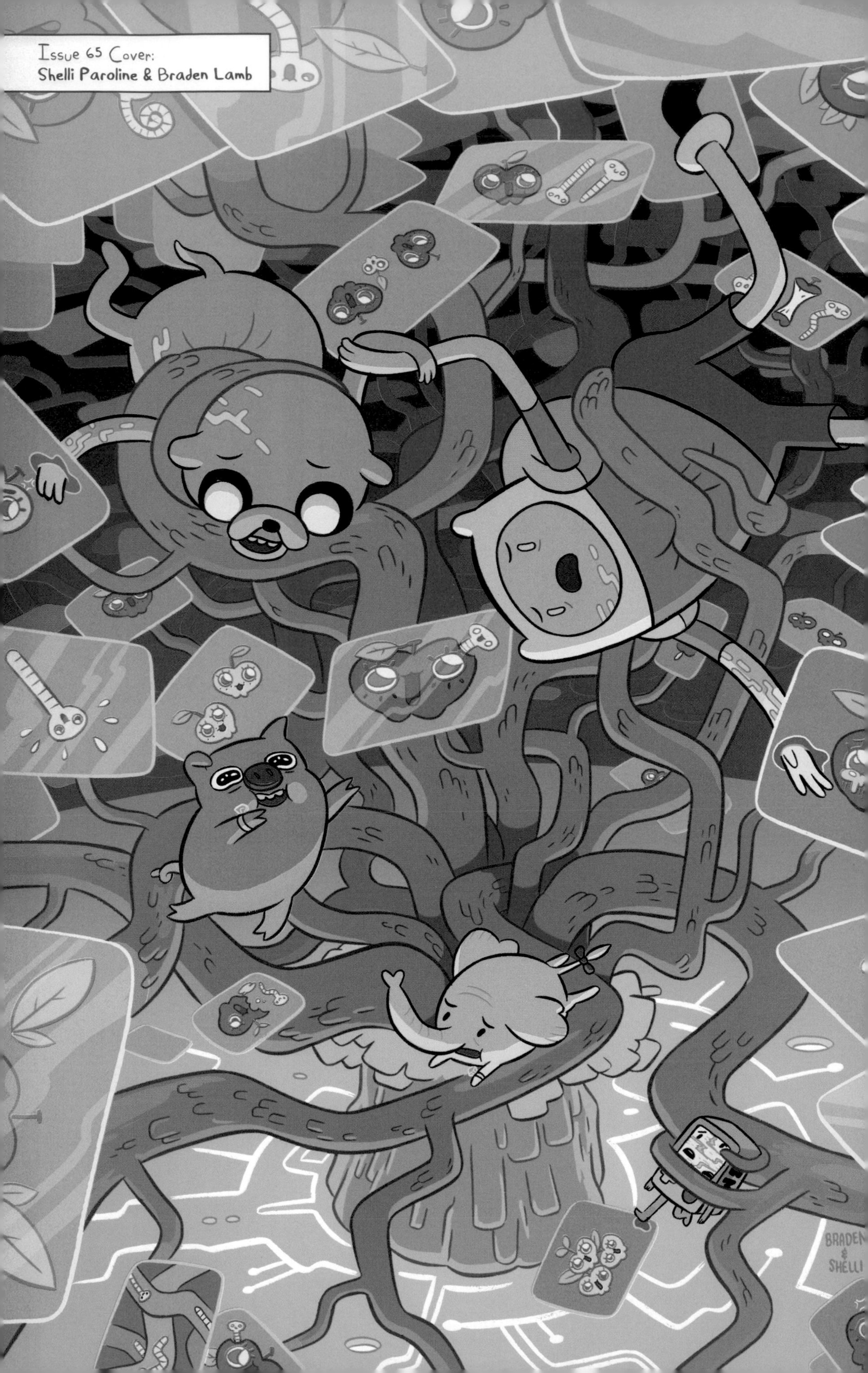
BRADEN
&
SHELLI

Issue 65 Subscription Cover:
E Jackson

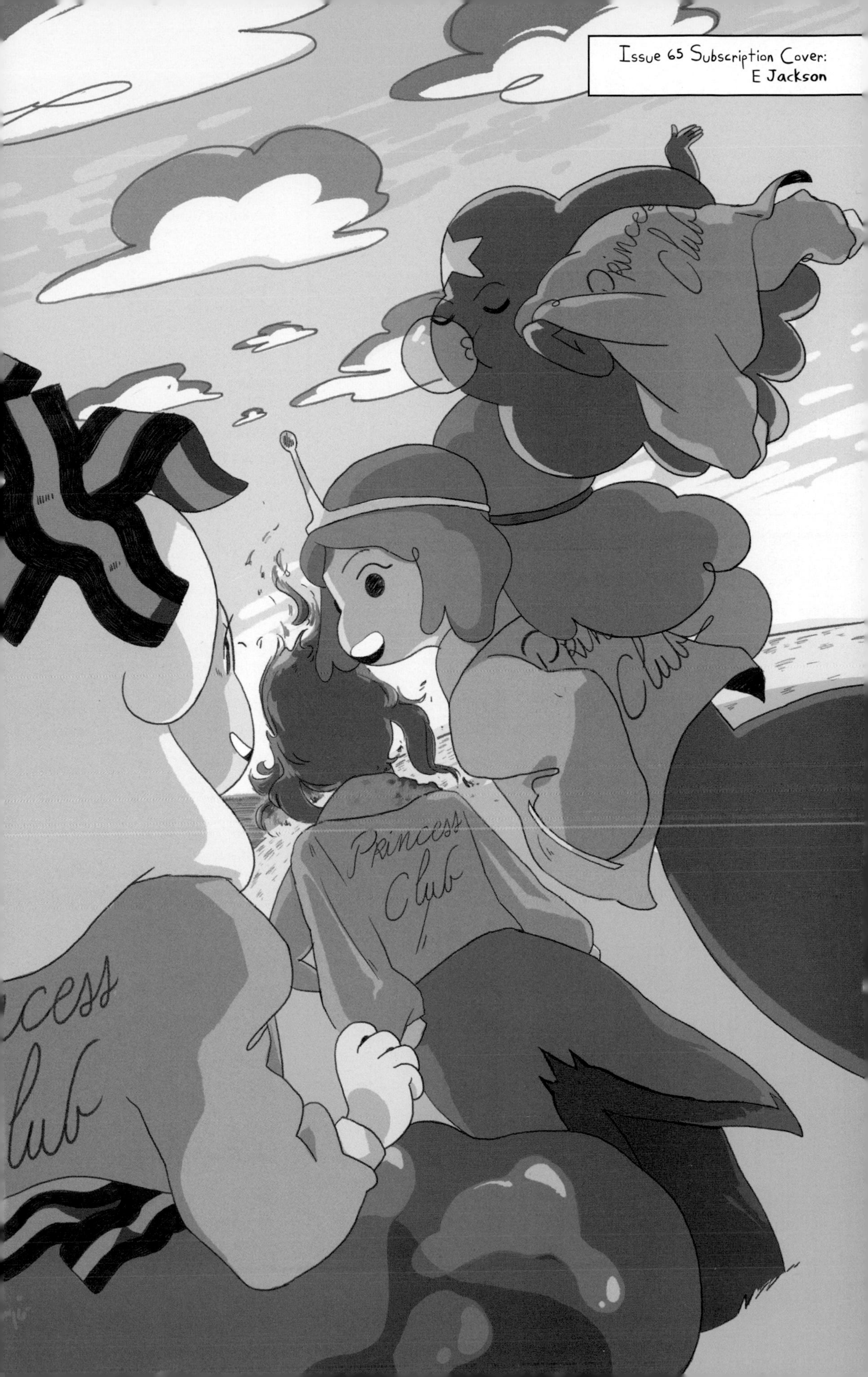
Princess Club
Princess Club
Princess Club
Princess Club

DISCOVER
EXPLOSIVE NEW WORLDS

Adventure Time
Pendleton Ward and Others
Volume 1
ISBN: 978-1-60886-280-1 | $14.99 US
Volume 2
ISBN: 978-1-60886-323-5 | $14.99 US
Adventure Time: Islands
ISBN: 978-1-60886-972-5 | $9.99 US

The Amazing World of Gumball
Ben Bocquelet and Others
Volume 1
ISBN: 978-1-60886-488-1 | $14.99 US
Volume 2
ISBN: 978-1-60886-793-6 | $14.99 US

Brave Chef Brianna
Sam Sykes, Selina Espiritu
ISBN: 978-1-68415-050-2 | $14.99 US

Mega Princess
Kelly Thompson, Brianne Drouhard
ISBN: 978-1-68415-007-6 | $14.99 US

The Not-So Secret Society
*Matthew Daley, Arlene Daley,
Wook Jin Clark*
ISBN: 978-1-60886-997-8 | $9.99 US

Over the Garden Wall
*Patrick McHale, Jim Campbell
and Others*
Volume 1
ISBN: 978-1-60886-940-4 | $14.99 US
Volume 2
ISBN: 978-1-68415-006-9 | $14.99 US

Steven Universe
Rebecca Sugar and Others
Volume 1
ISBN: 978-1-60886-706-6 | $14.99 US
Volume 2
ISBN: 978-1-60886-796-7 | $14.99 US

Steven Universe & The Crystal Gems
ISBN: 978-1-60886-921-3 | $14.99 US

Steven Universe: Too Cool for School
ISBN: 978-1-60886-771-4 | $14.99 US

AVAILABLE AT YOUR LOCAL
COMICS SHOP AND BOOKSTORE
To find a comics shop in your area, call 1-888-266-4226

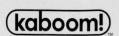

WWW.**BOOM-STUDIOS**.COM